The Stallions of Woodstock

Also by Edward Marston

In the Domesday Book Series

In the Nicholas Bracewell Series

The **Stallions** of **Woodstock**

Edward Marston

St. Martin's Press ⚏ New York

Library of Congress Cataloging-in Publication Data

Marston, Edward.
    The stallions of Woodstock / Edward Marston.
        p. cm.–(Domesday books ; v.6)
        ISBN 0-312-20021-8
        1. Great Britain—History—William I, 1066–1087—Fiction.
    I. Title. II. Series: Marston, Edward. Domesday books ; v. 6.
    PR6063.A695S7   1999
    823'.914—dc21   98-50733
                                                                         CIP

First published in Great Britain by Headline Book Publishing, a division of Hodder Headline PLC

First U.S. Edition: February 1999

10 9 8 7 6 5 4 3 2 1

To my beloved son
Prior Conrad
of the Abbey of St Catherine

Dominus illuminatio meo

The speaker observed in the disgusting lechery of the one, the chaste intention of the other, and he saw in that act not the conjunction of their bodies but the diversity of their minds. 'There were two persons involved and only one committed adultery.'

De Civitate Dei
Augustine of Hippo (AD 354–430)

Domesday Oxfordshire

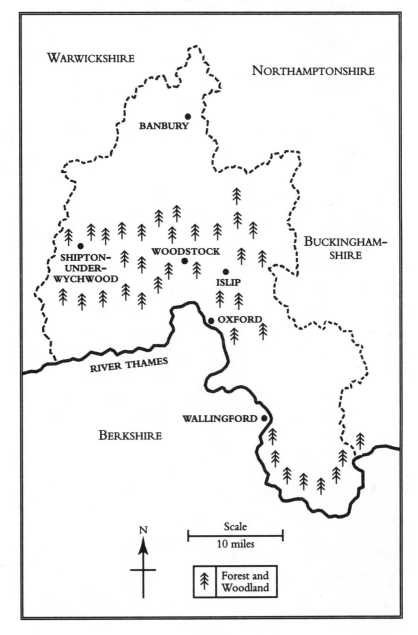

Prologue

Most of the riders were there well before the race was due to begin. They wanted to walk the course in search of potential hazards and have time to prepare their horses for the test ahead. All would be decided by a hell-for-leather gallop over uneven ground. It was no friendly contest. Far too much was at stake for that. A large amount of money and an even greater amount of pride were invested in the race. One of the parties involved was also prompted by a lust for revenge.

Wymarc made no effort to hide his bitterness.

'Let us start without him,' he declared.

'That would be unfair,' said Milo Crispin.

'When has he ever been fair with us?' argued Wymarc with sudden vehemence. 'His name is a byword for unfairness. He will seize any advantage in the most ruthless and unjust way. Bertrand Gamberell is not here at the appointed time and that is that. His horse must be disqualified. His share of the purse goes to the winner.'

'Not so fast, my friend,' cautioned the other.

'But he has failed to appear.'

'Be patient a while longer. The race is set for noon and we have not yet heard the bell for Sext. Until we do, we may not in all honesty proceed.'

'Even when it serves our purpose?'

'Even then, Wymarc.'

'But it would be a means to strike back at Bertrand.'

'We will do that in the race itself,' said Milo calmly. 'And without Bertrand, there *is* no race. He threw down

1

the challenge and we accepted it. As we have done on three previous occasions in the last six months.'

'Always to our cost!' said Wymarc ruefully.

'Fortune has favoured him thus far. His luck will not hold for ever. Win today and your losses are restored. That is the only way to strike back at Bertrand Gamberell. By beating that black stallion of his.'

'But Hyperion runs like the wind.'

'So do my horses, Wymarc. They have been in training.'

'Mine, too.'

'Then one of us will be the victor.'

A long sigh. 'I hope so. I would dearly love to wipe that arrogant smile from Bertrand's face and send him home with an empty purse. It would gall me to see him win again.'

'That will not happen today.'

'How do you know?'

'Rest assured of it,' said Milo with quiet confidence. 'This race will certainly not go the way of the others. Bertrand will be the loser here today.'

Milo Crispin was a slim, well-groomed, dignified man with an air of easy authority about him. A scion of the ancient aristocracy of Normandy, his military prowess and loyalty to the Conqueror had been richly rewarded. He was one of the major landholders in the county with over thirty manors in his strong grasp. The King had also given him the charge of Wallingford Castle, a key fortress in the south of Oxfordshire. So accustomed was Milo to the unimpeded exercise of power that he found any resistance to his will, however trivial, highly vexatious and swept it instantly aside.

Even in a horse race, he felt entitled to be the winner.

Unlike his companion, Wymarc was not able to hide his disappointment beneath a mask of composure. He wore his heart and his resentment on his sleeve for all to see. A short, stout man with piggy eyes set in a flabby face, Wymarc yielded to none in his appreciation of horses and he was forever trying to improve the quality of his stable. He had reason enough to dislike Milo Crispin but felt a kinship with him now, united as they were by a common hatred of Bertrand Gamberell and by a determination to humble him in the race.

'He is not coming,' said Wymarc irritably.

'Nothing would keep him away.'

'Why is he making us wait like this?'

'It is all part of his strategy,' decided Milo.

'Where *is* the man?'

Bertrand Gamberell gave his own answer to the question. Flanked by two of his knights, he came trotting briskly along on his destrier, towing the black stallion behind him on a lead-rein. He was an arresting figure, tall, rangy and possessed of a dark handsomeness that he knew how to exploit to the full. Over his hauberk he wore a white tunic emblazoned with the head of a black stallion. As he closed in on them he gave a cheerful wave of greeting.

'What did I tell you?' said Milo. 'Bertrand is here.'

'More's the pity!' groaned Wymarc, raising his voice as the newcomer rode up to them. 'You're late. That is unforgivable. I had half a mind to start without you.'

Gamberell grinned. 'You certainly have only half a mind. It is your most distinctive feature, Wymarc. But I beg leave to disagree about being late. I am here exactly on time.' He beamed at his black stallion. 'And so is Hyperion.'

On a nod from his master, one of his men dismounted from his own horse and hauled himself up into Hyperion's saddle. The stallion responded with a snort and some spirited prancing, then headed for the starting point at a gentle canter. Gamberell watched him with a proprietorial smile. Wymarc looked on with a mixture of envy and apprehension but Milo seemed unperturbed by the arrival of the celebrated Hyperion. He had faith in his own horses.

'Well, my friends,' teased Gamberell, gazing from one to the other. 'How much will I win off you today?'

'Nothing!' vowed Wymarc.

'You say that every time.'

'I have brought swifter legs with me today.'

'No horse can outrun Hyperion.'

3

'We shall see,' said Milo levelly.

'Do you really believe that you have a chance?' mocked Gamberell. 'In that case, you will be ready to increase the size of your wager. Is that not so, Milo?'

'Let it stand at the amount on which we settled,' replied the other. 'And let the race begin at the agreed time.'

'Hyperion is ready.'

'So are we, Bertrand.'

Milo Crispin gave a signal to the soldier who was acting as the starter and the latter began to marshal the runners into line. There were six horses in the race. Milo and Wymarc had entered two apiece against Hyperion. The other horse was owned by Ordgar, a Saxon thegn who had been robbed of most of his land after the Conquest and reduced to the status of a subtenant on Milo's estates, an ignominy he bore with surprising grace. Ordgar was a silver-haired old man, forced to come to composition with the invaders yet still ready to offer any legitimate check to their primacy if the opportunity arose.

Lacking the money for his share of the purse, Ordgar had collected it from a group of friends who were equally keen to see a Saxon competing with Norman riders, especially as the Saxon in question was Ordgar's son Amalric, barely sixteen but with the determination of a grown man. Young, strong and sinewy, Amalric was a fine horseman astride a speedy mount and his participation in the race had brought out a small and vocal group of supporters. The animal was a chestnut colt, stringy in appearance but pulsing with energy and lithe in movement.

When Gamberell saw him, he gave a derisive laugh.

'What, in God's name, is *that*?' he said.

'Ordgar's horse,' explained Milo.

'That creature intends to race against Hyperion?'

'Indeed he does. Ordgar's son is in the saddle.'

Gamberell sniggered. 'The boy would stand more chance of winning if he carried the horse instead of expecting that ridiculous skeleton to bear him. Is that foolish old Saxon so eager to throw away his money?'

'He is looking to increase it threefold, Bertrand.'

'Then he had better hobble Hyperion and the other runners because that is the only way he will have a hope of success. The horse is so thin and undernourished.'

'Yet hungry for victory,' observed Milo.

'Just like us,' added a scowling Wymarc.

The sound of a distant chiming silenced them. Midday was marked by the bell for Sext. The horses were prancing in a ragged line, but each time the starter raised an arm to set them off one or two broke mutinously away and had to be coaxed back into position. With each nervous second, the tension grew among riders and spectators alike.

Milo Crispin, Wymarc and Bertrand Gamberell were on a hillock a small distance away from the course. Each of the Norman lords was astride his destrier, sturdy animals bred for stamina, strength and reliability, but none had entered a warhorse in the race. They had carefully selected their best coursers, smaller horses with greater pace and nimbleness. Five riders had shed their armour to lighten the load on their mounts. Amalric, the sixth, wore his customary tunic and gartered stockings. He was the only bearded rider.

They were on the edge of the forest at Woodstock, part of a thick band of luxuriant woodland which extended almost without interruption from the hills above Burford to the forest of Bernwood in the neighbouring county of Buckinghamshire. Woodstock was part of the royal demesne and, as such, protected by savage forest laws. Only the privileged standing of the Norman lords allowed them to hold a race on land where anyone else would be accused of trespass and punished with severity.

As the riders struggled to bring their horses into line at the start, the noonday bell continued its sonorous boom in the background as if registering its disapproval of anything so frivolous as a mere horse race. The course was a straight mile long with enough undulations to test any rider. There was a leafy copse some two hundred yards before the halfway point. Onlookers had an excellent view of the race except for the fleeting seconds when the horses would be invisible in the trees. Two wooden stakes, set wide apart, marked the finishing line. Milo and Wymarc had each provided a man to act as judges in the event of a close finish. Ordgar and his friends also waited near the end of the course.

Recent rain had left the ground soft and treacherous. When the starter eventually brought down his raised arm to set the race in motion, two of the horses slithered in the mud before they sped away. Hyperion, by contrast, neighed loudly and rose up on his hind legs to pummel the air with shining hooves. By the time he condescended to join the race, he was thirty yards adrift of the others. Neither his rider nor his owner was alarmed by this state of affairs. They knew Hyperion's mettle. He would soon overhaul his rivals.

One of Wymarc's horses, a bay mare, was the early leader and it made him yell with joy. Milo was pleased to see his two runners close behind. Amalric's colt was also giving a good account of itself, covering the ground with long, graceful strides that belied its spindly appearance. After his delayed start, Hyperion was narrowing the gap remorselessly.

Wymarc only had eyes for the bay mare in the lead.

'I'm going to win!' he shouted, slapping his thigh.

'Do not celebrate too soon,' warned Gamberell.

'I'll beat you at last, Bertrand.'

'The race is not over yet. My money still rides on Hyperion. He will not let his master down.'

Milo Crispin said nothing. His face remained impassive.

When they reached the copse, Hyperion had almost caught up with them. The six horses plunged into the trees and were briefly lost from sight. Radical changes occurred before they reappeared. The bay mare had dropped back to third position. One of Milo's horses, a sleek grey with a slashing stride, now led the pack with Amalric's chestnut colt on his heels. Wymarc was distraught and let out a moan of disappointment as his mare lost even more ground.

But the most dramatic change concerned Hyperion. He flashed out of the copse with such speed and purpose that it was only a matter of time before he passed the others. The black stallion, however, had an advantage denied to his rivals. After his dash through the trees, he was now without a rider.

Bertrand Gamberell was jerked out of his complacence.

'My man has been thrown!' he protested.

'Then he is out of the reckoning,' said Milo.

'No! The race is void!'

'You have lost, Bertrand. Take defeat with good grace.'

'Hyperion has not been beaten fairly.'

'He has been beaten,' gloated Wymarc. 'That is what matters most. Your black stallion is not invincible after all.'

'I demand another race!' insisted Gamberell.

'Let us see who wins this one first,' said Milo.

They were approaching the last furlong now. The grey was still leading but the chestnut colt was slowly drawing level. Wymarc's bay mare was completely out of it. Surging past all three of them, Hyperion then swung off the course and galloped crazily towards the forest. Fearful that the animal might injure itself, Gamberell dispatched a man after him at once.

Under his skilful control, Amalric's mount was now racing neck and neck with the grey. From their vantage point on the hillock, it was impossible for the three men to tell which of the horses would pass the wooden stakes first, but Ordgar and his friends had no doubts. Exhorting their champion on over the final hundred yards, they let out such a collective cry of triumph that the result was all too evident. The chestnut colt had won the day. Five experienced Norman riders had been beaten by a Saxon youth.

Torn between delight at Gamberell's defeat and annoyance at his own, Wymarc did not know whether to grin or glower. Milo was irked by losing but gave no outward sign of this. Their companion ignored the result of the race. He was much more concerned to establish why Hyperion had thrown his rider and besmirched his hitherto spotless record. Kicking his destrier into life, Gamberell cantered towards the copse. Milo and Wymarc went after him at a more leisurely pace.

The sun was warm on their backs, the birdsong melodious

in their ears. As they picked their way through the trees, they saw that Gamberell had already dismounted. He was standing beside the fallen rider in a clearing. The man was lying on his back with his head at an unnatural angle to his body. His neck had patently been broken in the fall. Even Wymarc found sympathy stealing into his heart.

Bertrand Gamberell stared angrily up at them.

'The race is void!' he snarled. 'I refuse to pay.'

'It is a matter of honour,' reminded Milo.

'Honour!' He pointed to the corpse. 'What honour is there in this? My man was given no chance to win.'

Wymarc shrugged. 'He was thrown, Bertrand. It is very unfortunate but it does not invalidate the race. Your rider should have stayed in the saddle.'

'He did – until someone knocked him out of it.'

'What do you mean?' asked Milo.

Gamberell indicated the stream of blood that was trickling from beneath the prostrate figure, then used a foot to turn the man over. Milo and Wymarc reacted with horror at the sight. Gamberell cursed. The rider had clearly not been thrown by his horse in the copse.

Embedded in the middle of his back was a dagger.

Chapter One

They could not believe that it was still afternoon. It was more like the dead of night. The sky was so dark and menacing that it seemed as if it would drop down at any moment like a gigantic blanket to smother them in its unforgiving blackness and wipe out all memory of their existence. It was the worst possible time to be caught in open country. Ralph Delchard was leading the cavalcade at a brisk pace but there was no way that they could outrun the storm that was coming.

'How far is the next village?' asked Golde.

'Too far,' said Ralph, glancing up at the swirling clouds. 'We are going to get wet, I fear. Thoroughly and horribly wet.'

'Is there nowhere to shelter?'

'None that I see, my love.'

The first rumble of thunder set off a flurry of neighing among the horses. Their eyes rolled in alarm and their ears twitched apprehensively. When forked lightning suddenly ripped open the sky and caught them in the devastating brilliance of its glare, the animals were even more disturbed. Two bucked violently, a third tried to bolt and all had to be brought under control by their riders.

There were nineteen in the party. Behind Ralph and Golde were Gervase Bret, Maurice Pagnal, a new commissioner, and Brother Columbanus, their scribe. Ten of Ralph's knights rode in pairs with four from Maurice's personal retinue bringing up the rear. The escort was there to provide safety on the journey to Oxford and visible testament to the importance of the visitors

9

once they reached it, but the soldiers had no wish to ride into the town like so many drowned men on horseback. When Ralph increased his speed, they responded willingly.

There were no first warning drops of rain. The deluge was instantaneous. Stinging sheets of water fell out of the heavens, drenching them within seconds and turning the track over which they rode into a squelching quagmire. They splashed their way on until a stand of trees came into view. There was some cover under the branches but danger, too, from the lightning as it dazzled murderously again directly overhead. Spurning the dubious protection of the trees, Ralph took them round a bend and down a gentle slope. It was only then that hope beckoned.

The hamlet nestled in a hollow less than a quarter of a mile away. It was only a small cluster of mean houses but it held a promise of welcome hospitality to the travellers at that moment. With their spirits lifted, they quickened their pace even more and tried to ignore the driving rain and the capricious wind which had sprung up to torment them. Shelter was their sole concern. Relief was at hand.

As they got closer to the hamlet, however, they realised that it was a cruel illusion. Glimpsed through the downpour, it had looked like a dry haven in the midst of a roaring tempest. They now saw that it was a crumbling ruin, long deserted by its inhabitants and inconsiderately left to fend for itself against the depredations of time and sustained assaults from inclement weather.

Golde sighed with disappointment and resigned herself to a continued soaking but Ralph spied some comfort. Bringing the bedraggled column to a halt, he took a quick inventory of the settlement. Thatch on the hovels had perished or been burned but there was still a vestigial roof over the small barn, and, though many walls had started to tumble, enough remained to provide a modicum of defence against the storm.

Ralph barked a series of peremptory orders and jabbed at the buildings with his finger. Riders dismounted, horses were tethered, cover was sought. An arm around her shoulders, Ralph conducted Golde into the barn. When they were joined by Gervase and the grumbling Maurice, there was barely enough of the roof left to shield them all. Brother Columbanus stood in the open a few yards away with a benign smile of acceptance on his cherubic features. His tonsure glistened and raindrops ran freely from his nose, chin and ears.

'Come in under the roof,' invited Gervase.

'I am happy enough where I am,' said the monk.

'You will be soaked to the skin.'

'It will refresh me, Gervase. Rain is a gift from God and He does not mean us to flee from it in terror. It is something to be savoured.' He turned his face upward. 'We should offer a prayer of thanks for this blessing.'

'The fellow is mad!' exclaimed Ralph.

'Or downright stupid,' said Maurice. 'Look at the fool!'

'Come over here, Brother Columbanus,' urged Golde, moving closer to the barn wall. 'We have made room for you.'

'There is no need,' the monk assured her, closing his eyes as the water cascaded off his face. 'This rain brings joy. It will enrich the soil and stimulate new growth. It is all part of Nature's pattern. Even the thunder and lightning are sent by God for a purpose.'

'Yes,' said Ralph. 'To frighten the horses.'

'To signal His displeasure, my lord. We should take note of God's rebuke and strive to mend our ways.'

'We would rather strive to keep dry.'

'And so must you,' added Gervase.

Darting out into the rain, he took the monk by the arm and pulled him back under the roof. Brother Columbanus did not resist. He was a short, stocky man in his thirties with an unassailable buoyancy. While others might complain about the setbacks on their journey, Columbanus somehow managed to view them in a kindly and uncensorious light. Gervase liked him but Ralph was irritated by the monk's unrelenting optimism.

The other new member of the commission took a more

sceptical view of the world. Maurice Pagnal looked out at the storm and shook his head in bewilderment.

'What on earth am I doing here?' he wondered.

'Serving the King,' said Ralph.

'How can I serve anyone in weather such as this?'

'You are grown soft, Maurice. Have you so soon forgotten? We came to this country as soldiers, ready to fight in wind, rain, sleet or snow to achieve victory over our enemies. When did we let the weather get the upper hand over us?'

'Never, Ralph,' said the other with a chuckle. 'I recall a time in Yorkshire when we battled in a hailstorm. But my soldiering did not end here in England like yours. I saw service in Sicily and beyond. A helm and hauberk are rough companions in the baking heat. The sun roasted us like chickens on a spit.'

Maurice Pagnal was a grizzled warrior, a wiry man with a craggy face, who had spent most of his adult life in one army or another and had finally retired to his honour in Dorset. He had been asked to join the commissioners when Canon Hubert, their appointed colleague, was indisposed and, for all his protests, Maurice was a willing member of a team sent out to enforce the King's writ. Ralph found his cheerful gruffness infinitely preferable to the pomposity of the canon but Gervase was reserving his judgement on their new fellow. Maurice was a little too rough-hewn for him.

Deprived of the pleasure of attacking them on the open road, the storm intensified its fury, rattling the rafters with a fierce wind and blowing the rain vengefully in at them. Thunder and lightning tortured the horses afresh, and they grew ever more restless. Dispersed throughout the hovels, the soldiers found what cover they could. The hamlet was a poor refuge but it saved them from the worst of the wild afternoon.

Ralph moved his head to avoid a drip through the roof.

'What a dreadful place in which to lodge!' he said.

'I fear that you must take some blame for that,' observed Gervase softly.

'Me?'

'Indirectly.'

'I have never been near this God-forsaken spot before.'

'I think you have, Ralph,' said Gervase. 'Did you not tell me that Duke William led his invading army west along the Thames and crossed the river at Wallingford?'

'Why, so we did,' recalled Maurice. 'Cutting down everyone who stood in our way. Laying waste. You and I were comrades-in-arms, Ralph. We did our share of destruction.'

'Perhaps we did,' admitted Ralph, uneasy about a topic of conversation which would unsettle his Saxon wife. 'But I do not see why we should drag up such memories now. That is all in the distant past.'

'Not to us,' said Golde quietly.

Gervase took in the hamlet with a sweep of his arm.

'Here stands the evidence. Wallingford is no more than a mile or two away. This place must have been raided and its inhabitants killed or driven out. We shall find many such places in Oxfordshire, I believe.'

Golde nodded. 'And in my own county of Herefordshire.'

'War is war,' said Maurice dismissively. 'Resistance had to be put down and that is what we did. It needs no apology.' His face crinkled into a smile. 'And there were benefits to you as well, Golde. If you take the long view. Thanks to the ambition of Duke William, as he then was, you are now married to a Norman lord with fine estates in Hampshire. In some sense, you are a true beneficiary of the Conquest.'

'In some sense,' she confessed. 'But not all.'

Ralph shifted his feet. 'Enough of this idle banter.'

'Gervase has made a fair point,' said Brother Columbanus seriously. 'You and my lord Maurice were part of an army which left a trail of destruction across England. I sincerely hope that both of you did penance for the sins you committed during that time.'

'What sins?' said Maurice defiantly. 'We committed no sins, Brother Columbanus. We merely obeyed orders.'

'You cannot shuffle off responsibility like that.'

'We can do as we wish.'

'Bishop Ermenfrid imposed a series of penances,' said the

monk with disarming mildness. 'Slaughter on such a scale could not be ignored by the Church. That would be a sin in itself. Anyone who killed a man in the great battle of Hastings, for instance, was required to do penance for one year for each man he slew. Anyone who wounded a man . . .'

'Yes, yes,' interrupted Ralph. 'We know all this and do not need your recitation. Why talk of things which happened twenty years ago when we have enough to preoccupy us in the present?'

'Past and present meet in this hamlet,' said Gervase.

Ralph grew testy. 'If it is the only way to shut you up, I will concede your argument. Because a Norman army may – just may, mark you – have once marched through this place, we now have nowhere properly to shelter. If Maurice and I and the rest of us had had the sense to spare this hamlet, we would all be warm and dry at this moment in one of these dwellings. Will that content you, Gervase?'

'Admirably!'

Ralph's outburst broke the tension and they all laughed aloud at the absurdity of his words. He hugged Golde to him and she squeezed his arm affectionately. Marriage to a Saxon woman had made him see his earlier years in England in a different light and he did not like to reflect on them. Gervase was pleased with the way that Brother Columbanus had supported him but unsurprised by Maurice's blunt attitude. All shades of opinion were covered by the makeshift roof.

The five of them shook with inexplicable mirth. Huddled in corners or tucked hard against walls, the rest of the party looked on in blank amazement. What could anyone find to laugh at in the middle of a pelting storm?

Ralph's arm was still around his wife's shoulders.

'Your mantle is sodden, my love,' he noted. 'We really need a fire to get ourselves dry.'

'The sun will do that office in time,' said Columbanus, searching the clouds. 'It will not be long before it peeps through at us again, I fancy.'

Another rumble of thunder seemed to undermine this prediction but there was no lightning this time and the rain was slowly easing. The wind began to lose its bite. The horses were gradually calming down.

'I will be glad to get to Oxford,' said Maurice.

'So will I, my lord,' agreed Gervase, 'but I doubt if they will be as glad to see us.'

'Nobody likes tax-gatherers.'

'We are much more than that, Maurice,' corrected Ralph with a touch of pride. 'We are royal commissioners, empowered to investigate a number of irregularities in the returns from this county. Our task is to root out fraud and felony as well as to assign taxes to their rightful place. It is crucial work but it will not win us many friends.'

'What sort of town is Oxford?' asked Golde.

'A dull one, I hope,' said Maurice with a yawn. 'Dull and dreary. I am so desperately tired of excitement. From what I can judge, our work should be completed in less than a week. Then I can ride back home to Dorset where I belong.'

'Do not count on that,' said Ralph.

'But everything seems so straightforward.'

'It always does. But it never is.'

'Why do you say that?'

Ralph Delchard grimaced and heaved a deep sigh.

'Experience, my friend,' he said. 'Bitter experience.'

Hours later, Bertrand Gamberell was still seething with rage.

'The villain must be caught!' he exclaimed.

'He will be,' said Robert d'Oilly.

'It was foul murder.'

'The crime will be answered, Bertrand.'

'I will tear him to pieces with my bare hands!'

'That would be a ruinous folly on your part.'

'But he killed one of my men.'

'I know,' said the other, 'and I appreciate how you must feel. But do not let anger outweigh common sense. You will not cancel out one murder by committing another. It might assuage your ire but it will also bring you within the compass of the law. Leave this matter in my hands, Bertrand. I will deal with the assassin when he is apprehended.'

'If he is,' said Gamberell sourly.

Robert d'Oilly bristled. 'Do you question my ability and my strength of purpose?'

'No, my lord sheriff.'

'Do you presume to teach me my office?'

'No, my lord sheriff.'

'Then let us hear no more of your complaints.'

Bertrand Gamberell bit back a reply and lapsed into a brooding silence. The two men were riding side by side on their way to Oxford. Behind them was the rough cart on which the dead man lay, his body covered by some sacking, blood still seeping from his wound. Six of the sheriff's knights were in attendance and at the rear of the party, still shocked by the murder of his companion, Gamberell's other soldier pulled Hyperion along on a lead-rein.

Death enforced a slow pace and a sombre atmosphere. No words were spoken for the best part of a mile. Gamberell was fuming inwardly. To lose the race anyway would have been a severe blow to his self-esteem: to be cheated of victory by such vile means was quite unendurable. His mind was a hissing cauldron of retribution. Yet he did not wish to offend the sheriff. Robert d'Oilly was a big, solid man with the broad shoulders and rugged features of a veteran soldier. He held sway over the whole county and was merciless with anyone who sought to question his authority.

It was the sheriff who finally broke the silence.

'His name was Walter Payne, you say?'

'Yes, my lord sheriff.'

'What manner of man was he?'

'The best in my service,' said Gamberell sadly. 'Walter was brave, honest and loyal. A fine horseman, too. He knew how to coax the best out of Hyperion.'

'Hyperion?'

'My stallion. He has never been beaten in a race.'

'Until today.'

'Until today,' repeated the other grimly. 'Someone will be forced to pay for this outrage.'

'Have you any notion who that person might be?'

'None, my lord sheriff.'

'Did Walter have any enemies?'

'I'm sure he did but we do not need to search among them. We must look elsewhere. Walter's misfortune was to be in the saddle today. He was killed in order to stop Hyperion from winning the race. The assassin was really striking at me.'

'Why?'

'Hatred? Envy? Malice? Who can tell?'

'We will root out the truth of this, Bertrand.'

'I hope so, and speedily.'

'All that is needful has been done,' said d'Oilly firmly. 'My men searched the scene of the crime for clues and they are now combing the forest of Woodstock itself.'

'A man could hide for ever in there and elude capture.'

'We will flush him out. And then . . .'

'I'll hang him from the tallest tree.'

'No, Bertrand. He will stand trial in a proper manner. If his guilt be proved, he will not escape the direst sentence.' His voice darkened. 'Nor will you, if you attempt to take the law into your own hands. That is no idle threat but a stern warning. I will brook no meddling. Is that understood?'

Gamberell held back another heated rejoinder. Nothing would be gained by alienating the one man in the county who might be able to track down the assassin. He gave a reluctant nod of consent. The solemn procession moved on. Hyperion let out a long neigh of sorrow by way of an epitaph on his rider.

It was late evening by the time the commissioners reached their destination and Oxford was largely in shadow. That did not dismay them. They were not in the mood for sightseeing. With their bodies weary from the long ride and their apparel damp from the thunderstorm, their main priorities were food, rest and an opportunity to change into fresh clothing. All else could wait until a fitter time.

The only building which they were able to appraise to any degree was the one which opened its huge studded gates to them. Even in hazy silhouette, Oxford Castle was an imposing structure. Like other Norman fortresses which had appeared in such giddy profusion all over England, it followed the standard motte and bailey design, but it differed from most castles in two significant respects. It was built of stone and it was not set up on a commanding height to give it prospect and natural defensive qualities.

Robert d'Oilly, its first constable, had spent over fifteen years constructing and extending Oxford Castle. It stood at the west end of the town and guarded the river approaches with chilling effectiveness. Those in its massive keep or behind its high, forbidding walls were not simply well protected. Their castle was a declaration of Norman intent to maintain their supremacy over the Saxon population of the area. When they looked up at the four-storeyed tower of the church of St George's-in-the-Castle, the citizens of Oxford were not reassured by the presence of religion within a military compound. The fortress was to them a symbol of oppression and – as some of the bolder spirits in the community had discovered – a hideous place of imprisonment.

As they clattered in through the gates, the visitors paid no heed to the more sinister aspects of the castle. All that they saw was an end to a tedious and exacting journey. The steward was waiting to welcome the commissioners and to conduct them to their apartments. Brother Columbanus was taken under the chaplain's wing and guards helped the rest of the party to stable the horses before leading them to their quarters. The newcomers were pleased with their reception.

'This is better than being caught in a storm,' said Ralph.

Golde smiled. 'It is a relief to have a sound roof over our heads at last. I thought that we would never get here.'

'I determined that we would and we did. Are you not grateful to be married to such a masterful man?'

'Profoundly,' she said with a laugh.

'I have all the attributes of a perfect husband.'

'Save one.'

'What is that?'

'Modesty.'

'Perish the thought!'

'You are too ready to trumpet your virtues when they already go before you like lighted torches.'

'That was elegantly put, my love.'

'Take credit for that yourself, Ralph. It was you who instructed me in the finer points of your language. But only because you could not get your tongue around our Saxon vowels.' She began to undress. 'I so long to get out of these wet garments.'

'I will enjoy watching you do it,' he said with polite lechery. 'A day in the saddle with the others has made me yearn for some privacy with my wife.'

They were in a chamber high in the keep. Fresh rushes had been spread on the wooden floor and clean linen was on the bed. It was a serviceable lodging. The window looked out on the bailey but Ralph closed the shutters on the scene below. His attention was concentrated on Golde as she removed her chemise. Even with her back to him, she could read his warm thoughts.

'We do not have time,' she said pleasantly.

'Let us make time.'

'Later.'

'One minute, two minutes.' He ran his hands down her bare arms. 'I can wait that long, Golde.'

'You will have to be more patient than that.'

'Three minutes would test me to breaking point.'

'We are famished, Ralph. How can you even think about it?'

'By looking at you now and being reminded how beautiful you are, my love. And how fortunate I was to find you. You are the one good thing to come out of this ceaseless meandering I do at the King's behest.' He turned her to face him and pulled her close. 'I want you.'

'Stifle your desire until we have eaten.'

'Are you resisting your husband, Golde?'

'No, I am merely putting his empty stomach before my satisfaction.' Ralph gave a ripe chuckle. 'Now change into a dry tunic and you will feel more comfortable.'

'Is that an order?'

'A simple request.'

He kissed her on the lips and took her by the hips to lift her in the air and twirl her in a circle. When her feet touched the floor again she pushed him playfully away. While she dressed herself in fresh apparel, he began to take off his hauberk. There was a feeling of deep contentment between them.

'You have no regrets, then?' he asked.

'Regrets?'

'About riding with us to Oxford.'

'You invited me. I came.'

'But willingly, I hope.'

'Very willingly,' she said. 'I hate to be apart from you even for a short length of time. My only fear is that I will be a hindrance to you.'

'A most delightful hindrance.'

'You are here on urgent business. I am in the way.'

'That is not true at all, Golde.'

'Maurice Pagnal thinks so.'

'Only because he does not yet know you well enough.'

'Canon Hubert knows me well enough yet he is always uneasy in my company. Brother Simon is plainly terrified.'

'Neither of them is here, my love. If you want my opinion, this illness of Hubert's is a true benison. By losing him, we also rid ourselves of that walking cadaver, Brother Simon, who will not stir from his side. In their stead we have Maurice Pagnal and Brother Columbanus. An experienced soldier and a merry monk, sound fellows both, though I could do with less of that Benedictine's affability. I take them to be improvements on the canon and that corpse known as Brother Simon.'

'I still feel out of place, Ralph.'

'That feeling will soon wear off. It has troubled you in

20

the past at first. During our stay in York and then again in Canterbury. Yet in both places you proved your worth to us and rendered practical help.'

'I pray that I may do so again.'

'You will. I sense it.'

He reached across to cup her chin in his hand before placing another kiss on her lips. They looked deep into each other's eyes and forgot all else but their happiness. Marriage had changed both of them in ways they did not foresee and many compromises had been made on both sides. During a tender moment like this, all those compromises seemed a small price to pay for the resultant togetherness. Ralph enfolded her in his arms and held her tight.

The mood was soon shattered. A loving impulse had taken them into the embrace but a sudden commotion forced them instantly apart. Clacking hooves, jingling harness and raised voices seemed to fill the courtyard below. Ralph opened the shutters to look down. Golde stood at his shoulder to see what had caused the untimely tumult.

The castle gates had been flung wide open. Flaming torches had been brought to illumine the spectacle. Four knights in armour rode into the bailey with a prisoner whose hands were bound fast behind his back. The man had been dragged along by ropes and was obviously racked with pain and fatigue. When the prisoner fell to the ground, one of the knights dismounted to haul him roughly to his feet and to spit in his face.

There was harsher treatment to come. A powerful figure in a rich tunic and mantle swept down the steps of the keep with a sword in his hand. His bellowing voice echoed around the courtyard. Shaking with fear, the prisoner fell to his knees in supplication but the newcomer showed no mercy. He grabbed the man unceremoniously to lift him upright before howling an accusation into his face. The prisoner shook his head wildly in denial of the charge. His accuser wasted no more words.

Clubbing him to the ground with the hilt of his sword, he proceeded to kick the prisoner hard until his tongue stopped groaning and his body stopped twitching. On a command from their master, the four knights dragged the captive through the dust to the dungeon.

Golde was appalled by what she had witnessed. As she watched the figure in the tunic stride towards the keep, she was positively trembling with disgust.

'That was barbaric! Who is that man, Ralph?'

He took a deep breath before breaking the news to her.

'Robert d'Oilly,' he said apologetically. 'Our host.'

Chapter Two

Gervase Bret was kneeling at the altar rail when he heard the noise from the bailey. The thick walls of the church partially muffled the sound but it was still loud enough to interrupt his prayers. Lifting his head, he strained his ears to listen but he could make out nothing of what was being said by the angry voices. The distant clamour ended as abruptly as it had begun. A comforting silence invaded the church. Gervase lowered his chin, closed his eyes and surrendered himself once more.

The habit of prayer had been inculcated in him during his time at Eltham Abbey and, though he had elected not to take the cowl at the end of his novitiate, he did not abjure all that he had been taught. Prayer replenished Gervase. It stilled his anxieties, cleansed his soul, offered guidance and allowed him personal communion with his Maker. Prayer never let him down. His simple act of faith and humility was always rewarded with peace of mind.

It was only when he rose to leave that he realised he was not alone in the church. Standing in the shadows at the rear of the nave was a tall, slim figure who seemed to blend with the dark stone itself. The place had been empty when Gervase entered it so the newcomer must have slipped in unnoticed and that made the visitor wary. How long had he been watched at prayer? Why had his privacy been intruded upon? As Gervase walked back down the aisle, the man stepped forward to greet him and flickering candles disclosed his identity at once. He wore clerical garb and moved with the measured tread of someone at ease in the house of God.

'I am Arnulf the Chaplain,' he confirmed in a low and melodious voice. 'You, I believe, are Gervase Bret.'

'That is so.'

'Brother Columbanus spoke fondly of you. He much enjoyed your company on the ride to Oxford. You talked at great length together, I understand.'

'Brother Columbanus thrives on conversation.'

'So I have discovered. I look to have much debate with him myself. He holds you in high esteem.'

'I am flattered.'

'His portrait of you was clearly accurate.'

'In what way?'

'He told me what an unusual person you were.'

'Unusual?'

'Nineteen of you rode into the castle this evening. Tired, damp and hungry after your arduous journey. Apart from Brother Columbanus himself, you are the only member of the party who thought to come here in order to thank God for your safe arrival. That marks you out as very unusual.'

'Most of my companions are soldiers.'

'Say no more. This is a garrison church. I am acquainted with the difficulty of luring soldiers here for regular devotions. It is a problem with which I contend every day.'

He spoke without rancour. Arnulf the Chaplain accepted the role assigned to him and sought to discharge his duties as conscientiously as he could. There was no trace of reproach or self-pity in him. He was a pragmatic Christian.

Gervase's first impressions of the man were wholly favourable. Behind the chaplain's friendly smile, he sensed a keen intelligence and a deep commitment to his ministry. Arnulf had a long, thin, clean-shaven face that tapered towards the chin and positively glowed in the candlelight. Large, kind, watchful eyes were set beneath a high, domed forehead. Though in his early thirties, the chaplain retained an almost boyish enthusiasm. He was neither pious nor judgemental.

'Did you hear the disturbance?' said Arnulf, glancing over his shoulder. 'There was quite a commotion out there earlier on. It was deafening.'

'The noise reached me in here.'

'I thought that it might.'

'Do you know what caused it?'

'Yes. I was in the bailey when they brought him in.'

'Him?'

'The assassin,' explained Arnulf. 'Or so it is alleged. Earlier today, a man was murdered near the forest of Woodstock. My lord sheriff sent out a posse in search of the killer and they have captured him. The fellow now lies in the dungeon, awaiting his fate. If his guilt be established, no mercy will be shown to him.'

'And if he is proved to be innocent of the charge?'

'That seems unlikely. The posse are convinced that they have apprehended the man responsible for this heinous crime.'

'Who was the victim?'

'One of Bertrand Gamberell's knights.'

Gervase raised an inquisitive eyebrow. 'Gamberell?'

'You know him?'

'Only by name. He is to appear before us at the shire hall.' He ran a pensive hand across his chin. 'The timing of this murder is curious. It occurs on the very day that we arrive in Oxford.'

'An unfortunate coincidence.'

'Probably so.'

'What else could it be?'

'Nothing,' said Gervase. 'Nothing at all.'

But his mind was already grappling with another faint possibility. Bertrand Gamberell was locked into an acrimonious property dispute with two rival claimants, Wymarc and Milo Crispin. Gervase was bound to wonder if the murder was in some way connected with that fraught situation. He was not ready to confide in Arnulf until he knew the man better and until more facts about the crime were at his disposal. His suspicion might yet prove to be completely unfounded.

'I would hear more about this,' he said at length.

'Then I will tell you all I know,' offered the chaplain, putting a hand on his sleeve. 'But let us adjourn to the hall while we talk. A meal is waiting for you. Brother Columbanus tells me that you are all starving. You should not deny yourself a moment longer.'

He opened the door and led Gervase out into darkness.

Robert d'Oilly made only the briefest of appearances in the hall to welcome his guests and to assure them that they would want for nothing while they were in his care. He promised to spend more time with them on the morrow when his wife would return from a visit to her relatives and he himself might not be so weighed down with the cares of office. The castellan was unfailingly civil but there was little warmth behind that civility. When he took his leave of them, he did so with an undue alacrity. They felt unwanted.

A meal had been set out on the table for them and Arnulf joined in the repast, showing a genuine interest in them and supplying the cordiality that was so signally lacking in their host. Even Ralph Delchard, with his rooted distrust of all churchmen, began to warm to the chaplain. Golde found him a soothing presence and gradually pushed the memory of Robert d'Oilly's earlier display of brutality to the back of her mind. Arnulf somehow made Oxford Castle seem a more civilised place than she had at first feared. He would be a useful friend to her while her husband was preoccupied with his work as a commissioner, and he promised to act as her guide when she wished to visit the town.

Maurice Pagnal was more interested in the food than in anything else, munching his way noisily through his chicken pasties and flatbread, and washing them down with generous draughts of red wine. Brother Columbanus was the revelation. His predecessor as scribe, the shy, unworldly Brother Simon, rarely ate with the commissioners, preferring the more frugal fare and less boisterous company of a religious house, and never daring to venture an opinion of his own in public lest it bring down ridicule upon him.

Columbanus was an altogether more convivial Benedictine, fond of his food, even fonder of his ale and ready to enter any discussion with beaming eagerness. The more he drank, the more garrulous he became, and Gervase was left to speculate on the motives which had taken such a gregarious man into a closed monastic order. He would not have such freedom of expression when he sat in the chapter house with his brothers. It was almost as if the monk were using the meal to celebrate his temporary release from the cloister.

Arnulf, by contrast, ate little and drank only water yet showed no disapproval of Columbanus's voracious appetite. He encouraged the guests to call for anything they wanted from the kitchens. The strong ale eventually took its toll of the monk. He began to slur his words, sway on his bench and giggle ridiculously to himself. The chaplain took charge of him at once, helping him gently up and half carrying him off to his bed before another cup of ale nudged Columbanus into the realms of disgrace.

Ralph watched it all with a tolerant smile.

'A drunken scribe!' he said. 'That is all we need!'

'Columbanus will not be found wanting,' said Gervase.

'I am sure that he will not,' agreed Golde. 'Even though he differs in every imaginable way from Brother Simon.'

'Indeed he does,' said Ralph amiably. 'Columbanus downed more ale in one night than Simon drinks in a decade. There is a human being inside that black cowl. Brother Simon wears his in the same way that a snail carries his shell. As a place in which to hide from the real world.'

'I loathe monks of all kinds,' confessed Maurice through a loud yawn. 'They are forever trying to prick my conscience about my misdeeds. What misdeeds? Is bearing arms for my King a misdeed? I am not ashamed of anything I have done in my life. Let those sanctimonious brothers stay in their cloisters where they belong and leave us to manage the serious business of keeping the peace in this ungrateful land.'

He gave another involuntary yawn and his lids drooped. With a supreme effort, he lifted himself up from the table.

'Pray, excuse me,' he said to Golde. 'I did not mean to be so unmannerly. Old age is creeping up on me. I am exhausted.' He raised a weary arm. 'I bid you farewell, my friends.'

They waved him off and he staggered out of the hall.

'It is time for us to retire as well,' said Golde.

Ralph nodded. 'Go ahead of me, my love. I will not keep you long. Gervase and I need to speak alone for a moment.'

'Then I will steal quietly away.'

After an exchange of farewells, Golde went off on her own. As soon as she was out of earshot, Ralph leaned across the table towards his friend. His geniality vanished at once.

'What is going on here, Gervase?' he asked.

'Going on?'

'There was uproar down in the bailey earlier on.'

'Yes, I heard it.'

'Robert d'Oilly saw fit to batter some poor wretch senseless. Why? What had the fellow done? Golde was revolted by the sight. It took me an age to persuade her to come here to the hall. Having seen the way that our host dealt with his prisoner, she was refusing even to meet Robert.'

'I noticed that she was tight-lipped in his presence.'

'Thank heaven he did not stay to eat with us! Or Golde would certainly have called him to account. And that would not have advantaged any of us. I love her dearly but she can be outspoken at times.' He drained the last of the wine from his cup. 'Do you have any idea what this is all about?'

'Yes,' said Gervase.

'Well?'

'A horse race.'

Ralph's eyes widened. 'Horse race?'

'Close by the forest of Woodstock.'

'Can this be true?'

'I had it from Arnulf the Chaplain and have been biding my time until I could divulge all the details to you. It is too soon to be certain but they may well have a bearing on our work here.'

28

'How so?'

'Judge for yourself.'

Ralph listened intently as Gervase recounted all that he had heard. Arnulf had gleaned his information from Wymarc himself and it had the ring of truth about it. As the story unfolded, the cruel treatment of the prisoner took on a new meaning though Ralph could still not condone it and he knew that his wife would never forgive or forget it.

'Who is the man?' he asked.

'A slave called Ebbi.'

'And is he guilty?'

'So it is claimed.'

'Where was he taken?'

'In the forest of Woodstock,' said Gervase. 'After a long search they eventually picked up his trail and ran him to earth. He denied all knowledge of the murder but they pinioned him at once.'

'Why?'

'Ebbi was carrying a knife in his belt, not unlike that which was thrown at the rider on the black stallion. That was proof enough for the posse.'

'Do they have no other evidence?'

'They will look to beat a confession out of him in time.'

'And I am sure they will succeed,' said Ralph with a rueful sigh. 'Whether he is guilty or not. He was a small, skinny fellow in tattered clothing. I marvel that such a creature would have the boldness to commit this crime. What motive could he possibly have?'

Gervase shrugged. 'He is a Saxon.'

'So?'

'Look in the returns for this county and you will see motive enough for every Saxon to raise his hand against a Norman knight. They have been dispossessed, Ralph. Before the Conquest, this Ebbi was probably a *bordarius*, a smallholder. Or even a villager. Now he is a mere slave.'

'That may give him cause to resent us but it does not necessarily turn him into an assassin.' He became pensive.

'And why choose one of Gamberell's knights as his victim? A fitter target might have been Bertrand Gamberell himself. Or Milo Crispin. Or even Robert d'Oilly. They rule the roost in this shire. What could Ebbi hope to gain by killing this Walter? It does not make sense.'

'There is another question to ask.'

'Go on.'

'Consider the race itself,' said Gervase. 'Six horses galloping hell-for-leather. Flashing through those trees in a matter of seconds. It would have taken great skill to pick out the right man and hurl a dagger between his shoulder blades. Why choose such a difficult target when far easier ones must have presented themselves?'

'What are you saying?'

'I have grave doubts, Ralph.'

'You think that Ebbi is innocent?'

'I would need much more convincing that he is guilty.'

'The sheriff clearly does not,' said Ralph, recalling the scene he had witnessed. 'It will be a short trial, I fancy. All that we can do is await its outcome.'

'That is the last thing we must do,' argued Gervase.

'Why?'

'Because we are involved here, Ralph. Look at those who entered a horse in that race. Wymarc. Gamberell. Milo Crispin. All three are at the heart of our investigations here. They are contesting ownership of the same property near Wallingford. Could it not be that this murder is in some strange way linked to our business in Oxford?'

'That had not occurred to me.'

'Weigh the notion in the balance.'

Ralph pondered. 'Yes,' he said at length. 'It could be, Gervase. I am at a loss to see quite how. But it could be.'

'That would rule out Ebbi completely, unless he was hired by one of the others. It's conceivable, Ralph, but it seems unlikely. He has no place in our considerations. Put him aside for a moment.'

'Then you would have to find another assassin.'

'Consider what happened. Who stood to gain most by the death of Gamberell's rider?'

'Everyone else in the race.'

'That gives us five suspects immediately.'

Ralph was incredulous. 'One of the other riders was the assassin? Are you insane, Gervase? That is arrant nonsense.'

'Is it?'

'Yes – and plainly so!'

'Six men rode into that copse: only five rode out. Why?'

'Someone hurled a dagger at one of them in the trees.'

'Are you sure?'

'It is the only explanation.'

'I think not,' said Gervase, rising to his feet as he thought it through. 'A dagger can be used to stab as well as to throw. When a horse is running alongside you, it is more than possible to thrust a blade into its rider's back.'

'But according to you, most of the other horses were ahead of Gamberell's stallion at that point.'

'Most but not all.'

'It is a ludicrous idea.'

'Not if you are Wymarc or Milo Crispin. Not if you have placed a heavy wager on your own horses. Not if you are resolved that the black stallion will not beat them yet again.'

Gervase spread his palms. 'Is it really so ludicrous?'

Ralph pondered afresh. 'No,' he conceded after a long pause. 'Not ludicrous, perhaps. But highly unlikely. How could the assassin know that he would be alongside the black stallion as they plunged into those trees? How could he be sure that the other riders would be ahead of him and thus blind to his villainy?'

'He could not.'

'Then your argument must be discarded.'

'Must it? Could not this other rider simply have seized the opportunity when it offered itself? In a hectic race like that, his rivals would have no time to look back at him. Their eyes would have been fixed on the course ahead of them. I still contend that Gamberell's man may have been stabbed.'

'Then we must agree to differ.'

'Very well,' said Gervase. 'Let us move on.'

'To what?'

'The winner of the race. The chestnut colt.'

'That belonged to Milo's subtenant.'

'Ordgar. Once a proud thegn in this county. Reduced from his former glory. He might have the strongest reason of all to take the black stallion out of the race.'

'You surely cannot accuse him,' said Ralph with a mocking laugh as he got up from the bench. 'By all accounts, his horse was vying for the lead when they came out of that copse. Are you seriously suggesting that Ordgar's son tossed a dagger over his shoulder and that it somehow landed conveniently in the back of Gamberell's man?'

'Of course not.'

'It was a race. The son needed both hands on the reins.'

'All I am saying is that Ordgar may somehow be implicated. He stood to forfeit a lot of money if Gamberell won the race. Money which he could ill afford to lose. And he has twenty years of resentment against his Norman overlord to assuage. I think we should look closely at this Ordgar.'

'That brings us back to Ebbi then.'

'Does it?'

'Yes,' said Ralph. 'Perhaps he really did commit the murder. Perhaps we have been too quick to absolve him of guilt. Ebbi may have been Ordgar's hired assassin. Wymarc and Milo Crispin would hardly employ a creature like that to serve their ends. Besides,' he added, 'we should not be maligning respected men with our suspicions. On the evidence we have so far – and I know that it is patchy – there is no reason whatsoever to accuse either Wymarc or Milo. If they were ready to stoop to villainy in order to win that race at Woodstock, they would somehow have disabled Gamberell's black stallion instead of killing its rider. I rely on my instinct here, Gervase.'

'And what does it tell you?'

'Ordgar paid Ebbi to do the deed. That is my guess.'

'It would not be mine.'

'Why not?'

'Because Ebbi was caught too easily,' said Gervase. 'If you can plot such a cunning murder, you will also plan your escape with equal care. I do not believe that the man locked up in that dungeon is the assassin.'

'We shall see,' said Ralph wearily. 'We shall see. One thing is certain. We will not solve this crime by staying up all night and talking about it. We have shot enough arrows in the dark for now. Let us get some sleep. All may become clearer in the morning.'

'I hope so. But I doubt it.'

His companion gave a soulful nod.

'So do I,' he sighed.

'Still here?' gasped Milo Crispin. 'Did the man not go home?'

'He stayed here all night, my lord.'

'Where did he sleep?'

'We found him huddled on the staircase.'

'Old fool!'

'He is determined to see you, my lord.'

'I am far too busy to listen to his ramblings.'

'Ordgar will not be sent away.'

'Then he must be thrown out by force.'

'Is that your order?'

The steward waited patiently while his master took time to reflect. Milo Crispin had no wish to start the day by arguing with one of his subtenants. Ordgar was a nuisance and deserved to be turned away without compunction. At the same time, the problem which had brought the Saxon to Wallingford Castle had to be resolved sooner or later. Ordgar was persistent. He would lurk and harry until he was granted an audience with his overlord. One short discussion now might obviate a lot of irritation in the future.

'Very well,' said Milo, relenting. 'Send him in.'

'Yes, my lord.'

'But warn him to expect no more than a few minutes.'

'That is all he craves.'

33

The steward went out and Milo pored over the accounts on the table in front of him. He was in the hall, a long, low room whose timbered floor creaked beneath any footsteps. He did not look up when Ordgar shuffled into the room. An uncomfortable night had left the old man aching all over but he bore himself with as much dignity as he could muster. To remind him of his subordinate place, Milo kept him waiting for a long time.

'Well?' he said, finally turning his gaze on his visitor. 'Why have you come to bother me so early in the morning?'

'You refused to talk to me yesterday, my lord.'

'We had nothing to talk about.'

'But we did,' insisted the other. 'The race.'

'It has been declared void.'

'On whose authority?'

'Mine.'

'I ask you to think again, my lord.'

'There is no need.'

'But my colt won that race.'

'Only because Hyperion lost his rider.'

'We might still have beaten him,' urged Ordgar. 'Even if there had been no mishap, my colt might still have won. You saw the way he edged out your own horse. I think he would have beaten Hyperion as well.'

'That may be so,' admitted Milo, 'but it was not a fair race. A man was murdered in that copse. One of Bertrand Gamberell's knights. That was no mere mishap but a planned attack. Someone lay in wait for him among those trees.'

Ordgar weighed his words before speaking. He had learned the language of his masters but felt at a severe disadvantage when using it. His position was delicate. He had somehow to press his argument without upsetting his overlord. He ran a nervous hand through his silver beard.

'I regret what happened as much as anyone,' he said with slow deliberation. 'It was a vile murder. I hope that the killer is soon made to pay for his crime. I will do all I can to help to track down the man. But I am bound to ask myself this.' He licked his lips, then drew himself up to his full height. 'If my son, Amalric, had been the victim at Woodstock yesterday and one of *your* horses had won, would the race still have been declared void or would you have claimed the purse?'

Milo smouldered inwardly but kept his poise. There was a grain of truth in the accusation that made it sting even more. Much as he resented the charge, he had a sneaking admiration for the old man who made it. It took courage and that was a quality he acknowledged whenever he met it. At the same time, he was not going to be insulted by one of his subtenants.

'I will not even deign to answer that question,' he admonished. 'For the sake of amity between us, I would prefer to forget that I heard you put it to me.'

Ordgar backed away at once. By offending his overlord, he only weakened his case still more. In all their dealings, Milo Crispin would hold the upper hand. Nothing would change that. Ordgar's voice took on a placatory tone.

'All that I am asking for is fair treatment, my lord.'

'The race is void.'

'I accept that now. I was wrong to criticise your decision.'

'Then why waste my time arguing about it? And why did you spend a night on my stairs?'

'In order to reclaim my share of the wager,' said Ordgar, eager to get some recompense for his aching bones. 'You hold the purse for the race. Please return my stake and I will trouble you no further. Those who helped me to raise the money will want it back now.'

'Then they will have to be disappointed.'

'But we are entitled to the amount we wagered.'

'I will be the judge of any entitlement here, Ordgar. And I will not yield up one solitary coin from that purse. It stays under lock and key here in my castle.'

'But we need it, my lord,' pleaded the other, stepping forward. 'Desperately. We are men of limited means.'

'Then you should not have made such a rash investment.'

'It was a risk worth taking. Our horse won the race.'

'But lost his stake.'

'That is unjust, my lord!'

'The real injustice took place in those trees,' said Milo icily. 'A man was murdered. Bertrand Gamberell's knight may have been killed but his black stallion lives on to run another day. If you wish for your money, you will have to win it in the second race.'

'The second race?'

'Over the same course. Under the same rules.'

'We will need to think about that.'

'Withdraw,' taunted Milo, 'if you have no stomach for another contest. Take your colt out of the race and forfeit your wager.'

'That is a cruel condition to make.'

'The choice lies with you.'

'We will take part,' said Ordgar bravely.

'You may not enjoy such good fortune next time.'

'I have every faith in my horse.'

'He will certainly press Hyperion to the limit, I grant you. Especially with your son in the saddle. Amalric is a true horseman. He got the best out of his mount.'

'No other horse will outrun that black stallion.'

'That may be true. Your colt is fleet of foot.'

'None faster in the whole county, my lord.'

Milo sat back in his chair and regarded the old man through narrowed lids. He thought of the closing moments of the race when his own horse had been found wanting against the chestnut colt ridden by Amalric. And he remembered the size of the purse awaiting the eventual winner. An idea stirred.

'There is one way you may reclaim your money at once,' he said.

'What is it, my lord?'

'Take it in exchange for your colt.'

'In exchange?'

'I am minded to buy the animal off you.'

'But he is not for sale.'

'What use is a horse like that to you, Ordgar?' said Milo smoothly. 'He will be far better off in my stables. He will be well fed and properly trained here. I would be doing you a favour by taking him off your hands.' He gave a smile. 'Yes, I think the time has come for you to part with him.'

'He is ours, my lord.'

'You are getting a fair price for him.'

'We need him to win that race for us.'

'I am sure you do, Ordgar. But I, too, have my needs and I think you will agree that they take precedence over yours.' He waved a dismissive hand. 'Speak to my steward on the way out. He will give you your money.'

The old man was seized by a quiet terror.

Chapter Three

Brother Columbanus was so consumed by guilt at his over-indulgence during the meal that he spent an hour on his knees in the church next morning by way of atonement, vowing to fast throughout the whole day and to forswear ale in perpetuity. He was still chiding himself sternly when he stepped out into the bailey, hoping that the fresh air might bring him fully awake and help to ease his pounding headache. Through bleary eyes, he saw Gervase Bret striding towards the church. The monk's remorse took an even tighter hold on him.

'Good morrow, Brother Columbanus,' said Gervase cheerily. Then he noted the furrowed brow and the pale complexion. 'What is amiss? Are you not well?'

'No, I am not.'

'Do you need to be tended by a doctor?'

'Self-denial is the only medicine I require.'

'What are the symptoms of your illness.'

'A blinding headache and a deep sense of shame.'

'Shame?'

'Yes, Gervase,' said the other. 'My behaviour at table last night was quite unforgivable. I ate too much, drank too much and talked your ears off in the most intolerable way. You must all have been relieved to see the back of me.'

'Not at all. You were congenial company.'

'Gormandising like that? Gluttony is a sin.'

'You had earned a good meal after a day in the saddle. We ate and drank as heartily as you, Brother Columbanus.'

'That is your privilege. You are not bound by the strict

rules of the Order.' He clutched at his breast. 'Oh, what a poor ambassador I am for Saint Benedict! Half a pint of wine is his prescribed allowance for us yet I drank ten times that amount of ale. The only consolation is that Canon Hubert was not here to witness my derelictions. Had he still been a member of the commission, that holy man would have taken me to task for my gross intemperance.'

Gervase stifled a smile as he recalled the numerous occasions in the course of their travels when he had seen Canon Hubert feasting enthusiastically without ever feeling a twinge of conscience about his greed. Columbanus was a more penitent sinner and this was to his credit. Gervase was glad to hear that the monk had resolved never to touch intoxicating drink again. The scribe would certainly need to be sober and clear-headed while sitting alongside the commissioners.

Columbanus had lost much of his erstwhile liveliness. His head was bowed, his shoulders sagged and his confidence had been badly sapped. His manner was almost tentative now.

'Gervase,' he whispered, 'I sincerely hope that this will not rob me of your friendship.'

'There is no chance of that.'

'I value it highly. I would hate to lose your respect.'

'Have no fear on that score, Brother Columbanus.'

'You have my firm promise that I will endeavour to make amends for my conduct in the hall last night. You and your colleagues will have no further cause for complaint.'

'We have none now,' Gervase reassured him. 'You are being far too hard on yourself. Put the whole matter behind you.'

'That is what I will strive to do.'

'Good.'

'And you will not mention this incident to Canon Hubert?'

'I would not dream of it.'

Columbanus brightened. 'A thousand thanks, Gervase. I knew that you would show compassion. I said as much to Arnulf. You have lifted a huge weight from me. I am ever in your debt.'

After another burst of apologies, he excused himself and set off across the bailey. There was far more colour in his cheeks now and something of the old spring in his stride. Gervase was glad to observe these early signs of recovery. Contrition had taken all the ebullience out of Columbanus and crushed his spirit. Gervase preferred the animated companion of the previous two days.

He was just about to go into the church when a familiar voice hailed him. Gervase turned to see Arnulf the Chaplain sailing towards him. They exchanged a warm greeting.

'Did you sleep well, my friend?' asked Arnulf.

'Very soundly.'

'And your fellows?'

'They seemed well rested when we shared breakfast.'

'Brother Columbanus had a more troubled night.'

'So I hear.'

'I saw nothing in his behaviour to condemn,' said the chaplain with a wry smile, 'but he seems to feel that he committed seven deadly sins and danced naked with the devil. He was terrified that he would be given a sharp reprimand.'

'I put his mind at rest about that,' said Gervase. 'But I was hoping to see you before we left for the shire hall. I wanted to find out more about the prisoner.'

'Then you could not have come at a better time.'

'Why do you say that?'

'I have just visited him in his dungeon.'

'Ebbi?'

'He asked to see the priest from his parish church but my lord sheriff denied that request. Ebbi had to make do with me instead. My command of his language is uncertain but we did manage to have a conversation of sorts.'

'What did he want?'

'What anyone in his predicament wants, Gervase. Help. Kindness. Reassurance. Even a glimmer of hope.'

'Were you able to give him that hope?'

'Alas, no. His prospects are grim. He knows that.'

'Only if he was guilty of the murder.'

'Yes,' said Arnulf uneasily. 'Only then.'

'And that guilt has yet to be proved. From what you told me about this Ebbi, he seems an unlikely assassin. Was that the impression you formed when you spoke to him?'

'I did not discuss his crime with him.'

'His alleged crime,' corrected Gervase.

'Ebbi neither confessed his guilt nor pleaded innocence. And even if he had, I would not be at liberty to reveal to you what he said. He called for a priest for a particular reason.'

'What was that?'

'To ask a favour,' said the other softly. 'In the event of his being convicted – and he is fitting his mind to that dreadful probability – he begged me to carry a message to his family and friends. I could not refuse such an entreaty.'

'He must be in despair.'

'Completely.'

'What kind of man is he?'

'Old before his time, Gervase. Tired, scrawny, ragged.'

'Yet capable of this murder?'

'That is not for me to say.'

'Where does Ebbi dwell?'

'Close by the forest of Woodstock.'

'Who owns that land?'

'My lord Wymarc.'

'Has Ebbi fallen foul of the law before?'

'I have no idea.'

'Did you learn nothing of his past history?'

'Nothing,' said Arnulf with a shrug. 'It was a very short conversation. I have told you all that passed between us.'

Gervase studied him carefully. He could not decide if the chaplain was being totally honest or politely obstructive. Arnulf met his gaze without flinching.

'It is my turn to ask a favour,' said Gervase.

'What is it?'

'If you visit Ebbi again, take me with you.'

'But why?'

'I am curious to meet him.'

Arnulf stiffened. 'He is not a wild animal to be peered at

through the bars of his cage. Curiosity is an insufficient excuse, my friend.'

'My interest goes well beyond that. May I come?'

'Only my lord sheriff could sanction such a visit.'

'Will you speak to him on my behalf?'

Arnulf took a long time to consider the request.

'If you wish,' he agreed at length, 'but he is bound to question your motives.'

'Tell him that I wish to help his chaplain.'

'Help me?'

'Yes,' said Gervase. 'You had difficulty holding a proper conversation with Ebbi. I would not. My mother was a Saxon and I am fluent in the language. Ebbi will be able to speak more freely to you through me. That is what you can tell my lord sheriff. You need my assistance.' He flicked a glance towards the dungeons. 'Gervase Bret is your interpreter.'

Robert d'Oilly was giving instructions to his steward when Ralph Delchard came down the staircase in the keep. The sheriff dismissed his man at once and gave the newcomer a guarded smile of welcome.

'Well met!' he said with false affability. 'I am sorry to have been such an indifferent host thus far but you came upon us at a particularly awkward time.'

'So I observed.'

'A murder was committed at Woodstock yesterday.'

'We have heard the bare facts of the case.'

'A miserable slave had the sheer audacity to kill one of Bertrand Gamberell's men. A verminous Saxon killing a Norman knight. That makes the crime doubly heinous.'

'If the prisoner is indeed guilty,' noted Ralph.

'There is no doubt of that.'

'He has confessed?'

'Confession was not needed,' said d'Oilly irritably. 'He was found hiding close by the scene of the crime with a weapon about him identical to that used in the murder.'

'Identical, my lord sheriff? Or similar?'

'It amounts to the same thing.'

'Not quite.'

'What do you mean?'

'Have you examined the two daggers side by side?'

The sheriff bridled. 'Who is in charge of this inquiry?' he snarled. 'You or me?'

'You, of course.'

'Then I will thank you to let me get on with it. I need no prompting from you or from any other man. I speak for the King in Oxford. You would do well to remember that.'

'I am sure that I will have little opportunity to forget.'

The tart rejoinder made his host redden with anger. Ralph was a sturdy man but Robert d'Oilly towered over him. Their eyes engaged in a brief battle of wills and Ralph did not cede an inch of ground under the other's intimidating glare. The sheriff eventually calmed and tried to dispel the tension with a throaty chuckle.

'A host should not be arguing with his guest,' he said.

'I take my share of the blame.'

'Let us start afresh, shall we not? As true friends.'

'We are honoured by your hospitality, my lord sheriff.'

'I am delighted to offer it to you. The reputation of Ralph Delchard is not unknown here. It has gone before you. I have heard how sedulous you have been in your high office.'

'It is onerous work at times but someone has to do it.'

'The King chose well when he selected you.'

Ralph wondered why there was such a sudden change in his manner. A man who could move so swiftly from antagonism to flattery was not to be trusted. Something lay behind the surface bonhomie and Ralph soon learned what it was.

'I believe that you sit in session today,' said d'Oilly.

'That is true. I am on my way to the shire hall now.'

'You will no doubt be an upright judge.'

'We view each case on its individual merits.'

'That is as it should be,' said the other, moving closer. 'Justice must be paramount. I am sure you will apply that principle when the dispute concerning Islip comes before you this morning.'

'How do you know that it will be considered today?'

'Little of importance escapes my notice in Oxford.'

Ralph sensed what was coming. He realised that it was no chance encounter. Robert d'Oilly had been deliberately waiting to intercept him. A request was in the offing.

'Lady Azelina has the prior claim on that property,' said the sheriff airily. 'I can save you and your colleagues a lot of time and trouble here by giving my personal endorsement to her cause. If you wish, you may summon me as a witness on her behalf but I trust that this private word between us will carry enough weight in itself.'

'Any decisions we reach will be made in the privacy of the shire hall,' affirmed Ralph, 'and we have no reason to summon you to give evidence, my lord sheriff.'

'You know my mind,' said the other meaningfully.

'I hope you are not seeking to apply undue influence.'

'Advice is all that I have offered.'

'Then let me give you some in return,' said Ralph with a steely grin. 'We must be impartial at all times. The only reason we accepted your hospitality was that you are not involved in any of the disputes we have come to settle. It would have been quite improper for us to stay under the roof of Milo Crispin or Bertrand Gamberell or the lady Azelina or anyone else listed for examination. You appreciate that?'

'Of course,' grunted d'Oilly.

'It would have laid us open to charges of favouritism.'

'I accept that.'

'Then my advice is this. Refrain from giving any more yourself, my lord sheriff. If I thought you were trying to affect our decision in any way, I would quit the castle with the other commissioners and seek out a lodging in the town. Is that what you wish us to do?'

Robert d'Oilly accorded him a grudging smile.

'I wish you to carry out your duties unimpeded,' he said. 'I am sorry that you choose to misunderstand me. Just bear in

mind that I will still be here when you leave the shire. I will
have to live with the consequences of your judgements.'

'Do I hear a threat in that remark?'

The sheriff gave an elaborate shrug of the shoulders.

'What could I hope to gain by threatening Ralph Delchard?'

The question hung in the air between them.

When Ordgar returned to his house, his son was grooming
the chestnut colt outside the stable. The horse's coat shone
in the morning sunshine. Amalric began to comb his mane
with meticulous care. As he heard the approach of footsteps,
he broke off and turned to see his father.

'Where have you been?' he asked with concern.

'Wallingford.'

'All night?'

'He refused to see me until this morning.'

'Refused!' Amalric smarted at the insult. 'Milo Crispin kept
you waiting that long? Did you not protest?'

'Several times,' said Ordgar. 'And with vehemence. But all
to no avail. And so I refused to leave the castle until I had
talked to him. My lord Milo owes me some respect. I was not
going to be shrugged off by him.'

'You should have taken me with you. I would have ham-
mered on his door until he consented to speak to us.'

'That would only have annoyed him even more.'

'But we have right on our side, father.'

'It is not enough, Amalric.'

Ordgar lowered himself down on to the edge of the stone
water trough. The ride from Wallingford had taxed his already
depleted strength and the sad tidings he bore weighed heavily
upon him. Amalric, on the other hand, was young, alert and
bursting with energy. Ordgar thought wistfully of a time when
he had had his son's zest. The old man also had rank, property
and influence in the shire in those days. So much had changed
for the worse in the intervening years.

'Did you get the purse?' asked Amalric.

'No, son.'

'But it was ours. I won that race.'

'It has been declared void.'

'They cannot do this to us!'

'They can, Amalric.'

'It is sheer spite!' fumed the other. 'They are peeved because we beat the very best of their Norman horses.'

'All except Hyperion.'

'Had he stayed in the race, I'd have beaten him as well.'

'But he did not, Amalric, and that alters everything. It was not a fair race, they say, so the purse will not be awarded.'

'Did you not at least reclaim our share of it?'

'I tried,' said Ordgar with a sigh. 'I tried.'

'Then where is it?'

'My lord Milo would not yield it up.'

'But that money came from many hands. They expect it back. Our friends supported us. Are we to tell them that we won the race but lost their stake?'

'We have harsher news than that to pass on.'

Amalric started. 'Harsher, you say?'

'I fear so,' said the old man, shuddering at the memory of his ill-fated visit to Wallingford Castle. 'I was wrong to press my lord Milo so soon after the event. I should have let time elapse. He might not have been so vindictive then.'

'What did he say? What has he done?'

'Held on to the purse until the race is run again with a new rider in Hyperion's saddle.'

'This news is not so harsh,' said Amalric confidently. 'It gives us a second chance to win what is already rightly ours. Let me race again. We will beat Hyperion and any other horse they care to set against us.' He patted the colt's neck with a proud hand. 'Cempan is a match for anyone. When I am riding him, there is no way that we can lose.'

'But you will not be riding him in the race.'

'Why not?'

'Milo Crispin wishes to buy Cempan from us.'

Amalric was stunned. 'Buy him?' he echoed. 'Buy Cempan?'

'I fear so.'

'He is ours. We will never part with him.'

'We may be forced to, Amalric.'

'I'd sooner destroy the colt than sell him. Whatever price we are offered, we will turn it down. Cempan belongs to us.' He saw the pain in his father's eyes. 'You surely did not agree to this sale? That would be a betrayal.'

'I betrayed nobody,' said Ordgar with a flash of defiance. 'When I left Wallingford, I refused to take the money that was offered in exchange for Cempan. That was the worst outrage of all. Do you know what my lord Milo offered to pay? Nothing!' He spat contemptuously on the ground. 'Nothing, Amalric!'

'But you talked of refusing money.'

'That was only our wager in the race. Milo Crispin wishes to buy Cempan from us with money that is already our own. We would be letting him have the colt free.'

'He is robbing us!'

'That is why I stormed out of the castle.'

'He will not touch Cempan,' vowed Amalric, putting a protective arm around the animal's neck. 'Whatever happens, he will not steal our horse. Milo Crispin and his men will have to get past me first.'

'That is not the answer,' said a forlorn Ordgar. 'They are many, we are few. They have force on their side. We will have to find another solution.' He clutched at a last straw. 'Let us wait until Edric returns. He will know what to do. We must ask for Edric's help. He will be back any day now.'

Amalric was about to agree when a voice interrupted them.

'Father!'

Holding up the hem of her kirtle, the girl came bounding across to him from the house. Bristeva was only fifteen but she had the shapely figure of a woman allied to the bloom of youth. Long, lustrous, flaxen hair trailed down her back. Ordgar rose to take his daughter into a warm embrace.

'Where have you been?' she asked, tears in her eyes.

'To Wallingford.'

'We have been worried sick about you.'

'I am safely back home now, Bristeva.'

48

'Thank God! I did not sleep at all last night. I was afraid that something dreadful must have happened to you.'

Ordgar pulled her closer and stroked her hair.

'It did,' he whispered to himself.

Whatever reservations he might have about their host, Ralph Delchard had none about the town reeve. The man had acted with commendable efficiency. Warned in advance by letters of their arrival and their particular needs, the reeve had everything in readiness for them at the appointed time. The shire hall had been swept clean and four chairs had been set behind a table at one end of the room. Benches had been arranged in front of the table. There were even cushions on the front bench.

A pitcher of water and four cups awaited the commissioners as they trooped into the hall. A flagon of wine and a jug of beer had also been provided for their refreshment. Maurice Pagnal was especially pleased to see the wine but Brother Columbanus was dismayed by the sight of the beer. Gervase Bret moved it well away from him. The monk poured water into his cup and drained it at a gulp. His spirits revived.

The shire hall was a nondescript room with a low ceiling held up by thick beams and only limited natural light coming in through the windows, but it was more than adequate for their purposes. Even the musty atmosphere did not irritate them. Four soldiers stood at the rear of the hall and another four were on sentry duty outside.

When they took their seats with their documents in front of them, the commissioners were an imposing trio. Resplendent in a white tunic and red mantle, Ralph sat between Maurice, ever the soldier, in his hauberk, and Gervase in the sober attire of a Chancery clerk. Keen to impress them, their scribe reached for his quill long before it was required.

Ralph turned to the new and untried commissioner.

'Are you ready for the first assault, Maurice?' he said.

'More than ready, Ralph. The case is crystal clear.'

'We have not heard the disputants yet.'

'I am surprised that we need to. My mind already inclines one way. This will be a very brief session, I think.'

'Then you are wrong, my lord,' said Gervase pleasantly. 'The arguments are more finely balanced than they may appear at first. I'll wager that we reach no resolution today.'

'Then the sooner we start, the better,' decided Ralph.

He gave a signal and one of the guards left the hall. When the man returned, he was accompanied by two witnesses of strikingly different appearance and character. Azelina, wife of Roger d'Ivry, was a tall, gracious Norman lady with a mature beauty which arrested every eye. She wore a blue gown over a white linen chemise. Coiled at the back, her hair was covered by a wimple. Her girdle was a long silken rope, wound around her narrow waist, with its tasselled ends hanging almost down to the hem of her gown. She moved with exquisite grace.

Brother Timothy, by contrast, hobbled into the room as if his diminutive feet were tied together. The black cowl was tailored for a much larger monk and it made an already small man look absurdly tiny. Long sleeves hid his hands, his hem scraped the wooden floor and the thick folds obscured much of his chin and cheeks. When the commissioners took a closer look at him, they realised that the cowl might not, after all, be such a grave sartorial mistake, because Timothy had an ugliness that bordered on the grotesque.

A huge, bulbous nose sat right in the middle of a pasty countenance that was apparently assembled from discarded features of a dozen other misshapen faces. Nothing seemed to fit. Any garment which hid even part of his grisly visage was performing a valuable service. Beside a woman of such elegance and comeliness, Brother Timothy looked plainly ridiculous.

Ralph rose to his feet to welcome Azelina and to invite her to take a seat. While she lowered herself on to a cushion, Ralph suppressed the urge to stare in disbelief at Timothy and indicated that he, too, should be seated.

'I am surprised to see you here in person, my lady,' said Ralph, settling back into his own chair. 'I thought perhaps you would send your steward to speak in your stead.'

'I am well able to defend myself, my lord,' she said.

'We do not doubt it,' observed Maurice with gallantry.

'With my property under threat, I would not dream of sending a deputy to fight on my behalf. This is far too important a matter to be relegated to anyone else.'

Her voice was soft and compelling, a musical instrument in itself. Ralph had to force himself to look across at the monk.

'You, Brother Timothy, speak for the abbey of Westminster.'

'That is so, my lord,' said the other meekly.

'Then we have a case of Church versus State on our hands.'

After introducing himself and his colleagues, Ralph called upon Gervase to read out the relevant passage from the returns which had been sent to Winchester by the earlier team of commissioners who visited the county. Gervase first recited the information in its original Latin and gained an approving nod from Brother Timothy. Azelina was motionless.

'"Land of Roger d'Ivry's Wife,"' translated Gervase. '"Roger d'Ivry's wife holds 5 hides in Islip from the King. Three of these hides never paid tax. Land for 15 ploughs. Now in lordship 3 ploughs; 2 slaves. 10 villagers with 5 smallholders have 3 ploughs. A mill at 20 shillings; meadow, 30 acres; pasture, 3 furlongs long and 2 wide; woodland, 1 league long and 1½ leagues wide. The value was £7 before 1066; when acquired £8; now £10. Godwin and Alwin held it freely."' He glanced up at Azelina who was now listening carefully. '"Roger d'Ivry's wife also holds 3 hides and ½ a virgate of land in Oddington. She holds these two lands in commendation from the King."'

As soon as Gervase finished, Ralph turned to Azelina.

'Have you anything to add, my lady?' he asked.

'The document enforces my right to that property,' she said reasonably. 'If anyone challenges that right, the burden of proof lies on them.'

'Not so, my lady,' argued Brother Timothy. 'Our claim pre-dates yours and renders it invalid. That is why Abbot Gilbert has sent me here to present our case. There are aspects of this dispute which did not come to light during the visit of the first commissioners. What has just been read out to us was set down in error.'

'No error, I do assure you,' countered Azelina.

'An honest one but no less troublesome for all that.'

'The land was given to me, Brother Timothy.'

'The returns make that clear,' added Maurice helpfully.

'With respect, my lord,' said the little monk, 'they do not. They merely perpetuate a grave mistake.' He turned to Ralph. 'Do I have your permission to proceed at length?'

'State the case for the abbey,' encouraged Ralph.

'Then I will.'

Brother Timothy cleared his throat and took control.

'Islip is probably only a name on a document to you, my lords,' he began, 'and I feel that you should know something of its nature before you decide who rightly holds the land. It is a charming village. Islip straddles a hill that is undercut by the River Ray near its junction with the River Cherwell. The soldiers among you would appreciate its strategic value at once because, in floodtime, Islip Bridge is on the only dry route between north and south. In 1065, when the Northumbrians rebelled against Earl Tosti, they drove south across the bridge and caused hideous damage to Islip itself.'

'God's tits!' muttered Maurice, rolling his eyes upward. 'Is there much more of this homily?'

'But it has another special claim on our attention,' continued Timothy, well into his stride. 'Islip was the birthplace of King Edward of blessed memory and he was baptised in the font of the parish church there. As a gesture of kindness for which we are eternally grateful, the King gave the holding to his beloved foundation of St Peter's, Westminster, or, as it is now known, Westminster Abbey. There, in essence, is our claim. Islip came to us by royal decree and it is still legally and morally ours. Ten main reasons can be advanced in support of our claim.'

Brother Timothy was a remarkable advocate. His mild manner gave way to a driving confidence and his unsightly

52

features took on an animation that made them almost human. So cogent was his argument, so startling his control of language and so effortless the flow of his rhetoric that nobody else had an opportunity to speak for over an hour. Even the hitherto unsympathetic Maurice was forced to revalue the monk. In choosing Brother Timothy as his spokesman, Abbot Gilbert of Westminster had sent his most powerful weapon.

Azelina was neither cowed nor distracted by the skilful performance of her rival. She spoke with great feeling about her love for Islip and about the honour she felt when it was granted to her by King William. Her arguments tended to be emotional as well as legal but they were no less effective for that. Maurice found himself nodding in agreement with her as she contradicted the abbey's claim. Along with Ralph and Gervase, he put a number of questions to Azelina and found her resolute in her answers.

They were well into the afternoon before the two rivals finally paused to catch their breath. Maurice was impatient.

'The debate is over,' he said gratefully. 'All we have to do now is to reach our verdict.'

'There is no chance of that yet,' Ralph pointed out.

'Is there not?'

'No, my lord,' said Gervase. 'We have only watched the opening skirmish. The battle will not be properly joined until we have viewed all the documentary evidence from both sides.'

Maurice gasped. 'Documentary evidence?'

'I have brought a deposition from Abbot Gilbert himself,' said Timothy, patting the satchel beside him, 'and a collection of charters from our archives. They need the most careful perusal by you.'

'I, too, have royal charters to present,' said Azelina, not to be outdone. 'My steward has them. He stands without.'

'Then we will be pleased to have them along with the documents from the abbey,' said Ralph, on his feet again. 'All will receive our close attention before we can proceed. That being the case, I thank you both for appearing before us and adjourn this session until the same time tomorrow morning.'

Gervase escorted Azelina out of the hall while Brother Columbanus relieved Timothy of his satchel. Several hours of work remained for the commissioners. Maurice was dejected.

'Will every case be as interminable as this?' he moaned.

'No,' said Ralph with a grin. 'Most will be much longer.'

'This is Purgatory!'

'I thought we had a profitable day in here, Maurice.'

'Listening to that mad monk preaching a sermon?'

'He marshalled his argument well.'

'Yet Islip patently belongs to the lady Azelina.'

'That is a matter of opinion,' said Ralph, moving away, 'and I have no time to discuss mine with you now. I want to make best use of the light while I can. It is a tidy ride.'

'Ride?'

'To Woodstock.'

Chapter Four

It was late afternoon before Arnulf the Chaplain was able to fulfil the promise he had given to Golde the previous night. They met at the castle gates.

'I am sorry to keep you waiting,' he said. 'It must have been very tedious for you to be cooped up here all day without amusement or female companionship.'

'It was rather dull,' she admitted, 'but I cheered myself with thoughts of this walk through Oxford with you.'

'What would you like to see, my lady?'

'Everything.'

'Then let us begin.'

He led her out of the castle then swung right towards the centre of the town. Golde felt an immediate sense of release. All that she had learned about Robert d'Oilly made her want to keep well away from him and she could, in any case, never be entirely comfortable in a Norman garrison. Pungent smells from assorted trades wafted into her nostrils but it was still refreshing for her to be mingling with the ordinary citizens in the street even if her fashionable apparel set her apart from the Saxon womenfolk and induced some hostile glances.

Oxford was a loud, lusty, bustling town with a population of over three and a half thousand, enlarged by those who streamed in from the outlying areas to its thriving market. Dogs barked, children cried, horses whinnied and carts rolled to add to the general pandemonium. Arnulf had to raise his voice to be heard above the din of a blacksmith's hammer and anvil.

'What do you think of Oxford?' he asked.

'It is much bigger than I expected,' said Golde. 'It makes my own home town seem very small.'

'Where is that?'

'Hereford.'

'How many inhabitants do you have?'

'Barely a thousand.'

'Only London, Winchester and York are substantially larger than us,' he said with evident pride, 'and we think that Oxford is prettier than all three. I was born and brought up in Falaise myself but I have been here long enough to take the town to my heart. In time, I trust, we will come to blend in more harmoniously.'

'Why do you say that?'

'Look around you, my lady. Most of these people still view us as an army of occupation rather than as a source of protection for the whole community. After all these years, they have the same suspicion and resentment. That is why I have tried so hard to reach outside the castle walls to the local people.'

'In what way?'

'Visiting them, talking to them, helping them with their problems, showing fellowship, even nursing them through injury and illness on occasion, for I have some skill as a doctor. In short, my lady, doing exactly what a parish priest should be doing for his flock. Then, of course, there is the church choir.'

'Choir?'

'Yes,' he said, face aglow, 'it is a labour of love. Choral singing is the true perfection of Christian worship. I have devoted much time and effort to it. And since the garrison can hardly provide me with my choristers, I have come out in search of them.'

'Boys from the town?'

'Boys and girls, my lady. The female voice is every bit as beautiful as that of the young male. I had to endure much criticism when I first introduced girls as choristers but they have won over all but the most narrow-minded.'

'A mixed choir,' said Golde, excited by the notion. 'I wish I had been able to sing in church when I was a girl. I would have adored it. But it was not considered proper in Hereford.'

'Some of my young ladies sing like angels.'

She was drawn to him even more. Arnulf was a considerate man with natural charm. His easy companionship was the perfect antidote to her poisonous memories of Robert d'Oilly. The chaplain was the human face of Oxford Castle.

When they reached the crossroads, he guided her down the hill towards Grandpont, the stone bridge over which she had ridden on her arrival. Initiated by the sheriff, it was a solid structure which spanned the river at a critical point and provided a vital link with southern England. Traffic was crossing the bridge in both directions. Golde admired the work of the stonemasons then lent over the parapet to watch the rippling waters of the Thames. A rowing boat went past beneath her. Fishermen were walking along the bank. Birds abounded.

'A pretty place, indeed,' she remarked.

'And peaceful now, thank heaven! Oxford has had more than its share of bloodshed and suffering. All that is past.'

They went back up the hill and turned into the straggling High Street which ran eastwards down the slope. The crowd had thickened even more now and they had to dodge the jostling elbows with the same adroitness they showed in stepping over the occasional piles of refuse or excrement. Arnulf pointed out all the buildings of interest, especially the churches, but Golde was curious about those which were no longer there. Down each street and lane, she caught a glimpse of derelict houses and empty shops.

'Why are so many houses in decay?' she wondered.

'The scars of war, alas!'

'Here are some more,' she noted as they passed a row of five abandoned dwellings in the High Street. 'Did nobody think to rebuild these homes?'

'It takes time, my lady,' said Arnulf sadly. 'But your husband will be in the best position to tell the full extent of the spoliation here.'

'My husband?'

'Written in the Domesday Book, as it has come to be known, are the sorry details of the town's plight. There are almost a thousand houses in Oxford but you can see for yourself that a sizeable number are in such poor condition that no taxes can be levied upon them.'

'Were they in this state when Robert d'Oilly first came?'

'I was not myself here then,' he said evasively.

'Was he not responsible for some of this destruction?'

Arnulf became defensive. 'My lord sheriff has done a great deal for Oxford. He built the castle, constructed Grandpont and set in motion a number of other important projects.'

'Yet he allows these ruins to disfigure the town. What happened to all the people who once lived in these houses?'

'They moved out.'

'Or died in their homes,' she concluded.

Golde was in a more solemn mood as they headed towards the church of St Peter's-in-the-East. Oxford had clearly suffered greatly. The chaplain sought to rekindle her good humour.

'Your husband is a remarkable man,' he observed.

'Yes,' she agreed. 'Ralph is quite unique.'

'How did you first meet?'

'In the course of his visit to Hereford. He came to the town with the other commissioners to investigate some abuses that had come to light. Our paths crossed.'

'A fortunate encounter. You are well matched.'

Golde smiled. 'It did not seem so at first. I found him arrogant and uncaring beyond measure.'

'And now, my lady?'

The smile broadened out into an unashamed grin.

'I am married to the finest man in the world.'

Ralph Delchard enjoyed the ride to Woodstock. He and his two knights covered the seven miles at a steady pace, moving through open countryside that was dotted with small herds of sheep or cows. Men toiled in fields or tended animals or

worked in watermills. Laden with salt, a cart trundled past
them on its way to Oxford. After the mouldy atmosphere of
the shire hall, Ralph found the keen air bracing.

When they were close to their destination, they left the road
to cut across the fields and were soon accosted by four armed
knights from Wymarc's retinue, demanding to know why they
were trespassing on private property. Ralph introduced himself
and told them that he was staying with Robert d'Oilly in Oxford
Castle. The sheriff's name was a ready passport and the men
became more amenable. At Ralph's suggestion, one of them
went to summon his master from his nearby manor house while
the others obligingly conducted the strangers to the edge of the
forest where the race had taken place.

Seizing on the unexpected opportunity to ingratiate himself
with one of the commissioners, Wymarc spurred his horse
into a gallop. Ralph Delchard would preside over the property
dispute in which Wymarc was involved and the latter was keen
to gain any advantage over his rivals. He never stopped for a
moment to question Ralph's motives for wanting to examine
the scene of the crime. When he greeted his visitor, his manner
verged on the obsequious.

'How may I help you, my lord?' he asked, grinning helpfully. 'I understand that you have taken an interest in the foul
murder that was committed here yesterday.'

'That is so,' said Ralph.

'How much do you know of what happened?'

'Little beyond the bare facts and those were third-hand. The
account came indirectly from Bertrand Gamberell and I would
appreciate another version of events.'

Wymarc glowered. 'Bertrand's account is not to be trusted.
He is too incensed to give you a calm and accurate description
of what took place.' The slavish grin resurfaced. 'I will be glad
to correct any false information from Bertrand.'

'Please do,' invited Ralph.

He settled back in the saddle to listen. Wymarc launched
into his account of the race, introducing a lot of new details
but departing very little from the basic facts of the case

as they had already reached Ralph. What was plain was
Wymarc's deep hatred of Bertrand Gamberell. At no point
did he express the slightest sympathy for the dead man and
he took a grim satisfaction from the fact that Hyperion had
not won the race.

'Now you know the truth of it, my lord,' said Wymarc.

'You have given an exact chronicle of events,' said Ralph
with submerged irony, 'and I am grateful to you. When the race
was in progress, where exactly were you and the others?'

'I will show you.'

Wymarc took them across to the hillock from which he,
Gamberell and Milo Crispin had watched the race. The posts
were still in place to designate the course.

'You had an excellent view,' noted Ralph.

'We always chose this vantage point.'

'Always? Horses have raced over this course before?'

'Yes, my lord. When Bertrand first challenged us, I claimed
the right to designate a course on my land.'

'He did not object?'

'Not in the slightest. He was so confident of Hyperion's
ability to win over any course that he was happy to leave
the task to me. And so it proved,' he said with a frown. 'That
black stallion was unbeatable the first three times we put our
horses against him.'

'So yesterday was the fourth race over this course?'

'It was.'

'And the other three passed off without incident?'

'Completely.'

'When was the first race?'

'Six months ago.'

'The horses ran through that same copse?'

'Into it and out of it, my lord, on each occasion.'

'Who competed in the earlier races?'

'All three of us.'

'What about Ordgar?'

'No,' said Wymarc with contempt. 'We did not bother to
invite him. We only let him run yesterday because he begged

us to include his colt. Somehow he found enough for the wager so he was allowed into the race. Against my wishes, I may say.'

'Why?'

'I do not like the fellow.'

'Because he is a Saxon?'

'There are many other reasons.'

'Did you fear that his colt might defeat your horses?'

'Of course not!' declared Wymarc unconvincingly.

Ralph took another long look at the course below him.

'Where was Ordgar when the race took place?' he said.

'Near the finishing line, my lord.'

'Not beside you?'

'We did not indulge him to that extent.'

'So he would not have had the same view of Hyperion as you did when the horse was ridden into the trees?' Wymarc shook his head. 'Show me where you found the murder victim.'

'Follow me.'

Wymarc led them down the incline but Ralph asked him to dismount when they reached the edge of the copse. The two of them went on foot into the trees. Wymarc had no difficulty locating the exact spot where the body was found. On soft ground that was liberally marked with hoofprints there was a long smooth patch that came to an end in some tufted grass. Wymarc pointed to the dried blood still visible on the turf.

'That is where he lay, my lord.'

'But that is not where he was struck by the dagger,' said Ralph, looking over his shoulder. 'I think that he was back there when he was attacked, fell from his horse where we see that shallow dip in the ground and rolled along until he reached this point.' He knelt to inspect the bloodstains. 'You searched thoroughly for the assassin?'

'Behind every tree and under every bush.'

'No sign of him at all?'

'None, my lord,' said Wymarc. 'Hours later, they found him in the forest. He obviously fled there after commiting the deed.'

'Which way did he flee?'

He stood up to walk with his guide towards the rear of the copse. They came into an open field that was a hundred yards at least from the forest of Woodstock. Ralph assessed how long it would have taken the man to run from the cover of the trees to the safety of the forest. Doubts quickly formed.

'Why did nobody mark his escape?' he wondered aloud.

'We were unsighted. From our position on the hillock, we could not see this side of the copse at all.'

'You could not, but Ordgar might have.'

'Ordgar?'

'Yes,' said Ralph, pointing to the finishing posts. 'If he was standing there, he would have had a clear view of anyone dashing across to the forest.'

'That is true,' conceded the other.

'How then did he miss seeing the villain run away?'

'He was distracted, my lord. His colt had won the race. He did not look this way at all. We taxed him about that.'

'What did he say?'

'That his mind was filled with the joy of his win.'

'But there were others at the finishing line. They were not distracted. Why did none of them descry a man scurrying across this field?'

'I do not know.'

Ralph looked in every direction to check the sightlines. Between the copse and the forest itself, there was no means of concealment. He scratched his head in bewilderment.

'However did the assassin avoid being seen?'

'We will find that out from the rogue himself,' vowed Wymarc. 'My lord sheriff will squeeze the truth out of Ebbi. It pains me that this crime took place on my land, but I am not entirely surprised that Ebbi is the culprit.'

'You know the fellow?'

'He is a slave on one of my holdings. A surly creature, according to my reeve. Lazy and embittered. Quick to show his temper. We will be well rid of such a man.'

'What quarrel did he have with Bertrand Gamberell?'

'None that I know of, my lord.'

'Why, then, single out his rider for the dagger?'

'I am as anxious to learn that as you,' said Wymarc. 'It will lift the shadow of suspicion that hangs over me.'

'You?'

'Ebbi is one of my slaves. Bertrand has accused me of hiring him to commit this murder in order to prevent Hyperion from winning the race. It is a preposterous charge but that will not deter Bertrand from making it. That is why I am so relieved that Ebbi is now in the sheriff's hands.' He gave a grim chuckle. 'Robert d'Oilly will get at the truth if he has to cut it out of the man's heart.'

Ralph was still puzzled. Walking back into the copse, he tried to decide the most likely spot from which the fatal dagger was thrown. He took up a number of positions and imagined the six horses thundering past him. The killer would have only a second to discharge his weapon. He would need a hiding place from which he could emerge unencumbered in an instant. Searching through the undergrowth, Ralph did his best to put himself into the mind of the assassin.

'What are you looking for, my lord?' asked Wymarc.

'Clues.'

'But we already have the man in captivity.'

Ralph ignored the remark and moved slowly on. The copse consisted largely of hazel, cherry, maple and wych elm but it was beside an ash that he eventually paused. A man concealed behind it would have a good view of the horses from the start of the race to the moment they plunged into the copse. Ralph stepped behind the tree into the shadow of its overhanging boughs. He felt certain that he had the right place.

As he glanced down, he noticed some strange marks on the ground. He was still wondering how they had got there when Wymarc's podgy face came round the tree.

'What have you found, my lord?' he asked.

'Nothing.'

'We have been over every inch of the copse.'

'Then I will waste no more of my time here.'

Ralph led the way back to the horses. He was glad that he

had responded to the impulse to ride out to Woodstock. The visit had yielded far more than he had dared to hope.

Gervase Bret was given a chance to meet the prisoner much sooner than he expected. An hour after his return from the shire hall, he was summoned by a message from Arnulf and hurried down to the bailey to meet the chaplain. The latter was carrying a leather satchel over his shoulder.

'I have been asked to visit Ebbi again,' he explained. 'To tend his wounds.'

'Wounds?'

'My lord sheriff has been interrogating him.'

Gervase winced but made no comment. He could imagine what form the interrogation had taken. Arnulf touched the satchel.

'I have water to bathe and linen to bandage him.'

'What do you have to medicine his mind?'

'The mercy of God.'

Gervase doubted if it would be an adequate remedy. Ebbi was in a state of abject terror. Assurances from the chaplain would not calm his fears. He needed more practical help.

'Did you ask that I should go with you?' said Gervase.

Arnulf nodded. 'My lord sheriff opposed the idea at first but I represented how useful you might be to me and to him.'

'To him?'

'Yes, Gervase. Though I am an ordained priest, Ebbi will never fully trust me. In his eyes, I am a servant of Robert d'Oilly. You are not. If you win his confidence, you may be able to unearth facts which even my lord sheriff's close examination of the prisoner could not.'

Gervase contained his anger. The last thing he intended to do was to carry out an interrogation of the prisoner by more subtle means in order to assist Robert d'Oilly, but he knew how foolish it would be to make that declaration. Access to the prisoner had been granted. That was all that mattered.

Arnulf led the way to the dungeons.

'Did you have a profitable day at the shire court?'

'Interesting rather than profitable,' said Gervase.
'How did Brother Columbanus acquit himself?'
'Extremely well.'
'Still writhing with self-disgust?'
'He has shaken off his sense of guilt and returned to his more usual joviality. But he did spurn the jug of ale that was set out for us.'

They traded a quiet smile then descended the stone steps that led to the dungeons. The passageway at the bottom was lighted by a series of torches set in iron holders and an acrid stink pervaded the whole area. A guard rose from behind a rough table and took them across to the first of the cells. Opening the door with a key, he ushered them into the cell before locking them in with the prisoner.

The first thing which hit Gervase was the appalling stench. Thick straw covered the ground and it was clotted with the accumulated filth of previous occupants. No fresh air and no natural light reached the dungeon. Incarceration down there was like being buried alive.

Arnulf was less troubled by the noisome atmosphere. Two small candles flickered in the cell and he set them either side of the prisoner so that he could examine the man's wounds. Gervase recoiled when he saw the extent of the injuries. Ebbi lay motionless in the straw, hardly breathing. Blood streamed from his nose, his mouth and a gash on his temple. One cheek was hideously swollen. Dark bruises were a vivid reminder of his earlier beating by Robert d'Oilly.

The chaplain worked gently but firmly, bathing the wounds with a piece of linen which he soaked with water from the flagon in his satchel. It took time to stem the bleeding and to bind the wounds. Flinching from the pain, Ebbi rolled frightened eyes at them. Arnulf offered comforting words as he worked away but the prisoner did not even seem to hear them. It was only when the chaplain finished that Ebbi found the strength to murmur his thanks.

Arnulf introduced Gervase and the latter crouched down beside the figure in the straw. Ebbi eyed the newcomer with frank apprehension, like a desperate animal caught in a trap and at the mercy of his hunters.

'How do you feel now?' asked Gervase softly.

The man was surprised to hear his own language spoken so well but it did not diminish his suspicion of Gervase. He feared that this soft-spoken man was only a more cunning interrogator.

'I would like to help you, if I may.'

Studied silence. Ebbi's suspicion became a sullen glare.

'This may be your last chance to say what really happened in Woodstock,' continued Gervase. 'We would like to hear your side of the story.'

The prisoner closed his eyes and pretended to doze off.

'He will say nothing in front of me,' whispered Arnulf. 'I am the sheriff's man. That makes me tainted. Let me contrive to leave you alone with him awhile.'

'Thank you.'

Arnulf called through the grille in the oak door. The guard let him out and talked with him for a minute before agreeing to lock Gervase in alone with the prisoner. There was an air of finality about the thud of the door and Gervase had to remind himself that he would soon be released again. That was not the case for Ebbi. His situation seemed hopeless.

Gervase wasted no time. Kneeling beside the prisoner, he put out a friendly hand to touch the other's arm. The man drew back and opened his eyes once more.

'Leave me alone!' he hissed.

'I have come to help you.'

'Go away!'

'You need me, Ebbi,' said Gervase quietly. 'I am on your side. I do not believe that you committed this crime.'

Ebbi was unpersuaded. 'You are trying to trick me.'

'Why should I do that?'

'The sheriff has set you on me.'

'I answer to the King and not to Robert d'Oilly. I am here of my own accord, I do assure you.'

'Why?'

'Because I am a lawyer by training. I value justice.'

A low grunt. 'What kind of justice will I get?'

'That will depend on what you tell me.' He leaned in closer to the prisoner. 'Did you kill that man in Woodstock?'

'What is it to you?'

'I would not see an innocent man condemned.'

'Fine words!' sneered the other.

'I must know the true facts, Ebbi.'

'That is what the sheriff said.'

'Why did he beat you?'

'Because I did not tell him what he wanted to hear.'

'Then you must be a brave man,' said Gervase. 'To hold out against my lord sheriff took great courage. And it confirms me in my opinion. You are not the assassin, are you?'

'Do not pester me so.'

'Are you?'

'No,' said Ebbi with rancour, 'but I begin to wish that I had been. I wish I had killed all the Norman knights who plague our countryside!' The outburst taxed his strength. It was a minute before he could speak again. 'I am not the assassin. I would swear it on the Holy Bible.'

Gervase believed him but there were unresolved issues.

'Why did you run from those who searched the forest?'

'I thought they would accuse me of poaching. Do you know the penalty which that carries, Master Bret? Poachers either have their eyes put out or they are castrated. Of course I ran from them. Would not you?'

'What were you doing in the forest?'

'I was not poaching. I give you my word.'

'Something must have taken you there, Ebbi.'

A shake of the head. 'I am not able to tell you.'

'If you wish to come out of this alive, you must.'

The key was heard in the lock. Their conference was over.

'Tell me,' urged Gervase. 'It is your last hope.'

Panic descended on Ebbi and nudged him into a quick decision. Raising himself up on his arm, he whispered into his visitor's ear. Gervase heard all that was necessary before he was hustled out by the guard.

Bristeva knew that something was seriously amiss and she was hurt that they would not tell her what it was. Her father soothed her with gentle lies and her brother refused to answer any of her questions. Ordgar and Amalric were determined to keep the truth from her for some reason and she wished that she knew what it was. Since the death of her mother, Bristeva had become the lady of the house and that brought many responsibilities with it. She believed that it also entitled her to know everything that was going on.

The sound of an approaching horse took her to the window. Through the open shutters, she watched until a familiar face came into view. Edric the Cripple, steward to her father's depleted estate, had returned from his travels. Ordgar and Amalric went out to greet him warmly. All three were soon deep in animated conversation. Seeing her opportunity, Bristeva crept out of the house and ran to the rear of the stables. She inched along the wall until she came within earshot.

'We expected you back yesterday,' Ordgar was saying.

'I was held up in Warwick,' said Edric.

'We are so glad that you are home again.'

'Yes,' said Amalric. 'We need you, Edric.'

'Why? What has been happening while I was away?'

Edric the Cripple dropped from the saddle and balanced on one leg while he sought to untie the crutch which had been lashed behind the saddle. He was a tall, wiry man of middle years with a weathered face. Even with one leg cut off below the knee, he retained something of the swagger of a soldier. Edric was a capable and experienced steward, unswervingly loyal and with an instinct for making correct decisions. Both Ordgar and his son placed great faith in him.

With the crutch tucked under his arm, Edric was ready.

'Tell me all,' he encouraged.

Ordgar told the bulk of the tale but Amalric added frequent comments and embellishments. Hearing the story for the first time, Bristeva was shocked that they should keep something as important as this from her. When she learned of her father's excruciating night on the cold stairs at Wallingford Castle, she suffered his humiliation with him.

Edric listened in stony silence. He heard much which distressed him but little which actually surprised him. He scratched at a straggly beard before making any observation.

'There is one consolation,' he said at length.

'What is that?' asked Ordgar.

'Cempan won the race. Our belief in the colt was not misplaced. He was obviously the best horse on the day.'

'And I was the best rider,' reminded Amalric.

'Indeed you were. But your success was your undoing. Milo Crispin has seen that this famous Hyperion can actually be beaten. That matters a great deal to him.'

'I know!' said Ordgar ruefully.

'He wants Cempan for his own stable.'

'Never!' insisted Amalric. 'We will not part with him.'

'Suppose my lord Milo comes to take him?' asked his father. 'He will bring a troop of men to enforce his purpose. What then?' He turned to Edric. 'What then, old friend?'

Edric the Cripple hobbled to the water trough and perched on the edge of it. He thought long and hard. Unable to see the steward from her hiding place, Bristeva wondered what was going on. She mastered the urge to burst in on the discussion and claim her right to offer an opinion. More could be learned by staying where she was and listening.

'Well, Edric?' prompted Ordgar. 'What do you think?'

'I think we have one less Norman knight in Woodstock and that is a certain gain. Whoever killed the man is our benefactor.' He scratched his beard again. 'Unfortunately, he also landed us with a worrying possibility. The loss of Cempan. Stolen from us by Milo Crispin.'

'Is there no remedy?' said Amalric.

'I spy only one.' He turned to Ordgar. 'Has the time for the next race been set?'

'Not as far as I know.'

'Then we must delay it as long as possible.'

'Delay it?'

'Until the race is run, they will not need Cempan. We may be able to hold on to our colt a little longer.'

'But my lord Milo wants another contest soon.'

'So will Bertrand Gamberell,' said Amalric. 'His pride has been sorely wounded. He cursed me for winning a race that he thought belonged to Hyperion. He will want revenge.'

'In another race.'

'Yes, Edric.'

'Then there is our remedy.'

'Delay the race?'

'Make sure that it never happens.'

Ordgar and Amalric were completely baffled. They looked across at Cempan, grazing in the nearby field, then turned to look at each other. Both shook their heads in puzzlement. When they faced Edric again, they saw him chuckling to himself.

'Stop the race altogether?' asked Ordgar.

'That is my advice.'

'But how do we do that, Edric?'

The steward hoisted himself back up on his crutch.

'Leave it to me.'

Chapter Five

As soon as she returned that evening, the whole atmosphere at the castle underwent a subtle change. Edith, wife to Robert d'Oilly, was a rather plump woman with a fading beauty but she was treated with the utmost respect by the whole garrison. The guards greeted her with a polite wave, the soldiers in the bailey cut short their crude banter, the ostlers ran to take charge of the horses from the little cavalcade and the servants in the keep, from the humblest to the most exalted, went about their chores with a new zest. With Edith in residence, the castle was a different place.

But the most striking alteration was in Robert d'Oilly himself. A warmth came into his manner and the visitors noted a first spontaneous smile. Affectionate to his wife, he showed far more courtesy to his guests and invited them to feast in the hall with him that night. It was not a lavish occasion but Ralph and the others did not mind. They were delighted to be able to meet Edith and to watch the effect she had on those around her. The cooks excelled themselves under her direction and the meal was served with more alacrity. Seated beside his wife at the head of the long oak table, Robert at last began to remember the duties of a host. A convivial spirit soon spread throughout the hall.

Ralph could not resist baiting Brother Columbanus.

'Drink your fill,' he teased, pointing to the jugs of ale.

'I am content with water, my lord,' said the monk.

'There is water enough in ale. Sample it.'

'Do not tempt me.'

71

'Last night, you needed no temptation,' Ralph reminded him. 'You quaffed your ale so heartily that I thought you might burst asunder. Doff the cowl and drink until dawn. That seemed to be your rubric. Yet tonight you are telling Satan to get behind thee.' He gave the other a playful nudge. 'Drink, man. We will not tell on you. Have all the ale you wish.'

'Do not lead the poor man astray,' said a jocular Maurice Pagnal, raising his cup. 'You should not be thrusting ale at him. Introduce him to the taste of good French wine instead.'

Columbanus wore a brave smile but shifted uneasily on the bench. He was grateful when the conversation moved away from him. Out of the corner of his eye, however, he could still see the jug of ale and it exercised a strange fascination for him, at once attracting and repelling him, awaking a deep thirst yet frightening him with its inherent danger. The water began to taste increasingly sour upon his tongue.

Golde had no qualms about drinking the ale and she savoured its quality. Like most of those around the table, Edith sipped a cup of wine and she was intrigued by Golde's preference.

'Have you always had a liking for ale?' she asked.

'I had no choice in the matter, my lady,' said Golde. 'My first husband was a brewer and I was perforce apprenticed to the trade. When he died, I carried on after him and brewed ale for Hereford Castle until the day I left the town.'

'Have you taught Ralph to enjoy English ale?'

'Not yet, but I live in hope.'

'Robert will not touch it while there is wine to be had.'

'Both serve their purpose.'

'We can all see that,' observed Edith with a smile as Robert, Maurice and Ralph burst into laughter at a shared joke. 'I am so glad that you decided to accompany your husband on this visit, Golde. I will make it as enjoyable for you as I may. Rely on that promise.'

'Thank you.'

Golde had an immediate affinity with her. Like her, Edith was the daughter of a Saxon thegn who had lost his eminence and his property after the Conquest. Both had married Norman barons and learned to adjust to the new dispensation. It was a luxury for Golde to be able to talk in her own language to a woman of such rank.

'My father was Wigot of Wallingford,' said Edith with a wistful expression. 'Kinsman and butler to King Edward. I was born and raised in Wallingford.'

'We passed close by it on our journey.'

'An important town, Golde, even more so in those days. King Edward held some land there with a garrison of housecarls to protect it. My father talked so fondly of those days.'

'Everything has changed since then,' said Golde soulfully. 'In your life, as in mine. But those changes have not all been for the worse,' she added with a fond glance at Ralph. 'I have found a happiness that I never dared to imagine.'

'It is so with me. Robert has been a good husband.'

Golde found it difficult to believe. She could not understand how such a kindly and mild-mannered woman could bear to live with such a brutish man as Robert d'Oilly. Their host was genial enough now but Golde could not forget his treatment of the prisoner who festered in the dungeon. Nor could she shake from her mind the image of so many ravaged houses in the town over which the sheriff held sway. Oxford was an attractive place which had been ruthlessly pillaged. Golde suspected that she was sitting at the same table as its leading persecutor.

'Would you like to return to Herefordshire?' said Edith.

'I have done so a number of times,' replied Golde. 'My sister, Aelgar, is still there and I have many old friends to see as well.'

'I wondered if you would prefer to live there yourself.'

'There is no question of that. Ralph's estates are in Hampshire and it is a most pleasant county in which to dwell. In truth, I am relieved to have left Hereford. When I lived there, I was constantly reminded of all that had been lost of my father's manors. It must be so with you, my lady.'

'In some sort.'

'You live within an easy ride of Wallingford. Twenty years

ago, your father was a man of great consequence. Now his lands have been completely forfeited.'

'That is not quite true, Golde.'

'Indeed?'

'There are other ways to preserve an influence.'

'I do not follow.'

'The bonds of marriage,' said Edith with a gentle smile. 'Manors which formerly belonged to my dear father, Wigot of Wallingford, are now in the hands of Milo Crispin.'

'Is that not a cause for regret?'

'It was, Golde. Until Milo married my daughter.'

The two women remained in earnest discussion while Robert d'Oilly lapsed into soldierly reminiscences with Ralph and Maurice. Gervase Bret noted the way in which the feast had fragmented into three different conversations. He himself was seated between Arnulf and Brother Columbanus. The jug of ale was exercising a firm hold on the monk's attention.

Gervase swallowed a mouthful of grilled quail and turned to the chaplain.

'Golde tells me that you showed her the sights of Oxford.'

'That is so,' said Arnulf. 'She is a delightful companion and it was a joy to be her guide.'

'Where did you take her?'

'Almost everywhere. Her curiosity was insatiable.'

'She told me how much she enjoyed meeting the canons of St Frideswide's. From our point of view as commissioners, it is a privileged community. Land held by St Frideswide's is exempt from tax. It does not belong to any hundred.'

'The canons are duly grateful.' He looked beyond Gervase to Columbanus. 'But I marvel that you did not choose to stay with them rather than with us. You might have found a softer lodging there than at the castle.'

'I am happy enough here,' said the monk.

'You would be more than welcome at St Frideswide's.'

'I will pay my respects there at some point.'

'Brother Simon would certainly have stayed with the canons

while he was in Oxford,' said Gervase. 'He had but little tolerance of lay company.'

Columbanus grinned. 'I have a more forgiving nature.'

'It becomes you.'

The monk's eye twinkled and he seemed to be emerging from his repentance. He allowed a passing servant to pour him a first cup of ale and sipped it with only the merest trace of the guilt which had afflicted him earlier.

'Golde told me about your choir,' said Gervase to the chaplain. 'Is it true that you have female choristers?'

'One or two. I hope to recruit more.'

'From the town?'

'From Oxford and beyond,' said Arnulf. 'The best girl we had came from Woodstock. As pure a voice as any I have heard. Her talent was so remarkable that it was not confined to a church service. She sang in this hall at banquets for the delight of the guests.' He gave a sigh of regret. 'It was a pity to lose her.'

'Why did that happen?'

'To be honest, I am not quite sure, Gervase. I spent hours training her voice. Helene could not have been a more apt pupil. Then, one day, she told me that she was losing interest and wished to withdraw.' A deeper sigh. 'I could not force her to remain with the choir.'

'Did she say why her interest was waning?'

'No. And I believe that it was merely an excuse.'

'What was her real reason for leaving?'

'My guess is that it had more to do with her elder brother than with Helene herself. She lives in his house and must do his bidding. He was never happy about her being in the choir in the first place and Helene had many disagreements with him.'

'Could you not argue with him on her behalf?'

'I did so repeatedly, Gervase.'

'But without success.'

'Helene was taken away. Her voice can delight us no more.'

'It seems like an act of wilful cruelty.'

'Her brother, alas, does have a cruel streak.'
'Who is this man?'
'My lord Wymarc.'

Helene sat in the window of her bedchamber and stared
sorrowfully out at the garden below. Birds were heralding a
fine morning with full-throated relish and the sun was already
burnishing the trees and the grass. The sky was cloudless and
the wind a mere whisper. A squirrel darted up the trunk of
a beech tree. A frog explored the slime at the edge of the
pond. Insects were buzzing with early frenzy. A gardener was
ambling through the bushes.

Helene drew no pleasure from the tranquil scene. Its quiet
beauty only served to sadden her even more. She was a tall,
pale, willowy girl of fourteen with nothing of her brother's
ugliness or obesity. Her features were pleasant rather than
handsome and there was a childlike awkwardness about the
way she held herself. Still in her night attire, she ran a comb
absent-mindedly through her long, black hair and let her eyes
wander aimlessly around the garden.

A loud knock on her door brought her out of her reverie.

'Helene?' called a voice.

'Yes?' she said, crossing her arms protectively across her
chest. 'What do you want?'

'You have eaten no breakfast this morning.'

'I am not hungry.'

'You said that yesterday. Are you unwell?'

'No.'

'Are you sickening for something?'

There was no sympathy in her brother's enquiry. Wymarc
did not have a close relationship with his younger sister. Since
the death of their parents, the girl had been withdrawn and
secretive. Helene resented having to live with him and his
wife. After two years in their care, she had still not come to
accept him as her guardian. For his part, Wymarc found her
an irritating burden but she was his sister and duty prompted
him. Vows made to his parents had to be honoured. Besides,

his sister was a valuable commodity on the marriage market. Betrothed to the right man, Helene could bring her brother real advantage.

'Shall I summon a doctor?' he asked.

'No!' she protested.

'He may have a cordial to restore your appetite.'

'There is nothing wrong with me.'

'Then why do you keep refusing food?'

'I will eat in a while.'

Wymarc paused to consider his own diagnosis.

'You cannot deceive me,' he said. 'I know what this is all about. You are still angry with me, are you not? You are still hurt because I took you away from St George's-in-the-Castle.'

'That is not true.'

'It is, Helene. I remember how bitterly you railed at me. But I only did it for your own good. You will come to see that in time. While you were at the castle you were vulnerable, and it is my duty as your brother to protect you. That is why you had to leave the choir.'

'I will never go back,' she murmured.

'You still hold it against me.'

'No, I do not.'

'It had to end,' argued Wymarc. 'A certain person was starting to pay too much attention to my sister. You are only a child but that would not stop him. I know him too well. When I saw him at the race two days ago, he asked after you yet again, Helene. In a way that disgusted me. He hoped that I would have brought you out to watch his black stallion run. Can you hear what I am saying?'

'Yes.'

'And you understand my reasoning?'

'You did what you thought best,' she said dully.

'Then stop hiding up here from me. Come downstairs.'

'I am not hungry.'

'We would still like to see you, Helene. We are worried about you. Stop behaving like this.' A long silence.

He became brusque. 'Very well. I will send for the doctor.'

'There is nothing wrong with me.'

'I will let him be the judge of that.'

'No!' she protested. 'Please!'

'Then come out of there.'

Helene stood and made a forlorn gesture with her hands.

'Very well,' she capitulated. 'I will get dressed.'

Bertrand Gamberell did not have long to wait. On the following morning, he timed his arrival perfectly. He leaned nonchalantly against the trunk of a tree while Hyperion cropped the grass behind him. It was only when he heard the drumming of the hooves that he crouched down out of sight. There were five of them but his only interest was in the man who led them at a canter along the winding track. When they had ridden past, he stood up and slapped his thigh with satisfaction.

But he took no chances. Gamberell was far too wily and experienced to do that. Leaving his own horse tethered, he strolled up the wooded slope until he reached the summit of the hill. The vantage point allowed him to see a dim outline of Oxford on the distant horizon. He watched the five riders as they continued steadily on their way towards the town. When they were a mile or more away, he strolled casually back to Hyperion and mounted the horse.

'Come on, boy!' he urged. 'We must not keep her waiting.'

Ralph Delchard had to wait until after breakfast for the chance to speak to Gervase Bret alone and tell him about his findings at Woodstock the previous day. Alone in the hall at the castle, they spoke in subdued voices to cheat the echo. Gervase heard him out with rapt attention.

'What did you conclude?' he asked.

'That the assassin did not flee into the forest at all. Not at first. Too many eyes were against him. He was bound to be seen as he ran across that field.'

'Unless those eyes were deliberately blind.'

'That is a possibility but I think it unlikely.'

'Why?'

'Accomplices would not simply have ignored what they saw. They would have distracted everyone else's attention as well and there was no diversion. No,' decided Ralph, 'I think that there is another explanation.'

'The assassin remained hidden in the copse.'

'Yes.'

'But it was thoroughly searched, you say.'

'That is what Wymarc told me but I think they blundered about too hastily among those trees. They missed vital signs. I would like to have conducted a proper search myself but Wymarc was panting at my heels like a hunting dog. I need to go back to Woodstock when he is not around to hinder me.'

'What does he think?'

'That the murderer is here under lock and key.'

'Ebbi?'

'Yes, Gervase. According to him, Ebbi threw the dagger at his victim then hared across that field before the murder was discovered. But that is impossible.'

'Is it?'

'Only a fit and lithe young man would have risked a wild dash to the forest. Ebbi is none of those things. I only saw the fellow from a distance, but he looked too old and gaunt to have a turn of foot.'

'He is, Ralph. No question of that.'

'If Ebbi was indeed the assassin, I believe that he took refuge somewhere and remained hidden. It was only after everyone had left the area that he came out and made his escape to the forest. Except that it was no escape.' He pursed his lips and shook his head. 'I come more and more to doubt that Ebbi is involved at all here.'

'Of that I am certain, Ralph.'

'How?'

'I spoke with the man.'

'When?'

It was Gervase's turn to take over. He described his visit to the dungeon the previous day and explained how it helped to reinforce his earlier suspicions. Ralph was fascinated.

'And you accepted his word?'

'Why should he lie to me?'

'A condemned man will say anything to get off the hook.'

'That is not the case here. Ebbi is in despair. He has been beaten to a pulp by my lord sheriff and he knows there is worse to come. Yet he is not full of self-pity.'

'Who could blame him if he were?'

'He has resigned himself to his own fate,' said Gervase. 'But even in the midst of his own ordeal, he thinks of his family and friends. That is why he wanted Arnulf to carry a message to them from him. Does that sound like the action of some merciless assassin?'

'No, Gervase. And yet he was apprehended in the forest.'

'That was complete misfortune.'

'Why was he there in the first place? Poaching game?'

'No, Ralph. He swears it.'

'What, then, took him into the forest?'

Gervase was about to answer when he became aware that they were no longer alone. Standing in silence at the other end of the hall was the rotund figure of Brother Columbanus. When they both stared questioningly at him, he replied with his usual benign smile and they were left to wonder why he did not announce his arrival and how much of their conversation he had overheard.

There were eight of them in all. The piping trebles of the six boys mingled with the softer voices of the two girls and rose up to the ceiling of the little chancel. The choir of St George's-in-the-Castle was practising.

Sanctus, Sanctus, Sanctus,
Dominus Deus Sabaoth.
Pleni sunt caeli et terra gloria tua.
Hosanna in excelsis!

Benedictus qui venit in nomine Domini.
Hosanna in excelsis!

Arnulf took them through it three more times before he was satisfied with the result. He clapped gentle palms together. 'That is good,' he congratulated them. 'Very good.' The girls lapped up his praise like two kittens presented with a pool of milk but the boys, who were younger, more restive and more anxious to be at play with their friends, were merely grateful that the rehearsal was over. When the chaplain dismissed them, it was the boys who scuttled down the aisle and the girls who hovered for more approval. Arnulf waited until the others had left the building.

'Thank you,' he said feelingly. 'The boys were not at their best this morning. You redeemed their poor performance. Where the two of you led, they eventually followed.'

The younger of the girls giggled but the other simply gazed at the chaplain with admiration. In inviting her to join the choir, he had given her one of the most precious gifts she had ever received and she responded with total commitment. After garlanding them for a few more minutes, Arnulf let them go, then called back the older one at the door.

'Bristeva!'

'Yes?' she said, halting at once.

'There was something I wished to tell you. But not in front of the others. They will hear it from me in good time.' He glided down the aisle towards her. 'When we lost Helene, we lost the purest voice that we had.'

'Helene put us all to shame.'

'She was the heart and soul of the choir.'

'We miss her badly.'

'I was distraught when she decided to leave.'

'Is there no chance that she may come back?'

'No, Bristeva,' said Arnulf, hands clasped in front of him. 'Helene is lost to us. That is why I must look elsewhere for someone to set an example to the others.' Her face lit up in

81

anticipation. 'I think that you are the only one who could take her place. Does that idea excite you?'

'Very much, Father Arnulf!'

'It would mean a lot of work.'

'I am not afraid of that.'

'There would be rewards,' he promised. 'You would not only take the solo parts in church. On occasion, you might be asked to sing in the hall in front of guests and some of them can be very appreciative. Helene never went away empty-handed. Yes, you will certainly find that there are rewards.'

Bristeva did not even think of the money. Spending more time with the chaplain was reward enough for her. At home with her father, she was often neglected and always excluded from any discussion of significance, but she had achieved a mild importance in the little choir. It gave her a self-esteem which she had never had before and Bristeva could not have been more thankful to the chaplain. He chose her. His careful and patient training had turned a promising voice into one that was clear and mellifluous.

'I will speak to Ordgar,' he said.

'Father will not object.'

'I hope not, Bristeva. It took me a while to persuade him to let you join the choir. He was reluctant at first.'

'He is proud of my singing now.'

'And so he should be.'

'May I tell him what you said?'

'Please do, Bristeva. And ask him to talk to me.'

'I will, Father Arnulf.'

He smiled at her. 'Are you happy about this?'

'Yes!' she affirmed. 'Very happy!'

'So am I.'

When she left the church, she was suffused with joy.

The commissioners were still at the shire hall. Ralph and Gervase were calm but Maurice Pagnal was in an aggressive mood.

'What more do we need to debate?' he said testily. 'We

have heard both sides of the case and studied the documents which the witnesses produced. My mind is clear. Islip is legally the property of Azelina, wife of Roger d'Ivry. I have not the slightest doubt about that.'

'I have, my lord,' said Gervase firmly. 'Having read the deposition from the Abbot of Westminster, I have a number of doubts, especially about the way in which Islip first came into the hands of the lady Azelina.'

'It was a gift from King William.'

'Before that, it was a gift from King Edward.'

'If it is a choice between kings,' decided Ralph, 'I know which one I would support. The later surely supplants the former here.'

Maurice nodded. 'Thank you, Ralph. The matter is settled.'

'Not until we examine the disputants further,' said Gervase.

'What else can they tell us?'

'Certain points in the charters need clarification.'

'You are splitting hairs, Gervase.'

'Just like a lawyer!' added Ralph.

'May I say something?' interposed Brother Columbanus.

'No,' said Maurice contemptuously. 'You are only our scribe here and not a commissioner.'

'My opinion might be useful.'

'But not sought after.' He looked at Gervase. 'Our two votes outweight your one.'

'Only when we make a final decision, my lord.'

'We have just made it,' insisted Maurice. 'Ralph?'

'Let us hear the witnesses once again first.'

'God's wounds! We will be here until Domesday!'

'An appropriate date for this Survey,' said Gervase.

His mild joke produced a laugh which eased the tension considerably. Even Brother Columbanus joined in, chuckling happily and repeating the words aloud. Those waiting outside the shire hall wondered what had caused the mirthful explosion. Maurice waited until the laughter faded away then tried a different approach to win over his colleagues.

'Why lock horns over this?' he said reasonably. 'All three of us want the same thing. A just and fair settlement. I believe that we can reach that now without further debate or prevarication.' His manner became more confiding. 'I spoke with our host this morning. Robert d'Oilly was most insistent that the lady Azelina has the better claim here. The sheriff remembers the exact time and place when Islip and Oddington came into her hands. Our host vouches for her. What more proof do we need than that?'

'A great deal,' said Ralph with asperity. 'My lord sheriff has not been called as a witness and he is not speaking under oath. Discount his testimony at once.'

'But why?'

'Because he is the sworn brother of Roger d'Ivry and will naturally wish to offer support to his wife. When he tried to push me in her direction, I answered him roundly in spite of his rank. You should have done likewise, Maurice.'

'I knew nothing of this link with Roger d'Ivry.'

'You did not need to,' reprimanded Ralph. 'Impartiality is our touchstone. If someone tries to influence you in any way, you should give them a dusty answer and report them to me.'

'I am sure that the sheriff meant no harm.'

'He tried to affect your judgement.'

'It was no more than a casual remark.'

'I heard one of those from him myself, Maurice.'

'Robert d'Oilly is not a reliable witness,' said Gervase. 'That is why we did not call him before us. It is not simply because he has sworn brotherhood to Roger d'Ivry. He is also the father-in-law of Milo Crispin.'

Maurice shrugged. 'Milo Crispin does not figure here.'

'Indirectly, he does. He is kinsman to Gilbert Crispin, abbot of Westminster and the other claimant of this land. Whom does my lord Robert support? Church or State? The kinsman of his son-in-law or the wife of his sworn brother? He is bound to be prejudiced in one direction.'

'And we know what it is,' said Ralph.

'This is far too confusing for me!' groaned Maurice.

'I am as mystified as you. I never thought to hear myself

say this but I actually miss Canon Hubert's advice. Whenever there is a conflict between Church and State, he always seems to know how to settle it. Canon Hubert has insight.'

'I will pass on that compliment,' said Columbanus.

'He may choose to disbelieve it.' Ralph slapped a palm on the table. 'Enough of this bickering! We will hear both sides once more, then confer on our verdict.'

A guard was dispatched and soon reappeared with Azelina and Brother Timothy. Both were given a polite greeting and invited to sit on the cushions. There was an even greater contrast between them this time. The stately Azelina was glowing with confidence while the shuffling Timothy had a defeatist look about him. It was almost as if the verdict had already been given in her favour.

Ralph moved swiftly to counter that impression.

'No decision has yet been made by us,' he said firmly. 'Nor will it be until you have both had an opportunity to add to what you have already told us. We have examined the documentary evidence and each of you has a legitimate claim. What we need to know from you, my lady, is how Islip first came into your possession. And from you, Brother Timothy, why the abbey seems to have let it slip from its fingers.'

Azelina needed no second invitation to speak and her melodious voice rang around the hall with conviction.

'My husband, Roger d'Ivry, has been a loyal subject to the King and is held in high regard. When King William sought to reward his service, he granted him the manors of Mixbury, Beckley, Asthall and twenty more besides, now held from my husband by subtenants. At the same time, Islip was granted to me along with three hides and half a virgate of land in Oddington.' The recital was so smooth it must have been carefully rehearsed. 'Take note of the value of my holdings, my lords. Islip was worth seven pounds in 1066 and eight when I acquired it from the King. Thanks to my prudent stewardship, it is now worth ten pounds. That is an appreciable increase. The same is true of my land in Oddington.'

The facts poured out of her in a steady stream and her claim appeared unanswerable. When she finished, Brother Timothy looked more subdued than ever. Instead of leaping to the defence of Westminster Abbey as he had done so effectively during the previous session, he brought a hand out from a sleeve in order to signal withdrawal.

'I have nothing more to add, my lords,' he said meekly.

'Nothing?' echoed Gervase. 'Can this be so?'

'You heard him,' said Maurice, jumping quickly in. 'We may proceed to judgement without further impediment.'

Ralph agreed. He did not need to ask which way Maurice would vote and a glance from Gervase told him that the abbey was not unsupported. The casting vote lay with Ralph and he agonised for a few minutes before committing himself. All had seemed finely balanced on the previous day but Azelina had stolen the initiative now. After looking from one disputant to the other, he gave his verdict.

'Islip will remain in the hands of the lady Azelina.'

She gave a quiet smile of triumph but it did not stay on her face for long. Brother Timothy suddenly erupted into life. Jumping to his feet, he waved an accusatory finger at Ralph and issued his thunderbolt.

'I denounce this commission!' he yelled with passion. 'It has not dispensed justice here today. Instead, it has given way to bribery and corruption, making its verdict a travesty and a perversion. Unless the canker is removed from this tribunal, I will entreat Abbot Gilbert of Westminster to protest directly to the King himself to have this verdict overturned.'

The outburst ceased. Brother Timothy resumed his seat with studied calm but the rest of the shire hall was now in a state of consternation.

Chapter Six

Bertrand Gamberell lay on the bed in a state of joyful exhaustion. Long, luscious hours of exquisite pleasure had left him coated with perspiration and tingling with exhilaration. The woman in his arms was so gloriously sated that she dozed off to sleep. Gamberell ran a hand down her naked back and traced the curve of her fleshy buttocks. Her skin was like silk. She had a body of generous proportions and she had yielded it up to him unreservedly. It was their first time together and he resolved that there would be many other secret trysts. She was an eager lover but there was still much that he could teach her before he was done.

The thrill of a new conquest was always something to savour but Gamberell took a special delight from the seduction of a married woman. It added a piquancy and an element of danger. It also gave him an exclusive insight into the most private area of a marriage. When he took a man's wife to bed, he could see exactly what kind of lover the husband was and that gave him a perverse gratification.

In this case, the husband was an old, tired, neglectful man who was largely indifferent to his wife's needs and who had never fully explored the potentialities of her desire. What her husband lacked, Gamberell provided in abundance and she had groaned in ecstasy as he took her on a voyage of discovery. In place of a fumbling and inconsiderate old man, she now had a strong, sensitive, virile young lover who was seasoned in all the arts of pleasure. Her earlier fears and doubts had been burned away in the delicious heat of their adultery. She was a most willing victim.

The woman had provided more than just a few hours of calculated lust for Gamberell. She was his escape. Locked in her embrace, he could forget all about the grim events at Woodstock. The cold-blooded murder of his knight preyed on his mind even though the assassin had apparently been caught. It was no random action. Gamberell felt certain that someone had hired the killer to make sure that Hyperion did not win the race. The murder had been an indirect attack on Gamberell himself and he was determined to root out the villain who had instigated it.

As his excitement cooled, ugly memories began to flood back. Even the warmth of the woman's body could not block them out now. He recalled with a start that he had to be back in Oxford in good time for the funeral. In the service of his master, Walter Payne had been callously murdered. If he had not ridden Hyperion in the race, he would still be alive. The thought activated Gamberell's sense of guilt. He needed to be at the church to lead the mourners as they paid their last respects to a tragic victim.

When he tried to disentangle himself, she opened her eyes.

'Where are you going?' she asked dreamily.

'Back to Oxford, my sweet.'

'So soon?'

'I have important business there.'

She nestled into him. 'You have important business here, Bertrand. Or have you tired of me already?'

'I could never do that,' he murmured, nuzzling her cheek.

'Do you still love me?'

'You know that I do, my angel.'

'Prove it.'

'I have already done so.'

'Prove it again,' she coaxed, kissing him on the lips.

'If I had the time, I would. But I really must go.'

'Not yet.'

'I will come back another day. I promise.'

'Not yet!' she pleaded. 'Do not leave me just yet.'

He gave her a parting hug and tried to pull away but she held him tenaciously. Rolling on top of him, she started to kiss him with such ardour that his own passion was soon ignited again. He caressed her body until she was writhing with delight then he eased her on to her back so that he could take both breasts in his hands to suck the nipples in turn. As their pleasure swiftly heightened, he parted her thighs and made her gasp with joy as he drove deep inside her.

'Love me!' she begged. 'Love me, Bertrand!'

'I do, my sweet.'

'Show me how much.'

'I will.'

He rode her hard until her desire built irresistibly to the moment of release and she flailed about in ecstasy.

'My stallion!' she purred.

It was all over in minutes. Gamberell did not allow himself the luxury of rest and reflection this time. He rose from the bed and began to put on his apparel, gloating over the naked body that still lay so invitingly on the sheets. The woman stretched and sighed with satisfaction.

'When will I see you again?' she whispered.

'Soon.'

'Do not keep me waiting, Bertrand.'

'I will not.'

'Pine for me.'

'Send word when your husband is next away.'

'I have no husband now. Only a lover.'

'Your lover will return.'

She sighed again then drifted happily asleep for a short while. When she awoke, Bertrand Gamberell had gone and the bedchamber suddenly felt cold and empty. She went quickly to the window and was just in time to see him leaving by the back door of the house. He looked up, blew her a kiss of farewell, then headed for the stables. She was content.

Gamberell was making a swift departure. There was no point in taking unnecessary risks. Her husband was away and her servants had been diverted by their mistress with various chores but he was circumspect. He would not feel entirely safe until he was well away from the house. Only then could he relax and revel in his latest conquest.

Gamberell was still smiling to himself as he came round the angle of the stables. Everything had worked out well. There had been no problems. The smile suddenly froze on his lips and he stopped in his tracks. Hyperion was gone. He had tethered the horse to an iron ring in the wall of the stables but the animal was no longer there.

He looked around then darted into each of the stalls in a frantic search but all to no avail. He dashed into the bushes at the rear of the stables to widen his search but it still proved fruitless. Hyperion was simply not there. While one stallion had been rutting lustily in the bedchamber, another had completely vanished.

Ralph Delchard soon restored calm in the shire hall. When the shocking accusation was made by Brother Timothy, it was Maurice Pagnal who protested most vociferously but Azelina also made her disgust felt. Even Brother Columbanus joined in, calling upon his Benedictine brother to apologise for making such an unfounded charge. Gervase Bret alone held his peace. In the short time he had known him, he had come to respect Timothy's advocacy and doubted if the monk would make wild allegations out of pique at having lost the case.

When Ralph had persuaded Maurice to resume his seat, he asked Azelina to leave the room while the matter was sorted out. With a look of disdain at Brother Timothy, she rose to her feet and made a dignified exit. Controlling his own anger, Ralph turned to the lone figure on the front bench.

'Would you care to repeat that accusation?' he said.

'If you wish, my lord.'

'I do, Brother Timothy. Nobody can cast a slur on this tribunal with impunity. We are royal commissioners who have been sent to Oxford to look into a number of irregularities and disputed claims. The King appointed us because we are independent judges. None of us has holdings, ties of family, obligations of friendship or anything else in this shire which would influence our decisions. If we had,' he continued with emphasis, 'we would have been debarred from this commission.'

'I understand that, my lord.'

'Then why do you dare to denounce us?'

'Because it was my bounden duty to do so.'

'It is my bounden duty to stop this nonsense,' growled Maurice. 'Be grateful that you wear a cowl, sir, or I would ask you to back up this foul slander with your sword.'

'The sword of truth is my weapon.'

'We ought to use it to cut out your tongue!'

'Peace!' said Ralph. 'We will get nowhere with intemperate language. A serious allegation has been made. I am still waiting for it to be substantiated.'

'Do you censure all of us?' asked Gervase.

'No, Master Bret. There is only one culprit.'

'Which one?'

'He knows,' said Timothy. 'And his presence here makes the verdict of this tribunal invalid.'

'This is outrageous!' protested Maurice in a fit of indignation. 'Are we to let this minnow from the backwaters of Westminster vilify us like this? It is a disgrace. Let us hear no more of this calumny. Send him back to his abbot with a flea in his ear.'

'I will do much more than that if his charge proves groundless,' warned Ralph. 'Brother Timothy can look to be expelled from the Order at the very least.'

'I stand by my accusation,' said the other.

'Then name the man you accuse.'

The monk stood up again and pointed at Maurice.

'He sits beside you, my lord.'

'Let me at him!' roared Maurice, jumping up.

'Stay!' ordered Ralph, restraining him with a hand on his arm. 'Hear him out, Maurice. We owe him that right.'

'The only right he is owed is a rope around his neck!'

'Sit down again. This must be resolved calmly.'

With a menacing glare at the monk, Maurice took his seat.

'Speak your piece, sir,' he challenged. 'I am listening.'

'Yesterday,' began Brother Timothy, 'I presented the evidence in favour of Westminster Abbey's claim to Islip. I did so in good faith, firmly believing that the case would receive just, equitable and impartial consideration. When I left the shire hall, I took the trouble to ride out to Islip to view the land under dispute. While I was there, I chanced to meet the parish priest and fell into conversation with him.'

'Do we need to hear this gibberish?' grumbled Maurice.

'It is highly relevant, my lord.'

'How?'

'The priest was once chaplain to Hugh de Grandmesnil, sheriff of Leicestershire. He talked at length about that time and your name,' he said to Maurice, 'was mentioned more than once. I do not need to remind you why.'

Maurice glowered but there was no denial this time.

'I do not understand,' said Columbanus, baffled. 'What place has the sheriff of Leicestershire in a dispute that concerns a village in Oxfordshire?'

'Hugh de Grandmesnil is father to the lady Azelina,' explained Timothy. 'He would naturally support his daughter's claim to Islip as would anyone who had been in his household. My lord Maurice was once in that position. According to the priest, he might have looked to be deputy sheriff one day had he stayed in the county. At all events, he is a friend and confidant of the lady Azelina and thus not qualified to sit in judgement on this dispute.' He turned to Ralph. 'There is much more I can say on this subject, my lord. More evidence to support my charge. You will understand why I felt that our cause had been betrayed.'

'We have heard enough from you for the moment, Brother Timothy,' said Ralph through gritted teeth. 'I think that it is time my lord Maurice had a chance to defend himself.' He fixed him with a stare. 'Were you so acquainted with Hugh de Grandmesnil?'

'It was a long time ago,' said Maurice evasively.

'But you did serve him?'

'We fought together. It forged a friendship.'

'Why did you conceal it from us?'

'I did not think it had a bearing on our work.'

'It had a most profound bearing!' hissed Ralph before reining in his temper. He turned to Timothy. 'We need to discuss this in private for a time. Bear with us until we send for you, Brother Timothy.'

'Gladly, my lord.'

'The same applies to you, Brother Columbanus.'

'But I am your scribe.'

'No record need be kept of this conversation,' said Ralph pointedly. 'Besides, the language may grow warm in here and offend more cloistered ears.'

Columbanus nodded and followed Brother Timothy out. On a signal from Ralph, the four guards also quit the hall. There was a strained silence. Elbows on the table, Maurice leaned forward with his head bowed. Ralph stood over him.

'Can you deny this?' he demanded. 'Have you really been deceiving us all this while, Maurice? Working in collusion with the lady Azelina and her father?'

'She has the stronger claim to Islip,' retorted Maurice. 'You believed that, Ralph. Your verdict favoured her.'

'That is immaterial.'

'We did not know of your personal interest here,' said Gervase coldly. 'Your action has tainted us, my lord.'

'That was not my intention.'

'Then what was that intention?' yelled Ralph, quivering with rage. 'To pull the wool over our eyes while you showed favour to your friends? To pervert the course of justice? We have built our reputation on fairness and integrity. In one flawed judgement, you have put that reputation under threat.'

'Do not take this so personally, Ralph.'

'Can you not see what you have done?'

'Is it so serious a matter?'

'Yes, my lord,' affirmed Gervase. 'Extremely serious.'

'Awarding land to someone who legally owns it?' Maurice gave a hollow laugh. 'Where is the crime in that?'

'You prejudged the case.'

'When you had no right even to be a member of this tribunal,' said Ralph. 'Now I begin to see why you contrived to get yourself appointed. You pretended that the work was an imposition but you came to Oxford with a purpose. To help your friends at the expense of honesty and justice. Hell and damnation, man! This is rank corruption!'

'Come,' said Maurice, rising to his feet, 'which of you would not help a friend in the same circumstances?'

'Neither of us, my lord,' said Gervase.

'Do not be so pious.'

'You must have known that this dispute would come before us or you would not have agreed to join the tribunal. Did the lady Azelina make contact with you?'

'Or was it Hugh de Grandmesnil?' added Ralph.

'Roger d'Ivry, perhaps?'

'How was it done, Maurice? We will find out in time.'

'The King himself will wish to look into it.'

Maurice Pagnal was cornered. He could not wriggle or browbeat his way out of the situation. Only one possible escape remained and he seized on it with grinning desperation.

'We three are men of the world,' he said, reaching out to touch both of them. 'Nobody else needs to know of this. I will find a way to silence that infernal Brother Timothy. Let us resolve the matter here behind closed doors. Between friends.' He licked his lips before making his offer. 'Someone did appeal to me for help. When the ownership of Islip was to be contested, I was asked to use what influence I might have with the commission. We bore arms together, Ralph, so I hoped that friendship might carry the weight of a favour.'

'That hope was shipwrecked before it set sail.'

'Chance contrived better than I could myself,' continued Maurice. 'Canon Hubert fell ill and a replacement was sought. I used what connections I had at Court to have the name of Maurice Pagnal pushed forward. Others, too, had influence which was used subtly to secure my appointment. Thus it stands, my friends.' He looked from one to the other before blurting out his offer. 'Handsome payment was made for my help. The money is meaningless to me. I was prompted only by old ties. Take the money and divide it between you. Let it buy your silence. I will excuse myself from this commission and it can then continue with its reputation untarnished.'

'Untarnished!' howled Ralph. 'Untarnished! You offer us a bribe and tell us that our integrity will remain intact!'

'In the eyes of everyone else.'

'But not in our own, my lord,' said Gervase sharply.

'Do not be fools!' urged Maurice. 'You throw away a rich reward. Give yourselves some recompense for the tedium of sitting through this dispute. Share the spoils.'

Ralph's anger took over. Grabbing him by the shoulders, he hurled him to the floor with such force that Maurice slid for yards along the wooden boards. Ralph was on him at once. As Maurice pulled his dagger from its sheath, it was kicked away from his grasp. Fury was Ralph's weapon and Maurice knew that he had nothing to match it. He listened to his sentence.

Ralph was on fire. 'By the power vested in me as leader of this tribunal,' he said, looming over him, 'I strip you of your rank as a commissioner. The King will hear a full report of your crimes. You will be duly arraigned.' Taking him by the throat, he hauled Maurice upright. 'You have caused enough damage in Oxford. Leave by sundown, Maurice. Or answer to me.'

After a show of defiance, Maurice Pagnal slunk away in disgrace. Ralph watched until the door was closed behind him, then his rage slowly ebbed. He looked at Gervase and gave a hopeless shrug.

'Where do we go from here?'

'We summon Brother Columbanus and dictate a letter to Canon Hubert,' said Gervase. 'A fast horse would reach him in Winchester some time tomorrow. Hubert may have recovered his health by now. And even if he has not,' he added, 'I am sure that he would respond to your call.'

'Wise counsel. I'll act on it.'

'The dispute over Islip can be left in abeyance. We will look at it afresh when Hubert gets here.'

'And until then?'

'We suspend our investigations, Ralph.'

'We have to, I fear, though it will extend our stay here.'

'Let us make virtue of a necessity.'

'What do you mean, Gervase?'

'Someone else is in desperate need of justice,' said the other, 'and there is no tribunal to mete it out to him. Will you ride with me to Woodstock?'

The warm sun encouraged them to leave the drab interior of the keep and descend to the bailey where they perambulated slowly around the perimeter by way of gentle exercise. Golde kept in step with Edith in every sense. A friendship which took root on the previous night was growing apace as they discovered a wealth of shared interests and common experience. As they strolled amiably along, Golde shed all her reservations about Oxford Castle. It was no longer a place of such menace and discomfort. Edith made it seem homely.

'Do you have any children?' asked Edith.

'No, my lady.'

'It is still not too late.'

'I have no hopes in that direction.'

'Oh?'

'Ralph's first wife died in childbirth,' explained Golde. 'I would not put him through that suffering again. Such a tragedy is not certain to happen again, I know, but it is always at the back of my mind. We are happy in each other, my lady. Even without the blessing of children.'

'They are not always a blessing,' admitted the other with a sigh. 'Childbirth is a trial enough but raising a family can also be something of an ordeal in itself. It is such a responsibility to educate the young. I am glad all that is behind me now.'

'I'm sure that you were an excellent mother.'

'I tried, Golde. Within my limitations.'

Arnulf the Chaplain came out of the great square tower of the church and waved a greeting to them before heading for the castle gates. Edith looked fondly after him.

'Life is so ironic at times,' she mused.

'Ironic?'

'Arnulf would have made an ideal parent. Kind, loving and endlessly patient. He would have been a perfect father and yet he will never have children of his own.'

'It is the choice he made, my lady.'

'Yes,' said Edith. 'When he became ordained, he committed himself to a vow of celibacy. I teased him once and he said that he did have children. In his choir. They are his family and he dotes on them like any father.'

'I am looking forward to hearing them sing.'

'They are a positive delight, Golde. Even though they have lost their young soloist.'

'The chaplain told me about Helene.'

'He lavished so much time and care on that girl.'

'Perhaps he will find someone to take her place.'

Golde halted involuntarily as they came to the entry to the dungeons. An armed guard stood on sentry duty outside it. She remembered the prisoner who had been beaten to the ground by Edith's husband before being dragged down into the twilight of the dungeons. Golde wondered if the man was still alive down there.

Taking her by the elbow, Edith led her gently away. She seemed to know exactly what Golde was thinking. Neither of them spoke a word but they were at that moment closer than they had ever been, two compassionate women in a world that was dominated by the coarse brutality of men, one pretending not to notice while the other was denied that choice. They, too, Golde now saw, were trapped in a larger and more comfortable dungeon. The sweet sense of freedom which they had been enjoying was circumscribed by the high walls of the castle.

When they reached the gates, a sturdy figure came lumbering towards them. Maurice Pagnal was too preoccupied to greet them. His jaw was tight, his eyes staring, his head drooping with shame. Before they could detain him, he pushed roughly past them and went off towards the stables.

Edith was shocked by his blatant rudeness.

97

'What is amiss with him?' she wondered.

'They cannot have finished at the shire hall so soon,' said Golde. 'Ralph told me that they would not possibly be back until this evening.'

'Then why is my lord Maurice here?'

'They will not sit in session without him.'

Maurice was ordering one of the ostlers to saddle his horse. His knights were running to him to see why he was making such an unforeseen departure. Golde grew fearful.

'Where are Ralph and Gervase?' she said.

They tethered their horses on the fringe of the copse and stepped into the trees. Learning from his earlier visit to Woodstock, Ralph had brought them by a slightly different route to avoid being seen by Wymarc's men and thus hampered by the deferential companionship of their master. To conduct a proper search, they needed to be alone.

Gervase was shown the spot where the dead body had lain and surmised how it must have tumbled along the ground. Like Ralph, he decided that the assassin must have lurked near the point where the six horses in the race first entered the copse and were thus lost from sight to the spectators. After a careful examination of potential hiding places, he decided that a wych elm had offered the man the best cover.

'He stood here, Ralph. I am sure of it.'

'Then I am just as certain that he did not.'

'Why?'

'Borrow my dagger and you will find out.'

Ralph handed it over and Gervase moved behind the tree.

'Stand ready!' warned Ralph. 'The six horses are here.'

When Gervase stepped out to throw the dagger, he realised what Ralph had known instinctively. The wych elm was on the right of the horses as they galloped into the copse. To hurl the dagger after them with his left hand, Gervase would only have needed to move out a foot or so.

'But you are right-handed,' said Ralph, taking the dagger from him. 'Like most people. A right-handed assassin would never choose that side of the copse or he would have to come out into the open to throw his weapon.'

'Where do you think he lay in wait?'

'Let me show you.'

Gervase followed him to the ash and saw the advantages of cover and prospect which it afforded. Ralph drew his attention to the strange marks in the ground which he had noticed earlier. They were small, round indentations in the soft earth. Neither of them could decide how they had come there. Ralph grinned.

'My turn to be the assassin in the greenwood,' he said. 'It is as well for Maurice that he is not about to ride past for I would surely loose the dagger at him.'

'He certainly tried to stab us in the back.'

'Too true, Gervase. We were easily misled.'

'Brother Timothy did us good service in unmasking him.'

'Yes,' said Ralph uncomfortably. 'But I do not like to be beholden to monks. They are an unnatural crew.'

'Columbanus is an exception.'

'Only when he is drunk.' Ralph eased him back. 'Stand aside and I will show you how the murder was committed. Here come the horses and I pick out my man.'

One stride was enough to bring him half clear of the tree. Ralph threw the dagger with vicious force and it spun through the air until it sank into the trunk of a hazel.

'That was the easy part, Gervase. Now for the hard one.'

'What is that?'

'Disappearing.'

'Where?'

'That is what we must find out,' said Ralph, looking around behind the ash. 'But I would certainly not be stupid enough to race across open ground to the forest. A fleeing man is a form of confession.'

'Ebbi discovered that.'

'This is not his doing. You need a strong arm to throw a dagger with enough force to knock a man from the saddle. I am a more likely assassin than that poor wretch.'

'So where would you hide?'

'In the last place they would expect to find me. My guess is that he would have only a couple of minutes to conceal himself before they came in search of the fallen rider. It would be long enough to climb a tree.'

After reclaiming his dagger, Ralph led the hunt, picking his way through the undergrowth and assessing every tree as a possible refuge. Only three were high enough and leafy enough to provide adequate cover. After scrutinising their trunks, Ralph shook his head.

'How can you be so sure?' said Gervase.

'There are no marks upon them. A man shinning up those trees would leave some sign of his passing. He would be in a hurry, remember, so it would have been a scramble.'

'Unless he climbed up on a rope which he had earlier secured to one of the higher boughs.'

Ralph nodded appreciatively. 'We will make an assassin of you yet. I never thought of a rope. Climb up and put your theory to the test.'

'Climb up?'

'Of course. You are lighter than me and far more nimble. Come, Gervase. Try this tree first. I can easily bear your weight on my shoulders but you would collapse if I tried to use you as my ladder.' He knelt down. 'Step on to me and I will lift you up.'

Gervase obeyed his bidding, standing on his friend's broad shoulders and bracing himself with his hands against the trunk of a beech. Ralph rose up without effort and Gervase was able to grasp a bough and clamber into the heart of the tree.

'Find a branch strong enough to take a rope,' urged Ralph. 'Look for the marks that will surely be there. Then get yourself out of sight of the soldiers who will be standing exactly where I am now.'

'It cannot be done, Ralph.'

'Then you are up the wrong tree. Try another.'

Gervase had grave misgivings about the venture but it was important to eliminate all the possibilities. Ralph's strength hoisted him up into the other two trees but neither showed signs of a rope's bite on their branches and it was impossible wholly to vanish behind the foliage. Descent was somehow more hazardous than climbing and Gervase was glad when he dropped down from the last tree.

Ralph was perplexed. 'He must have had a hiding place,' he insisted. 'Unless he simply changed himself into a bird and flew away. But where? If not up a tree, was it under a bush?'

'I think not, Ralph. The soldiers would have flushed him out with their swords. From what you told me, there were enough of them searching in here.'

'Yet the assassin eluded them.'

'Apparently.'

'Up a tree or under a bush.' Ralph gave a low chuckle. 'There is only one other place it could have been, Gervase.'

'And where is that?'

'Beneath the ground.'

The funeral of Walter Payne was held at the parish church of St Peter's-in-the-East. It was part of a manor which comprised fifty houses, both inside and outside the town wall, owned by Robert d'Oilly. The benefice was in his gift and it had been bestowed on a stout, stooping priest of middle years with a keening voice and eyes which were forever searching the heavens for some kind of inspiration.

The sheriff himself was in the congregation with his steward and some of his knights. Milo Crispin was also present to see the unfortunate rider consigned to his grave. Wymarc was a reluctant mourner but feared that his absence would be noted and wilfully misinterpreted. Ordgar had also felt the need to attend and was accompanied by his son Amalric and by his steward, Edric the Cripple. What puzzled all of them was that there was no sign of Bertrand Gamberell at the funeral of his own man.

Minutes before the service commenced, there was a mild commotion outside and Gamberell finally appeared. He looked flushed and harassed as he slipped into his place near the front of the nave but his lateness was quickly forgotten by the congregation. Mass was sung and a short sermon about Walter Payne was delivered by a priest who had never really known him but who nevertheless contrived to move the hearts of all but a few. Gamberell was visibly distraught and tears moistened many otherwise hardened eyes.

When the coffin was borne out to the churchyard, a long file of mourners followed and arranged themselves in an arc around the grave. Walter Payne was laid to rest and the priest tossed in a prayer for his soul before the first handful of earth was cast by Gamberell. He stood there in watchful silence as the mourners gradually dispersed.

Gamberell was surprised to see Ordgar and faintly touched that the old Saxon had come to the funeral. He was annoyed to see Wymarc and relieved when the latter skulked guiltily away. But it was Milo Crispin who really aroused his ire. He sensed a deep complacence behind the poised manner. Milo was among the last to leave and the very act of lingering seemed to Gamberell like a deliberate taunt. Unable to suppress his rising anger, he followed Milo and grabbed his shoulder to spin him round. Gamberell stared accusingly.

Milo was unperturbed. 'You were late, Bertrand.'

'And you know why.'

'Do I?'

'You stole Hyperion.'

'Now why should I want to do that?'

'Out of sheer spite. You could not bear to lose another race to him. You stole my horse. Where is he, Milo?'

'I have no idea, my friend. But I hope you find him soon.'

'Why?'

'I have a horse of my own to beat him now.'

Turning on his heel, he left Gamberell speechless.

Chapter Seven

It took them the best part of an hour to find it. The hiding place was so carefully chosen and so cunningly disguised that they walked past it a dozen times without ever suspecting that it was there. Gervase Bret eventually stumbled on it by mistake. He noticed the fresh earth which had been scattered over a wide area among the bushes. When he knelt to take up a handful for closer examination, he felt the ground give way slightly beneath his weight.

'Ralph!' he called.

'Have you found something?'

'I may have.'

'Where?' asked Ralph, emerging from the thick shrubbery. 'I hope that this is not another false trail, Gervase. We've had a dozen of those so far.'

'This time, we may have more fortune.'

With both palms on the ground, he pushed down with his full weight and the turf gave way. Ralph let out a whoop of triumph and knelt beside him, using his dagger to probe further into the cavity. It was less a hole than a natural depression in the ground which had been hollowed out then covered over with the turf which had been lifted from it with such painstaking care. Twigs, bramble and small logs had been stuffed into the cavity to hold the turf in its original position, but they could not withstand the pressure from Gervase. Overhung by a thick bush, the hiding place was quite impossible to detect with the naked eye. Only a combination of patience and good fortune had finally brought it to light.

After removing the segments of turf, Gervase began to scoop out the wood and bramble which had supported it. The cavity was gradually exposed. Ralph Delchard began to have doubts about the find.

'Are you quite sure that this is it, Gervase?'

'Yes.'

'It's not big enough to conceal a man.'

'Not someone of your size and solidity, perhaps. But a slighter frame could easily be concealed in there.'

'Ebbi has a slight build.'

'So do I,' said Gervase. 'Let me try it for size.'

Ralph was horrified. 'You're going to crawl in there?'

'Why not?'

'You will get filthy.'

'It is in a good cause.'

'What about all those insects?'

'Someone who wanted to evade capture would not be troubled by a few ants. Nor even by the odd worm or two. Stand back.'

Gervase lay face down on the edge of the cavity then slowly rolled over until he toppled into it on his back. It was just wide enough and deep enough to accommodate him.

'Replace some of the turf,' he said.

'Are you mad, Gervase?'

'I want to be absolutely certain.'

'First, you drop into a hole in the ground. Now you want to be buried alive.' Ralph was aghast. 'How will you breathe?'

'That is what I wish to find out.'

'Then you are a braver man than I. Give me a sword and I will fight all day against superior odds without a qualm. But you would never get me to rehearse my own funeral like this.'

'It will not take long.'

'*Hic iacet Gervase Bret. Requiescat in pace.*'

He collected the segments of turf and replaced them in the order in which they had been lifted off the cavity. Gervase's legs and body would soon be completely hidden. Ralph picked up the final square of turf and hesitated.

'You are my dear friend. I cannot do this to you.'

'You have to, Ralph.'

'What if you suffocate?'

'I will not stay down here long enough.'

'Gervase, I hate this.'

'Cover my face.'

After further protest, Ralph acceded to his request and Gervase vanished from sight. The turf fitted so neatly that Ralph was astounded. Had he not known, he would never have guessed that a grown man lay inches beneath the surface.

'Can you hear me, Gervase?' he called. 'Do you want me to dig you out of there? Gervase!' A long silence. He became alarmed. 'Are you in trouble down there?'

Before he could grab the first section of turf, the whole patch suddenly erupted into life as Gervase sat up. He was caked in dirt and insects were crawling over him but there was a smile of satisfaction on his face.

'That was how it was done, Ralph. I have proved it.'

'All you have proved is that Gervase Bret could have been the assassin. Give me your hand.' Ralph hauled him upright in one fluent move. 'Look at the state of yourself.'

'It will brush off,' said Gervase, dusting vigorously with both hands. 'We have solved the mystery. We now know how it was done.'

'Could you breathe down there?'

'Not very well. Until I lifted the edge of the turf that lay across my face. Did you observe that?'

'No.'

'Then neither would that search party. We cannot blame them for not finding the man. He outwitted them. Then quit his hiding place when it was safe to do so and covered it up again so that nobody would discover his ruse.'

'Until we came along.'

'Yes,' said Gervase, detaching a worm from his hem.

'We have learned how he evaded capture. All we have to do now is to track the villain down.'

'There is someone else we must track down first, Ralph.'

'Who is that?'
'Ebbi's saviour.'

Robert d'Oilly listened with growing impatience to the demand. He raised a hand to silence the bitter recriminations.

'Enough, Bertrand,' he decreed. 'I will hear no more.'

'But you must, my lord sheriff.'

'You rush to judgement without proper evidence.'

'Milo covets Hyperion. Milo has thrice been humiliated by Hyperion. Milo has sworn revenge. What more evidence do you need? My horse has been stolen and I name Milo Crispin.'

'Then you do not deserve one more second of my attention. Milo is my son-in-law and a more upright man does not dwell in this county. Accuse him and you attempt to stain my family. Is that your intention?'

'No, my lord sheriff.'

'Did you see Milo steal the animal?'

'Not exactly.'

'Did you witness any of his men committing the crime?'

'The theft occurred privily.'

'And what clues were left behind?'

'None, to speak of.'

'In short, you have nothing beyond your own hostility towards Milo to indicate that he is involved here. False accusation is a crime in itself, Bertrand. Withdraw this charge against my son-in-law or he will call you to account and I will back him to the hilt. Do I make my purpose clear?'

Bertrand Gamberell's temper began to cool. He was coming to regret his premature confrontation with Milo Crispin. He believed that Milo might still be in some way responsible for the theft of Hyperion but it had been wrong to challenge him at the funeral. The stone-faced Robert d'Oilly reinforced the point with a wagging finger.

'Your own man lies in his grave and all you can do is bicker about a piece of horseflesh.'

'Hyperion is an exceptional animal.'

'That may be, Bertrand, but an animal is all that he is. Not a human being like Walter Payne. Can you not show some respect for your knight? Riding your horse cost the fellow his life. Does that not trouble your conscience?'

'Of course.'

'Then forget about the horse.'

'Hyperion has been stolen. We must find him.'

'The crime has been reported and I will look into it. In time. But I will not disrupt a funeral service to arrest my son-in-law on a charge that arises solely out of your blind rage.'

Gamberell felt slightly ashamed. They were standing outside St Peter's-in-the-East as the last of the mourners departed. The priest lurked beside the grave. Having ridden to Oxford on a borrowed horse, Gamberell had all but missed the start of the funeral and found it impossible to concentrate fully during the service. He was certain that Walter Payne's murder and the theft of the black stallion were interrelated crimes and he persuaded himself that both could be laid at the door of Milo Crispin.

Robert d'Oilly regarded him with frank distaste.

'Why did you make such a ludicrous allegation?' he said.

'I acted on instinct.'

'You are far too impulsive, Bertrand. As always.'

'Time will tell if I am quite so far from the mark.'

'Milo is no horse thief!'

'If you say so, my lord sheriff.'

'I do say so!' growled d'Oilly. 'What you claim about my son-in-law could equally well be said of Wymarc. He, too, is a rival of yours with a score to settle against you. Why not heap your accusations on him? Or even on Ordgar? He put a horse into that race alongside your black stallion. Could not he have plotted to steal the horse out of envy?'

'Ordgar would never dare and Wymarc would be too inept.'

'Then look elsewhere for your culprit.'

Gamberell nodded. His obsessive concern for the horse had blotted out all else from his mind and committed him to rash actions. Robert d'Oilly had rightly scolded him. Gamberell tried to bank down his wrath so that he could take a calmer view of the situation. His priority was to trace Hyperion as quickly as possible and he needed the sheriff's help.

'When was the horse taken?' asked d'Oilly.

'Earlier today.'

'Where was it?'

'In the stable.'

'At your manor?'

An awkward pause. 'No, my lord sheriff.'

'Then which stable?'

'It does not matter.'

'Of course it matters. If we are to pick up the trail, we must begin at the point where the horse was taken. Where was Hyperion at the time?'

Gamberell's hesitation was an explanation it itself. Robert d'Oilly burst into laughter then put a hand to his mouth to speak in a mock whisper.

'Who is the lady this time, Bertrand?'

'I have no idea what you mean.'

'The horse was stolen when you were bare-arsed in some bedchamber. There is your most likely thief. Do not drag Milo into this. You have one obvious suspect.'

'Do I, my lord sheriff?'

'Yes. Her husband.'

The laughter become more raucous as d'Oilly strode away.

She saw them from a long way off and scurried back to the hovel at once, diving inside and barring the door before running to close the shutters on the solitary window. Alone in the gloom, she crouched down behind the rough wooden table and waited. The hoofbeats eventually came within earshot. When a fist banged on the door, she shivered with apprehension.

Ralph Delchard pounded even harder on the door before trying to open it. The wooden bar held against his shoulder.

'There is nobody at home,' he concluded.

'There has to be,' said Gervase. 'Unless the door locked itself from the inside. You frightened her off.'

'Me?'

'She took one look at you and fled indoors.'

'You are more likely to have scared her off, Gervase. Look at the state of your attire, man. Scuffed and dirty. You rose from that grave like Lazarus and that is enough to put the fear of God into anybody. It terrified me.'

Gervase grinned and dismounted from the saddle.

'Leave this to me,' he suggested.

'I was about to kick the door in.'

'That is not the way, Ralph. Frighten her further and we will not get a word out of the woman.' He looked over his shoulder. 'When we came over the brow of that hill, I thought I saw movement down here. I was right. She must have espied us and gone to ground.'

'Not another one who burrows like a rabbit!'

'Move further off.'

'Why?'

'So that I may speak to her in her own tongue and try to win her trust. She will not come out if she sees a figure of such authority standing before her door.'

'I do not even wear a sword.'

'You do not need to, Ralph.'

A moment's reflection convinced him that Gervase was right. Ralph could only yell at the woman in a language which she had learned to hate even though she did not understand a single word of it. Compulsion would achieve nothing. Only gentle persuasion would succeed and that meant yielding control to Gervase. Taking both horses by the reins, Ralph led them a short distance away and tethered them to some bushes. He folded his arms and watched his friend in action.

Instead of belabouring the door, Gervase tapped softly.

'Leofrun!' he called. 'I wish to speak with you.'

The woman was astounded by the sound of her name and the kindness in his voice but it was not enough to draw her out of hiding. If they had come to arrest her, they would use any trick to ensnare her.

'My name is Gervase Bret,' he said. 'Ebbi has sent me.'

Her curiosity was aroused but she remained cautious.

'Can you hear me, Leofrun?'

There was a long pause and she hoped that he might have gone away. When he spoke again, his voice came through the shutters directly behind her. She spun round in alarm.

'We need to talk, Leofrun,' he said. 'Come to the window.'

Instead, she backed away and huddled in a corner.

'Ebbi told me about you,' he continued. 'He is in grave danger and only you can help him. He lies in a dungeon at the castle and will soon be tried by my lord sheriff for a murder that he did not commit. You know that he is innocent and so do I. Will you help him, Leofrun?'

'Who are you?' she croaked.

'A friend.'

'One of my lord sheriff's men?'

'No,' he explained slowly. 'We are strangers in the town. We have come to Oxford at the King's behest on important business. But this murder has interrupted our work and we would see it solved before we can continue.'

'Ebbi is no killer,' she averred. 'He is a good man, a kind man. Ebbi could never kill anybody.'

'I believe you.'

'Why?'

'Because I spoke with him myself. In his dungeon.'

'Have they hurt him?'

'He is not in good health.'

'They were cruel,' she said with spirit. 'I saw the way they treated Ebbi. Four soldiers against one man. They bound his hands tight then beat him black and blue. Ebbi had no chance against them.'

'He will suffer worse if you do not help him.'

'What can I do?' she wailed.

'Open the door and I will tell you.'

She was reluctant even to budge from the corner.

'Very well,' he coaxed. 'Look at me through the crack in the shutters and judge for yourself if I am friend or

110

foe. I will stand a few yards off. Will that content you, Leofrun?'

It took her a long while to pluck up the courage to respond to his suggestion. Rising to her feet, she crept across to the shutters and applied a wary eye to the crack. Gervase was standing away from the house. His smile was friendly and his manner unthreatening but she wondered why his garb was so covered in dirt. He gave an apologetic shrug.

'Forgive the state of my apparel,' he said. 'We have been searching in the undergrowth and this is the result. We were looking for clues that might help Ebbi.'

She angled her head so that she could appraise Ralph for the first time. A Norman baron was a more disturbing presence. Leofrun was worried that he might have soldiers within call.

Gervase seemed to read her thoughts once more.

'We have come alone,' he promised. 'My lord sheriff's men would have battered down your door without a second thought but they do not even know that you exist. Ebbi has shielded you once again. It has cost him dear.'

'What does he want of me?'

'The truth, Leofrun. That is all.'

'Who would listen to it?'

'I would. So will my lord Ralph here. We have influence at the castle and will speak in Ebbi's defence, but our word is worthless without your testimony. Will you give it?'

The latch was lifted on the shutters and they were flung wide. Leofrun was framed by the window. She was a short, swarthy, round-shouldered woman whose pleasant features bore the stamp of time and the drudgery that went with it. She wore a kirtle of homespun material and her hair was hidden beneath a torn hood. Smudged with grime, her face was still puckered in suspicion. Words came out slowly and painfully.

'Why should you wish to help Ebbi?' she said.

'Because he is plainly innocent.'

'How do you know?'

'The same way that you do, Leofrun,' said Gervase. 'When

Walter Payne was murdered during a horse race, Ebbi was here with you. No man can be in two places at the same time.'

Ebbi lay in the fetid straw, too weary to move yet unable to reach for the solace of sleep. Since his arrest in the forest of Woodstock, his life had been a continuous torment and he was coming to think that death, however agonising, might be a blessed release. His spirit had been broken. He no longer had the strength to despise Robert d'Oilly and to rail against the rank injustice of his situation. Ebbi had heard all the stories. Few people imprisoned in the castle dungeons ever came out alive again. Why should he fare any better?

The jingle of keys made him turn bloodshot eyes towards the door. When it creaked back on its hingers, Arnulf the Chaplain stepped into the cell. The door was locked behind him. The visitor knelt beside the wounded man.

'How do you feel now?' he asked.

'No better.'

'Take heart. All is not yet lost.'

'I feel that it is.'

'Have they fed you at all today?'

'All that I am given is foul water.'

'I am sorry to hear that,' said Arnulf, moving in closer to him. 'I am not permitted to relieve your hunger or I surely would. You do know that?'

Ebbi felt something being pressed into his hand. When he glanced down, he saw that he was holding a hunk of bread.

'God bless you!' he murmured.

Then he took a first desperate bite of the food.

Bristeva watched her brother put the horse through its paces. Bolt upright in the saddle, Amalric took his mount at a steady trot in a wide circle, gradually increasing Cempan's speed by judicious pressure with his heels. The chestnut colt was mettlesome and needed to be kept on a short rein. Edric the Cripple looked on with satisfaction. He had taught the boy to ride and was pleased with the skills that were

112

now second nature to him. Horse and rider belonged to each other.

Using his crutch, he moved across to Bristeva. They were in a field at the rear of the stables and the soft ground bore countless examples of Cempan's signature. As he broke into a canter, the horse left even more clods in his wake.

'Would you like to ride him?' asked Edric.

'No,' said Bristeva. 'He is too spirited for me. I am happy enough with my pony.'

'Your brother is a fine horseman.'

'Amalric will practise all day.'

'The only way to improve, Bristeva,' said the steward. 'At his age, I was often in the saddle from dawn until dusk. There is no greater pleasure for a man.'

'I prefer other delights.'

'So your father has been telling me.'

Bristeva liked the steward but she could never be as close to him as Amalric. Her brother looked upon him as a favourite uncle and often forgot that Edric was not a member of the family. In some ways, he was closer to the steward than he was to his own father. Edric certainly spent more time with him than Ordgar was able or inclined to do.

There could never be the same bonding between Bristeva and Edric. He was always polite to her but far more at ease in male company and a slight friction had crept into their relationship. It surfaced once again.

'Why do you bother with this choir?' he said, keeping his eyes on the circling horse. 'It is a waste of your time.'

'I like singing.'

'Then sing at home so that we may all enjoy your voice.'

'I only sing at the church.'

'For the benefit of the garrison.'

'Some of the townspeople come to hear us. Father Arnulf is always trying to invite more and more of them in.'

'Who wants to venture into that castle?'

'I do, Edric. They have been kind to me.'

'Normans are never kind to us, Bristeva,' he said with muted hostility. 'The most they will do is condescend. That is what Arnulf the Chaplain is doing to you.'

'No, he is not.'

'I spoke to your father about it.'

'About what?'

'This church choir. I think he should stop you going.'

'But I get so much pleasure out of it,' she said with a vehemence that surprised even her. 'Father Arnulf has been wonderful to me. He has taught me to appreciate music. He has turned me into a chorister. Nobody bothers with me here but he has shown a real interest in me.'

'I wish that were true,' said Edric, turning to look at her, 'but you are deceiving yourself, Bristeva. The chaplain is looking down his nose at you. Yes, he may have one or two Saxon children in this choir of his but not because he cares about you. To him, you are just performing bears hauled in to amuse the garrison.'

She was wounded. 'That's a terrible thing to say!'

'I'm only trying to warn you.'

'Father is glad that I'm in the church choir.'

'We've had many arguments on that subject. I see it very differently from Ordgar. He, too, is being misled.'

'Father Arnulf is my friend!'

'Then I will say no more.'

Amalric came trotting up to them and brought the horse to a halt. He looked at his sister's flushed cheeks.

'What ails you, Bristeva?'

'Nothing,' she said.

'We had an argument,' confessed Edric. 'It is over now.'

'What was the argument about?'

'It does not matter,' said Bristeva but her stomach was churning. 'I will go back indoors.'

'Wait!' said Edric, wanting to appease her. 'I am sorry I spoke out of turn. I had no right to do so.' He took the horse's reins. 'Let me show you what Cempan can really do.'

Amalric dismounted and the steward handed him his crutch. Grasping the pommel, Edric bounced on his foot then hauled himself into the saddle with remarkable ease. He disdained the stirrup and used his knees to control the horse. They set off across the field. It was no steady canter in a wide circle this time. Edric the Cripple was putting on an exhibition for them, zigzagging at a gallop and showing a control over Cempan that even Amalric could not match.

He brought the horse to a skidding halt then made it spin sharply on its heels three times before urging it on again. Cempan was soon racing once more and describing complex patterns in the field. The horse made so many sudden switches of direction that they felt giddy watching it.

Amalric was suffused with enthusiasm.

'I will ride like that one day!' he boasted. 'Edric will teach me. I want to be as good as him. I know I can do it.'

'Then you will be able to show off in the same way.'

'That is horsemanship of a high order, Bristeva.'

'Edric is making sure that we know it.'

He looked at her. 'What did he say to you just now?'

'I would rather forget it.'

'Do not fob me off,' he said. 'I could see that he upset you. Edric speaks his mind. What did he say to offend you?'

'He does not think I should be in the church choir.'

'No more do I.'

'Amalric!'

'Why do their bidding at the castle?'

'I enjoy singing.'

'You are out of place there, Bristeva. They laugh at you.'

'That is not so!' she said hotly. 'I am respected. Father Arnulf told me that I have improved beyond his expectations.'

'I am at one with Edric on this. Leave the choir.'

'Never! It is the most important thing in my life. I will never give it up. If you and Edric think it clever to ride a horse around a field, then go to it. I will not stand in your way. So please do not stop me doing what I want.'

'I am entitled to an opinion.'

'And I am just as entitled to ignore it, Amalric,' she said

with her eyes flashing. 'The choir means much to me. I have been given an education at the castle far beyond anything I could have hoped for. Father Arnulf now wants me to lead the choristers. That is a real honour. Think of it.' Her face shone with pride. 'I have been chosen to take over from Helene.'

Helene waited until the house was completely empty before slipping quietly upstairs again. It had been an effort to make conversation with the others and she was relieved to be on her own once more so that she could lose herself in her thoughts. She had already decided what she must do. When she got to the bedchamber, she locked the door then dragged the heavy wooden chest against it to barricade herself in. Then she closed the shutters and flicked the latch into place.

Sitting on the edge of the bed, she brooded endlessly in sombre silence. Weeks before, she had danced around the room and sung at the top of her voice but all that was in the past. There was no choir in her life any more. It could never be the same again. As memories crowded in upon her, she became more convinced that her decision was the correct one. There was no alternative. Helene was trapped.

She crossed to the chest and lifted the lid to examine her wardrobe. Her brother was a reluctant guardian but not without impulses of generosity. As she sifted through the various garments in the chest, she saw how much he had spent on her to turn her into an elegant young woman. But the very apparel which was intended to enhance her had proved her downfall. In a fit of sudden anger, she grabbed a tunic and tore it into shreds before being seized by a burning regret at what she had just done and trying, pointlessly but with pathetic determination, to stick the strips of material back together again in order to recapture associations which she had so recklessly destroyed.

It was hopeless. She discarded the torn fragments and slammed the lid of the chest shut once more. Then she moved to the bed and knelt down to feel beneath the mattress. Her hand closed on a tiny stone jar. It was cold to the touch. Helene brought it out to examine it, rubbing it between her palms for several minutes before removing the stopper and holding it beneath her nostrils. It had no aroma.

She looked around the bedchamber for the last time. A tide of regret swept over her. Helene closed her eyes tight and lifted the bottle to her lips. She had bought it from an apothecary in Oxford, telling him that she needed a strong poison to kill vermin. The contents of the bottle were drained in a second and her tribulations were almost at an end.

They were all there. Milo Crispin sat in the front row and waited with unruffled patience. Wymarc was a more restive spectator, shifting about on his seat as if it were on fire and darting glances at every person who entered the hall. Ordgar was not invited but came along as an interested party nevertheless. Still fuming at the loss of his horse and still harbouring grudges against all three of the others, Bertrand Gamberell stood at the window to catch an early glimpse of the man who had first set his misery in motion. When he saw the prisoner being brought up from the dungeon, his hand went straight to his sword.

'Take a seat, Bertrand,' ordered a curt Robert d'Oilly. 'And stay there throughout the proceedings. I am the judge here and you would do well to remember that.'

Gamberell schooled his rage and crossed to his seat. Milo, Wymarc and Gamberell were now in a straight line, separated by the knights who had watched the race at Woodstock and were thus additional witnesses. Ordgar sat alone at the rear of the hall, knowing that his evidence would never be sought. The fact that his horse had actually won the race was an embarrassing accident for his three rivals. They wanted a man to be convicted of the murder so that they could erase the memory of the fateful race from their minds.

The hall in the keep had been transformed into a courtroom. Robert d'Oilly sat behind the long table which had been turned sideways to face the witnesses. A scribe sat beside him to keep a record of the trial and the chaplain was next to the scribe, retained to act as an interpreter for the Saxon prisoner and looking distinctly uneasy with that role. Armed guards were on sentry duty at both doors. A room which had reverberated to the laughter of his guests on the previous night was now a chamber of death. The atmosphere was chill.

When the prisoner was brought in, he could barely stand. Swathed in bandages, Ebbi was dragged across to a stool to the right of the table and forced to sit. His hands were tied behind his back and he was patently in considerable distress. Temples pounding, Gamberell glared with hatred at the man. Wymarc, too, directed a blistering hostility at Ebbi. Milo was more detached from the whole thing and Ordgar, peering over their shoulders for a first proper look at the prisoner, felt a rush of sympathy for him. Guilty or not, the man would get short shrift from Robert d'Oilly. Ordgar had seen too many examples of Norman justice in Oxford to expect either fairness or clemency. Ebbi was doomed.

The sheriff banged a fist on the table to stifle the loud murmur which had started. With the funeral of the victim out of the way, he saw no reason to delay the trial. The sooner retribution was set in motion, the sooner he could shake Bertrand Gamberell from his back. Robert d'Oilly believed that summary justice was a useful instrument. It sent out a clear and unequivocal message that crime would be dealt with swiftly and savagely.

On the table in front of the sheriff was a copy of the Holy Bible but it induced no spirit of Christian charity in him. His voice boomed out with rasping authority.

'This court has been convened to try a man for the foul murder of one Walter Payne, knight, cut down at Woodstock but two days ago.'

He paused while Arnulf translated for the benefit of the prisoner. Then Robert d'Oilly surged on with his preamble.

'The slave, Ebbi, from the manor of my lord Wymarc, stands accused of this crime. The law is clear. If anyone breaks the King's peace, given by his hand or seal, so that he kills a man to whom the peace has been given, his limbs and life shall be in the King's decision.' His back straightened and his chest swelled. 'I represent the King in this shire.'

The chaplain took more time to translate this time and there was no indication that Ebbi even heard what was being said. The sheriff signalled to one of his men.

'Take the Bible to him so that he may take the oath.'

'How can he when his wrists are tied, my lord sheriff?' said Arnulf reasonably. 'May I suggest that his bonds be loosened so that he may place a hand on the Bible?'

'If it is held before him,' snapped the other, 'that will suffice. Explain to him the significance of the oath. God himself will be his witness here in this hall.'

Arnulf acted as an interpreter once more and Ebbi took the oath in a faltering voice. The Bible was replaced on the table and the sheriff consulted the document in front of him. He did not foresee a long trial. All the witnesses told the same story. He switched his gaze to Ebbi.

'How does the prisoner plead?

But there was no time for the words to be translated by Arnulf the Chaplain. Voices were heard outside, then the door was flung open and Ralph Delchard burst in. Everyone watched in stunned silence as he took a moment to look around before striding purposefully across the hall. Ralph stationed himself beside the cowering prisoner and put a compassionate hand on his shoulder. He spoke with quiet certitude.

'This man is innocent, my lord sheriff.'

119

Chapter Eight

Mild uproar greeted Ralph's announcement but it was quelled immediately by a peremptory command from the sheriff. Robert d'Oilly mustered all the righteous indignation that he could and directed a withering gaze at the newcomer.

'How dare you interrupt these proceedings!' he said. 'You have no place in this court and I demand that you withdraw.'

Ralph held his ground. 'I am needed here.'

'Leave now or I will have you removed by force.'

'That would be very foolhardy, my lord sheriff.'

'You are in contempt of court.'

'I have come to defend the prisoner.'

'Depart, sir!'

'Not until you have heard me out.'

'Away with him!'

He gave a gesture and four guards converged on Ralph but his bold rejoinder made them stop dead in their tracks.

'Stay!' he warned. 'Lay hands on me and you will have to answer to the King himself. He will ask stern questions about the administration of justice in this shire. King William already has cause to be displeased with Oxford. I came to the town bearing a royal warrant and accompanied by two other commissioners.' He aimed his words directly at the sheriff. 'One of those colleagues, Maurice Pagnal, whom you entertained as your guest at the castle, and with whom you discussed one of the cases that came before us, has been sent home in disgrace because he succumbed to bribery and tried to influence our verdict to the benefit of his paymaster.

Maurice Pagnal will face the wrath of the King. Am I to tell his grace that injustice runs much deeper here in Oxford?'

The four guards looked helplessly across at their master. Ralph Delchard exuded such authority and spoke with such fearlessness that they were reluctant to carry out the sheriff's order. Robert d'Oilly rescinded it with a flick of his hand and they returned gratefully to their positions.

Ebbi could not understand a word that was said but he sensed that he now had a friend. In a place where he had been treated with such cruelty, it was an unexpected bounty. He looked up at Ralph with pathetic gratitude.

Bertrand Gamberell saw only a mischievous interloper.

'Who are you?' he demanded.

'My name is Ralph Delchard and I am a royal commissioner.'

Realising who the newcomer was, Gamberell showed a modicum of respect. 'That gives you no right to interfere here,' he said with slight deference. 'This crime is outside your jurisdiction.' He rose to his feet to introduce himself. 'I am Bertrand Gamberell. My name will already have significance for you. Two days ago, one of my men was murdered in Woodstock during a horse race and I am here to make certain that his killer pays dearly for his crime.'

'First, make certain that you catch the right man.'

'He sits beside you, my lord.'

'Ebbi is innocent. We have the proof of it.'

'You know nothing whatsoever about this case.'

'That is not true,' said Ralph. 'My lord Wymarc showed me the scene of the crime and explained in great detail what happened. Is that not so?'

'Yes, my lord,' agreed Wymarc, enjoying a rare chance to dumbfound Gamberell. 'You expressed great curiosity and I was able to show you all that you needed to see.'

'Not quite all. There was a vital element missing. I have just returned from a second visit to Woodstock with fresh evidence.' He touched Ebbi again. 'And it exonerates this man here, who has been most shamefully abused.'

'Do not listen to him, my lord sheriff,' urged Gamberell.

'I believe that we should,' countered Wymarc.

'Your opinion was not sought.'

'Neither was yours, Bertrand.'

'Whose knight was killed out there in Woodstock?'

'On whose land did the murder take place?'

'Stop this bickering!' snarled Robert d'Oilly.

'Let me make a suggestion,' said Milo Crispin, who had preserved his composure throughout. 'If there is indeed new evidence, it should be taken into account but not before it has been sifted properly and that is best done in private. My advice is this, my lord sheriff. Adjourn the case until all the facts relating to it have been scrutinised then reconvene the court at your discretion. This answers all.'

'Well spoken, friend,' said Ralph.

'My name is Milo Crispin.'

'I had a feeling that it might be.'

'Milo talks sense,' endorsed Wymarc.

'We have delayed this trial long enough,' said Gamberell. I recommend that you proceed with it now, my lord sheriff. We have the guilty man before us. What more do we need?'

'The truth,' affirmed Ralph.

All heads turned to Robert d'Oilly. The decision lay with him and a great deal was hanging on it, not least his own reputation. If he let his authority be undermined by Ralph Delchard, then he would lose some of the respect in which he was held by the other barons and knights in the hall. On the other hand, were he to try the case without even examining the alleged new evidence, he would be incurring the displeasure of a royal commissioner and, through him, the anger of the King.

Two factors weighed most heavily with him. The trial was to have been a mere formality. He had pronounced sentence on Ebbi the moment the man was dragged before him and he had never doubted his guilt nor allowed Ebbi any chance of pleading his innocence. A Saxon villain suited his purpose in every way. If the prisoner were somehow exonerated and –

it did not bear thinking about – acquitted and released from custody, then his handling of the case would be shown to be seriously at fault. What he saw as legitimate force used to question an assassin would instead become mindless brutality against an innocent man. Robert d'Oilly needed a verdict of guilt. That prompted him to continue.

A second factor held him back and that was the dismissal of Maurice Pagnal. He was the one amenable member of the tribunal, impelled by an old loyalty and rewarded by a hefty bribe. The sheriff and he were kindred spirits. Yet Maurice had been exposed and instantly discharged from the tribunal. Ralph Delchard had asserted himself to great effect. There would be severe repercussions when the King heard the grim tidings, and the more Robert d'Oilly obstructed the royal commissioners, the worse those repercussions would be for him.

Ralph chose that moment to reinforce the point.

'No man is above the law,' he reminded. 'The greatest landholder in this county was the King's own half-brother, Odo, Bishop of Bayeux, Earl of Kent and one of the richest men in the kingdom. Where is he now? Languishing in prison, his lands forfeit.' His gaze moved from d'Oilly to Milo Crispin. 'Three men in this shire own between them one-fifth of its land. Two of them sit in this hall, the third, Roger d'Ivry, is presently in Rouen where he holds the Tower. None of those men is above the law. Let them remember Odo. If they try to thwart justice, they will bring the law down upon their own heads.'

Robert d'Oilly caught his son-in-law's eye and wished that he could appear as calm and detached as Milo, whose advice, as always, had been sound though uncomfortable. There was no easy way out of the predicament. Hiding his misgivings behind a show of authority, the sheriff banged the table once more and enforced absolute silence.

'This case is adjourned until tomorrow,' he said.

Coming to Oxford was in the nature of an ordeal for Leofrun. Crowds frightened her. She was a simple countrywoman who had rarely travelled more than a few miles from the place where she was born. In a town as big as Oxford, even with two men to escort her, she felt lost and threatened. Only the thought of helping Ebbi kept her from leaping down from Gervase Bret's horse and running back home. Leofrun was quite overwhelmed.

The sense of menace pressed down upon her even more when she rode through the castle gates. She clutched Gervase's shoulders tighter than ever, unused to being on any horse, still less on one ridden by a royal commissioner. Guards looked at her with derision, wondering why a scraggy old Saxon woman was being brought into the castle with such undeserved courtesy. She was humiliated by their sneers.

Gervase spent all his time trying to reassure her.

'You will not have to stay here for long,' he said.

'Take me back now.'

'No, Leofrun.'

'Then let me walk home. I cannot stay here.'

'You must. Until you are called.'

'I am afraid.'

'That is understandable.'

'They will hurt me.'

'Nobody will lay a finger on you.'

'I should never have come.'

'Would you desert Ebbi?'

She gave a despondent shrug. 'What can I do? Who would listen to an old woman like me? Nobody will believe me.'

'They will if you speak under oath.'

'I will not know what to say.'

'The truth.'

She began to sob and he put a consoling arm around her.

They were in an ante-room in the keep and Gervase was having doubts about her value as a witness. Leofrun was the only person whose evidence could save Ebbi but that evidence had to be offered clearly and confidently. If she was tearful now, when they were sitting alone on a bench, how could she possibly survive in a courtroom where she would have to face some searching questions? It had been embarrassing enough for Leofrun to have to confide in a stranger like Gervase. To make the same confession in front of more hostile listeners would be a continuous agony for her.

'It will not be as bad as you fear,' he said.

'I will let you down.'

'No, Leofrun.'

'I will let Ebbi down. He will hate me for it.'

'He will thank you with all his heart.'

A fond smile slowly spread across the moist cheeks.

'Do you think so?'

'I know it,' he promised. 'Ebbi sent me to you.'

'That is true.'

'He spoke so warmly of you, Leofrun.'

'Did he?'

'You are all that he has.'

Her voice cracked with emotion. 'Ebbi is all that I have. I cannot bear the thought of what he has suffered here.'

'Then help him, Leofrun.'

'Do you really think I can?'

'Be schooled by me and all will be well.'

She grasped his hands and squeezed them gratefully.

'Why are you being so kind to us?'

'I will not see an innocent man convicted of this crime.'

'Ebbi trusted you. I see why.'

'Put your own trust in me, Leofrun.'

She nodded and made an effort to collect herself.

'Will you be in there with me?' she asked.

'I will not leave your side.'

'How will I understand what they say to me?'

'I will act as your interpreter.'

'Will they deal harshly with me?'

'Not while I am there,' he said firmly. 'I am a lawyer by training. The court is my home. You will be safe.'

'Will I?'

Leofrun was unconvinced. She sat there in trepidation without saying another word. Several minutes passed. When the door opened without warning, she gasped in alarm. Gervase steadied her with a touch on her arm, then rose to speak to the guard who had just entered. The message was short. When the man went out again, Leofrun looked questioningly up at Gervase.

'The court has been adjourned,' he explained.

'What does that mean?'

'We got here in time.'

'Ebbi has been sentenced?'

'Not yet. My lord Ralph managed to stop the trial before it reached a verdict. He is now talking to the sheriff about you.'

'Me? Why?'

'He has to persuade the sheriff to admit your evidence.'

'And if he fails?'

Gervase did not attempt to conceal the truth from her.

'Ebbi will die.'

Robert d'Oilly was in a truculent mood. He did not like to be balked at any time. To have his authority questioned in so public a way was intolerable to him. When he conducted Ralph to a private apartment in the keep, he slammed the door behind them and confronted his guest.

'That was unforgivable!' he stormed. 'You barged into a court when a trial was in progress and had the audacity to claim that I am slack in my duties.'

'I made no such claim, my lord sheriff.'

'Take care how far you go!'

'There was no personal attack on you.'

'Oxford is mine,' declared the other. 'All mine. I have been castellan here for twenty years and kept this town under strict control. It is the only way to get respect from these people. Show one sign of weakness and you are lost. Rule by force and they learn to obey.'

'There is another way to earn their respect.'

'And what is that?'

'By dispensing justice.'

'I always do.'

127

'A trial such as this one? Hastily convened when the murder victim is still fresh in the ground? Why the unseemly rush? What time has there been to gather all the evidence?'

'The man confessed. That was evidence enough.'

'He admitted his guilt in so many words?'

'Well, no. Not exactly. But he did not deny it.'

'The fellow has been beaten to a pulp and scared witless. What credence can you place on anything he tells you? I saw Ebbi in court. Is that how you treat your prisoners before they are convicted?'

'He was insolent and unhelpful.'

'That means he did not admit his guilt.'

'Whose side are you on?' demanded the other.

'Yours. If you deal justly.'

Robert d'Oilly turned abruptly away and marched to the window. Down in the bailey, he could see an armed guard escorting Ebbi back to his cell. Arnulf the Chaplain was walking beside them, talking to the prisoner and reaching out to steady him when he stumbled. The sheriff waited until Ebbi disappeared from sight before swinging back to face Ralph.

'What is this new evidence?' he said sceptically.

'First, let me tell you how the murder was committed.'

'I know that already. The assassin hurled a dagger at Walter Payne's back then made his escape into the forest.'

'You are wrong, my lord sheriff.'

'Every man present has vouched for those facts.'

'Did any of them see the assassin run to the forest?'

'No,' conceded the other.

'Let me tell you why.'

Ralph gave a brief account of their search of the copse and discovery of the hiding place. The sheriff showed a grudging admiration for their pertinacity.

'You and Master Bret have been very thorough.'

'Gervase deserves the real credit,' said Ralph. 'He found the hole in the ground and lay hidden in it himself.'

'You have learned how the assassin eluded capture but that does not absolve Ebbi from blame. He may still have committed that murder before concealing himself in the hiding place.'

Ralph was scornful. 'You have met the man, my lord sheriff. Would Ebbi really have the strength and skill to hurl a dagger with such accuracy? Never! Nor would he have the guile to devise such a cunning hiding place in the copse. And there is another telling detail. When he was taken, did your men find Ebbi coated with dirt?

'They made no mention of it.'

'Then there is further evidence in his favour. Wait until you see Gervase. He was only in that hole for a minute or two yet his face was besmirched and his attire was covered with filth. Had Ebbi been under the ground much longer, he would have come out in a far worse state before he raced to the cover of the forest.'

'That is a fair point,' admitted d'Oilly.

'There is one final question to be asked.'

'What is that?'

'*Why* should he kill Walter Payne?'

'A random act of violence.'

'There was nothing random about this. It was planned with great care. The assassin chose his target and worked out his means of escape in advance. Ebbi has never met Bertrand Gamberell's knight.' Ralph spread his arms. 'Why go to such lengths to kill him?'

Robert d'Oilly was forced to bow to the inexorable logic of the argument but he was reluctant to loosen his grasp on the prisoner. A lesser crime could be attributed to him.

'What was Ebbi doing in the forest?' he challenged.

'I was coming to that, my lord sheriff.'

'At the very least, my men caught a poacher. Forest law is there to be enforced. Ebbi may yet hang on to his life but we'll castrate him for that offence.'

'Was he caught with game in his possession?'

'No, but he may have hidden it so that he could retrieve it at a fitter time. When my men hunted him down, he made a run for it. If he committed no crime, why should he flee?'

'Leofrun will explain that.'

'Who?'

'The witness we brought with us, my lord sheriff. Leofrun may seem like an ill-favoured old woman to us but Ebbi sees her through different eyes. That is why he ran from your men. To divert their attention and spare the blushes of a lady.'

'What are you talking about?'

'An assignation,' said Ralph with a grin. 'Ebbi and Leofrun had a secret tryst. He is single, she is a widow. They lack the marriage vows which would make their love valid so they have to resort to stolen moments of pleasure.' He gave a confiding chuckle. 'Come, my lord sheriff. Which of us has never dallied with a lady in the greenwood? We might not choose such an unsightly lover as this Leofrun but that does not alter the case. If we were surprised in the long grass with a lady, would not our first instinct be to protect her from discovery and shame?'

'This is some ruse,' decided the sheriff.

'It is God's own truth.'

'The woman is lying. She will say anything to save his balls from the knife.'

'She has a vested interest in those balls, I grant you. But ask yourself this. Would any woman admit in open court that she was copulating in the forest with a man to whom she is not wed unless she knew that he was completely innocent and that her confession could save him from a death sentence?'

Robert d'Oilly took time to consider Ralph's argument.

'Where is the woman?' he said at length.

'Here at the castle.'

'I will need to hear the story from her own lips.'

'Gervase will be a ready interpreter.'

'Fetch her in at once.'

'I will,' said Ralph. 'But first brace yourself.'

'Why?'

'Leofrun is a most unlikely enchantress.'

When Arnulf came back up the steps from the dungeons, he

saw Ordgar crossing the bailey and moved to intercept him. It was important to secure a father's approval.

'Has your daughter spoken to you?' he asked.

'Yes,' said Ordgar. 'Bristeva is thrilled.'

'What about you?'

'I am pleased with your decision, if somewhat surprised.'

'Surprised?'

'Can my daughter really deserve this honour?'

'She has a fine voice, Ordgar.'

'I know,' agreed her father, 'and I love to listen to her. But I have also heard the other girls in your choir, Father Arnulf. Much as I love my daughter, I must admit that Bristeva will never compare with my lord Wymarc's sister.'

'Helene did have an exceptional talent, it is true. But her brother has, alas, taken her from us. We miss her dreadfully. However, there is no point in dwelling on the past. We must look to the future and find a replacement for Helene.'

'And can Bristeva be that replacement?'

'I believe so.'

'She will need much help from you.'

'That is why I am glad of this chance to speak to you,' said Arnulf politely. 'I want your permission before we go any further. Bristeva will have to spend more time here at the castle from now on. Are you happy for her to do that?'

'Very happy. I will not hold her back.'

'You have no reservations about this?'

'None at all, Father Arnulf. You have surely seen that?'

'What I have seen is a loving father doing all he can to encourage his daughter. That is as it should be. But you have not always been the one to escort Bristeva to and from the church. When your son has brought her, I have sensed a strong disapproval.'

Ordgar stiffened. 'Has Amalric been disrespectful?'

'He has expressed a low opinion of the choir.'

'Let me speak to him. I'll chide him for his rudeness.'

'You might also have a word with your steward.'

'Edric?'

131

'Yes,' said Arnulf with mild embarrassment. 'I am sorry to have to report this to you. Your son has shown disapproval but it is your steward who has been openly hostile. On the few occasions when he has come to collect Bristeva from a choir rehearsal, Edric has been very resentful of the time she spends here. When I asked him why, he told me that your daughter had no place in the choir of a garrison church.'

'Then he spoke wildly out of turn.'

'It is a relief to hear you say that.'

'From now on, I will escort Bristeva to the castle. I will not have my son or my steward causing any upset. I am proud of my daughter's talent and will do all I can to let you develop it.'

'That brings me to the banquet.'

'Banquet?'

'I did not dare to mention this to Bristeva herself until I had first discussed it with you.' Arnulf glanced across at the keep. 'A banquet is to be held in the hall on Saturday in honour of an illustrious visitor. Geoffrey, Bishop of Coutances is to stay here as a guest and a lavish entertainment has been planned.'

'How does this affect me?'

'I want Bristeva to take part in that entertainment.'

Ordgar had immediate doubts. 'To sing before such a large gathering? My daughter is surely not ready for that.'

'She would be with careful rehearsal.'

'My lord Wymarc's sister would be a more suitable choice.'

'Helene is no longer available to us,' said Arnulf sadly. 'And I would hate to miss such an opportunity to display one of my choristers. Bristeva would only have to sing two songs. The bishop is known for his generosity.'

'The occasion might overwhelm her.'

'Not with me there to guide her and you to support her.'

'Me?'

'You would be invited to the banquet. When such an honour is bestowed on Bristeva, her father must be there to enjoy the moment. Will this persuade you?'

Ordgar required only a minute to reach his decision. By

singing at the banquet, his daughter would not only achieve some personal glory. There would be a tangible reward at a time when the family was sorely in need of money. A further inducement was the fact that Ordgar would for once be on equal terms with the Norman aristocracy as a guest at the banquet.

'Bristeva will sing for you.'

Arnulf the Chaplain gave a benevolent smile.

Apology was anathema to Bertrand Gamberell. It was an article of faith with him that he did what he wished and never had to explain or excuse his actions. The need for apology was something which only lesser mortals encountered. Gamberell had always been above it until now but the time had finally come when he himself was obliged to say that he was sorry. He was so unaccustomed to the process that he did not know where to begin. It made his discomfort even more intense.

'A word in your ear, Milo,' he said.

'I have heard enough from you for one day.'

'That is what I wish to discuss with you.'

'Save it until another time,' said Milo Crispin with a foot in the stirrup. 'I have to ride back to Wallingford.'

'This will not wait.'

'It will have to, Bertrand.'

Milo hauled himself up into the saddle but he was not allowed to leave. Gamberell held on to the horse's bridle. He searched desperately for the words which would assuage his rival without involving his own loss of face.

'Are you turned ostler now?' taunted Milo.

'I spoke too hastily at the funeral.'

'That is ever your fault, Bertrand. One of them, I should say, for you have many defects. Your words outrun your sense.'

Gamberell cleared his throat and shifted his feet awkwardly. His smile of apology was more like a grimace of pain.

'I was vexed beyond endurance,' he explained.

'That was plain.'

'Hyperion was stolen from me today. That was a terrible

shock. It put me in a choleric mood. When I arrived at the funeral, I was still pulsing with anger.'

'We all saw that.'

Gamberell clenched his teeth. There was more shifting of his feet and negotiation with his pride before he finally blurted it out.

'I was wrong to direct my anger at you, Milo. I was under great strain at Walter's funeral. Losing him in such a tragic way was a vicious blow. When Hyperion was taken from me as well, I could not at first handle my despair. Now I can.' He released the bridle and lowered his head. 'I am sorry to have accused you like that.'

'I would prefer to forget it, Bertrand.'

'Thank you.'

'On one condition.'

Gamberell looked up. 'What is that?'

'When you have found Hyperion again,' said Milo, 'and realised that I had no part in his disappearance, you must let me pit my own horse against your black stallion for double the original stake.'

'Gladly!'

'Wymarc, too, will be invited to take part.'

'What of Ordgar?'

'He will be unable to compete again, I fancy.'

'Why is that?'

Milo was impassive. 'It does not matter,' he said evenly. 'The first priority is to find Hyperion. Such a distinctive horse will be difficult to hide. I am sure that your men are already conducting a search. If you need help, I will put some of my own retinue at your disposal.'

'You take an uncommon interest in Hyperion.'

'I want him returned so that I may beat him.'

'You have no hope of doing that,' said Gamberell with a touch of his old bravado. 'Nor does Wymarc. You will both be throwing your money away yet again.'

'We shall see, Bertrand.'

'Do not delude yourself. You do not have a horse in your

stables to touch Hyperion. Wymarc's stables are even less equipped to compete with my stallion.' He gave a callous laugh. 'The only thing Wymarc has worth riding is that comely sister of his. Helene. I would be happy to saddle her myself.' He was still laughing as Milo Crispin rode away.

Leofrun shook like a leaf throughout the entire interview. She was terrified of the sheriff and humiliated by the position in which she found herself but she knew that she held the key that might unlock Ebbi and she tried desperately hard not to drop it. Robert d'Oilly questioned her closely and Gervase Bret was a deft interpreter. It seemed incredible that such an unprepossessing woman could arouse such ardent love in any man but Leofrun gave a clear testimony.

'We met in the forest every week,' she explained in a quavering voice. 'Always the same place, always the same time. Nobody suspected for a moment. What harm were we doing? In the sight of God, we may not have been man and wife. In our own hearts, we were. And always will be.'

It was a touching act of devotion. Even the sheriff came to accept that she was giving an honest account of what happened. Leofrun had no reason to lie. Her evidence and the discovery of the hiding place in the copse had complicated the murder inquiry. Suspicion was slowly lifting from Ebbi.

'It is a case of wrongful arrest,' argued Ralph.

'He should not have fled from my men,' said d'Oilly.

'Ebbi feared being mistaken for a poacher.'

'He should have stood his ground and explained.'

'A lady's honour was at stake.'

The sheriff wrinkled his nose in disgust.

'That is not what I would have called it,' he said. 'She stinks to high heaven. If I had been rolling in the grass with this revolting old Saxon sow, I would have run a mile sooner than own up to such bestiality!'

Although the insult was not translated for her, Leofrun gathered something of its import and looked deeply hurt. Gervase leapt swiftly to her defence.

'That remark was uncalled for, my lord sheriff,' he said with controlled anger. 'Leofrun has shown courage in coming here today and no little dignity. Before you sneer at her again for being what she is, you might remember that both you and my lord Ralph have chosen Saxon ladies as your wives.'

'And I could not have chosen better!' attested Ralph.

'Leave my wife out of this,' said d'Oilly. 'There is a world of difference between a gracious lady and a foul slut like this one before us. If she is Ebbi's woman, his five senses must be sadly lacking for nobody in his right mind would willingly touch, taste, smell, look at or listen to this creature with any hope of pleasure.'

'That is not the point at issue,' Gervase reminded him.

'No,' added Ralph. 'Whatever her shortcomings, she has spoken with great sincerity and her evidence clears Ebbi.'

'I am not so sure,' said the sheriff.

'You have examined her at length,' said Gervase.

'True. But I am not entirely satisfied with her answers.'

'Then press her even more on the subject.'

'What else can she tell us?'

'The situation is plain,' said Ralph, trying to nudge the sheriff towards a decision. 'Leofrun's evidence has changed everything. She has provided Ebbi with an alibi. You can either exercise your right to act upon her testimony and release the prisoner forthwith, or reconvene the court tomorrow and call her as a witness. Then we will have to go through the whole thing again.'

Robert d'Oilly contemplated the idea without enthusiasm. Ralph pressed home the advantage he felt that they had gained. He first nodded to Gervase and the latter took Leofrun out of the room. Then Ralph moved in close to his host.

'Well, my lord sheriff,' he asked, 'which is it to be? A quick decision in private or a long and tedious trial in public that will end in an acquittal? Set the prisoner free. Then we can join forces to hunt down the real killer.'

Ebbi was more confused than ever. Resigned to his fate, he

had fully expected the trial to end in his conviction. Ralph Delchard's intervention had delayed the proceedings and even raised the faint possibility of a reprieve. According to the chaplain, there were definite grounds for hope. Yet Ebbi was still shut away in a reeking cell, denied food, daylight and companionship, and treated in every way like a condemned man. The hope which had stirred in the courtroom was soon supplanted by his earlier despair.

When he heard the sound of voices, he did not even look up. Guards might be coming to mock him again, or Robert d'Oilly to interrogate him with even more ferocity. His body would not be able to withstand further torture. If confession would spare him, he was now ready to offer it without resistance. A key scraped in the lock and the door swung open. Footsteps rustled in the straw. The prisoner shrank defensively into a corner.

'Do not be afraid, Ebbi,' said Arnulf softly. 'It is over.'

'Over?'

'Your ordeal. The sheriff has signed your release.'

'Can this be true?' cried Ebbi, clutching at him.

'God has answered our prayers.'

'But what has changed the sheriff's mind?'

Arnulf helped him to his feet and guided him out.

'Her name is Leofrun. She is waiting for you.'

137

Chapter Nine

With four of his knights at his heels, Wymarc rode north-west out of Oxford towards his manor. He had much to occupy his mind on the seven miles home. Ralph Delchard's sudden arrival in the courtroom had been at once annoying and pleasing to Wymarc. He was irritated that the trial had been extended beyond the short time he had expected it to last, but he was gratified at the way in which Ralph had allowed him to secure a momentary advantage over Bertrand Gamberell by indicating that Wymarc had assisted the commissioner during the latter's visit to Woodstock. In his long battle of attrition with Gamberell, every successful blow which Wymarc landed on his enemy was to be relished.

Their rivalry had long roots. It grew partly out of Wymarc's envy of someone who seemed to enjoy an effortless superiority in almost every area of life. Where Wymarc had to sweat and struggle to achieve his aims, Gamberell did so with a studied nonchalance. Close in age, they were far apart in appearance and ability. All the advantages undoubtedly lay with Gamberell and, as a handsome bachelor, he could explore myriad pleasures that were for ever beyond the reach of an ugly married man like Wymarc.

It was when Bertrand Gamberell turned his plausible charm on Helene that her brother's hatred of him reached new depths. The girl was young and immature but that did not deter a seasoned voluptuary. When he learned that Helene was in the church choir, he took to lurking around the castle when she was due to leave, seizing a few minutes with her to flirt and entice and ensnare. Wymarc had broken up their conversations a number of times but no amount of dire warnings from him had held his sister back from further association with Gamberell. After singing the praises of God in church, she went out to play with the devil. Wymarc's only remedy was to take her out of the choir altogether.

The sky was slowly darkening as they neared the end of their journey and they kicked more speed out of their horses for the final mile. The house eventually came into sight and Wymarc envisioned a warm welcome from his wife and a hot meal prepared by his cook, compensatory comforts after a long day away from home. Disappointment awaited him. In place of the warm welcome, he rode into a scene of fear and tension. His wife and two of the servants were waiting outside the house to waylay him with their anxieties.

'Thank heaven you are come!' exclaimed his wife.

'Why?'

'It is Helene.'

'What is wrong with her?'

'She has barricaded herself into her room.'

'Not more tantrums!' he sighed.

'Helene refuses even to speak,' said his wife, taking his arm as he dropped from the saddle and hustling him towards the front door. 'She has not said a word for hours.'

'Is her door locked?'

'Locked and bolted. And the shutters are also closed.'

'Leave her to me.'

'She has not eaten all day.'

'This has got to stop!' insisted Wymarc, heading for the stairs. 'I'll stand no more of it.'

As he pounded up the steps, his wife, a short, thin-faced woman with a febrile prettiness, trotted behind him with the servants bringing up the rear. All four were soon standing outside Helene's bedchamber. Wymarc gave the door a hard and uncompromising kick.

'Helene!' he ordered. 'Come out at once!'

There was no sound from within. He kicked out again.

'Open this door or I'll force my way in. Do you hear?'
He interpreted the silence as deliberate insolence.
'This is your last chance, Helene!'

When there was still no reply, Wymarc's patience snapped and he put his shoulder to the door. The lock held at first but it could not withstand the repeated assaults of his beefy frame as he hurled himself against the timber. There was a splintering noise as the door finally surrendered its position but it retreated only a couple of inches. Something heavy was jammed up against it on the inside. Wymarc used the combined strength of himself and the two servants to dislodge it with a concerted shove.

The chest slid back, the door flew open and the hideous truth was at last revealed to them. Helene was lying spreadeagled on the bed, her limbs contorted, her face paler than ever, her eyes staring sightlessly at the ceiling and her mouth wide open to utter a cry of agony that nobody would ever hear.

'Helene!' yelled Wymarc.

His wife screamed, the servants gasped and everyone else in the house came running to see what had happened. Wymarc cradled his sister in his arms and tried in vain to revive her with profuse kisses and redundant words of love. He was so shaken by fear and afflicted with guilt that it was minutes before he even noticed the tiny stone bottle beside her.

In the capacious kitchen Edith was taking an inventory of their stock. Game of all kinds hung from hooks in abundance. Golde was amazed by the number of geese, chickens and other birds waiting to be plucked and she had never seen so many dead rabbits before.

'Twenty years ago, they were unknown,' she observed.

'Rabbits were brought over from Normandy as a delicacy. They breed quickly so they soon spread. We will certainly serve rabbit at the banquet. And venison,' Edith added as she looked around. 'We will need more. Far more. It is as well that Robert has hunting privileges in the forests.'

'How many are you expecting on Saturday?' asked Golde.

'Fifty at least. Probably twice that number.'

'A hundred guests!'

'We had even more the last time the bishop stayed at Oxford Castle. Geoffrey has a large entourage. He likes to do things in style.'

'So I can see.'

'He is a power in the realm, Golde.'

'I know that.'

'Robert wants me to spare no expense. Everything must be in perfect readiness. We have only a few days.'

As the two women walked between the tables and ducked under the swinging carcasses, the cooks and their assistants watched in obedient silence. A banquet would involve an immense amount of work for them but they did not complain. It brought Edith down to the kitchen and that was always a source of delight. She consulted them, directed them, cajoled them and generally made them feel that they were performing a vital service to the inhabitants of the castle. Under her careful supervision, any banquet would be a feast to remember.

'Is there anything I have forgotten, Golde?'

'Ale.'

Edith laughed. 'I will leave that in your hands.'

'The bishop will assuredly prefer French wine.'

'He drinks nothing else.'

'A moderate amount of English ale, then.'

'At your discretion.'

Golde's friendship with her hostess had been enriched even more. Edith put her so completely at ease that she felt they had known each other for years instead of merely a matter of days. Edith ran a discerning eye over some sides of pork and nodded in approval. They moved on to a table laden with fruit and cheese. Edith examined it with the utmost care.

Golde stood beside her and inhaled the various aromas.

'I am sorry we are an extra burden, my lady,' she said.

'Burden?'

'Ralph led me to believe that the work of the tribunal would be completed by the weekend. We should have ridden out of Oxford on Saturday and left you in peace to cope with your other guests. But the commission has had to suspend its work until Canon Hubert arrives.'

'I am delighted that you are able to stay, Golde.'

'The delay has been forced upon us.'

'So I understand.' She probed gently. 'Why did my lord Maurice quit the town so abruptly?'

'He and my husband had some sort of disagreement.'

'Do you know its exact nature?'

'Ralph does not confide in me, my lady,' Golde lied.

'No more does Robert in me and rightly so. Well,' she said with a smile, 'let us leave the affairs of the world to our husbands and concentrate simply on feeding them properly. This is where real power resides, Golde. In the kitchen. Important decisions can only be made on a full stomach.'

Golde laughed and followed her across to the serried ranks of fish, shimmering monsters laid out on stone slabs for their perusal and giving off the most arresting odours. Golde held her breath and took a couple of steps back.

'You made mention of entertainment,' she recalled.

'It would be a dull banquet without it, Golde.'

'What form will it take?'

'The details have yet to be finalised by our steward,' said Edith, prodding at a salmon. 'But we will certainly have music, dancers, tumblers and clowns. Minstrels will be hired and Arnulf has promised us a girl from his choir.'

'The celebrated Helene?'

'Alas, no. She is lost.'

'Who has taken her place?'

'A young Saxon girl.'

Golde grinned. 'I am all in favour of that.'

'Arnulf says she has considerable promise.'

'He is the best judge.'

'The girl will be sparingly used at the banquet but it will be a valuable experience for her.'

'And a pleasing one for us.'

'I am certain of that, Golde.'

'What is her name?'

'Bristeva.'

She arrived not long after dawn and he was there to greet her and to thank Ordgar for bringing her so early. Arnulf the Chaplain helped the girl down from her pony then tethered it to a rail outside the stables. When they had waved her father off, Bristeva followed her teacher eagerly into the church of St George's-in-the-Castle.

He could see that she was brimming with excitement.

'Your father has obviously told you.'

'Yes.'

'And what was your reaction, Bristeva?'

'At first, I was overcome with fright.'

'Why?'

'I have never sung in front of so many people before.'

'You will soon get used to that,' said Arnulf with an avuncular hand on her shoulder. 'Geoffrey, Bishop of Coutances loves choral singing and he will almost certainly wish to attend a service here to listen to you. As an additional treat, I want him to hear my best pupil at the banquet.'

Bristeva was diffident. 'Am I really the best?'

'Easily.'

'I do not feel it, Father Arnulf.'

'You are getting better all the time.'

'Helene had a far more beautiful voice.'

'Forget Helene,' he said with uncharacteristic sharpness, taking his hand away. 'She is gone, you are here. Helene let us all down, you will not. Will you, Bristeva?'

'No, Father Arnulf.'

'Do as I say and you will have nothing to worry about.'

She nodded dutifully and walked down the nave beside him.

Bristeva had been in a state of exhilaration from the moment she set out from home. Amalric had mocked her and Edric the Cripple had been cynical about the choir, but their comments had not dimmed her pleasure, and she was encouraged when her father upbraided both of them sharply for trying to upset her. On the ride to Oxford, he told her how proud he was of his daughter and how hard she must be prepared to work to meet the chaplain's high standards. In performing at the banquet, she would be representing her whole family.

When they stopped at the altar rail, she realised that she had never been alone in the church with him for a private rehearsal. Bristeva had always been one member of a choir before. Now she had been singled out and that filled her with the most unspeakable joy. Arnulf, too, seemed pleased to have a new soloist to whom he could impart his love of singing.

'I want you to be happy, Bristeva.'

'I am, I am.'

'Singing is an expression of joy.'

'I know, Father Arnulf.'

'You have that joy bubbling inside you and it is my task to draw it out. But I cannot do that without your help. We must share that joy together, Bristeva.'

'We will.'

He gave her a smile then indicated that she should kneel.

'Before we begin, let us pray together.'

'Yes, Father Arnulf.'

'We will ask for God's blessing on our endeavours.'

Bristeva knelt at the rail with her hands gently closed together. With his back to the altar, the chaplain stood facing her and enclosed her hands between his palms. She was deeply comforted. When Arnulf began to chant the prayer in a soft, caressing voice, Bristeva felt that she was almost listening to the voice of God Himself.

It was well past midnight by the time the doctor finally arrived. Wymarc's man had ridden several miles to summon him, only to find him absent on another call. A long wait ensued. When the two of them eventually reached the house in the pitch dark, Wymarc berated the doctor for keeping them waiting then rushed him upstairs to his sister's bedchamber. By the light of the candles, the weary doctor examined Helene. As soon as he realised what had happened, he cleared the room so that he could work in private.

145

Time trickled past. Wymarc began to wonder if the man had fallen asleep through fatigue. He himself had difficulty in staying awake. His wife had taken to her bed and the servants had been packed off to their rooms. Wymarc kept a lonely vigil in his parlour, hoping ridiculously that Helene could somehow be brought back to life yet knowing such a miracle was well beyond any doctor's skill. What hurt him most was the ranting discourtesy he had shown at the end. Helene lay dead and all that her brother could do was yell at her before smashing his way into her chamber. It was a kind of defilement.

Exhaustion finally claimed him. Wymarc fell into a deep and troubled sleep. When he was awakened at cockcrow, he saw that the doctor was sitting opposite him. Wymarc sat up with a start and rubbed his palms into his eyes.

'How long was I asleep?' he said.

'An hour or two.'

'Have you been here all this time?'

'For most of it.'

'Why on earth did you not rouse me?'

'You needed the sleep, my lord,' said the doctor quietly. 'You will get precious little of it when you hear what I have found out about your poor sister.'

Wymarc was on his feet. 'Was there no hope at all?'

'None, my lord.'

'If only you had got here earlier.'

'It would have been no use, my lord. Helene was dead long before you burst into the chamber. I know the signs. Her body is very eloquent.'

Baldwin the Doctor was a small, wizened, inoffensive man with an almost permanent smile of apology on his lips. A skilled physician, he was also kind and tactful when it came to passing on bad news about a patient to family members. The present situation, however, would tax even his discretion and he had been glad to find Wymarc asleep. The delay gave him time to come to terms with the tragedy and to frame the explanation he would have to give.

'Well?' said Wymarc.

146

'Helene died from a fatal dose of poison. Until a proper postmortem examination is carried out, it is impossible to say what type of poison it was though the rash on her skin would incline me to think that belladonna was a constituent element.'

'Would she have died in pain?'

'I fear so, my lord.' He saw the other wince. 'The position of the limbs suggests she had some kind of spasm.'

Wymarc was stunned. 'Helene? Poison? I cannot believe it, Baldwin. I *will* not believe it.'

'The evidence is unmistakable.'

'But who could have given her such a hideous concoction? Who could have tricked her into taking it?' He became furious. 'There's villainy at work here. I'll hunt down the culprit, no matter how long it takes. Helene has been murdered!'

'No, my lord.'

'Someone has poisoned my sister!'

'She took her life with her own hand.'

'Who could do such a thing to her?'

'Nobody else was involved.'

'This must be reported to the sheriff at once.'

'My lord,' said Baldwin, rising wearily from his seat. 'I am sorry to be the one to break the sad tidings to you but the truth must be faced. Helene committed suicide.'

'Never!' yelled Wymarc, seizing him by the arms. 'That is a hideous charge to make against my sister. Take it back at once. I will not listen to such calumny. Take it back!'

'If only I could.'

'Helene would never kill herself.'

'She did, my lord. Send for another doctor, if you do not believe me. Every physician in the land will tell you the same thing. Helene deliberately swallowed the contents of that bottle.'

'She was forced to drink the poison.'

'By whom?'

'The villain who procured it.'

'But there was nobody else in the bedchamber with her. It

was locked from the inside.' Baldwin grimaced. 'Please let me go, my lord. You are hurting me.'

Wymarc relaxed his grip and the doctor stepped back a precautionary yard, rubbing his arms to relieve the pain. He waited as Wymarc slowly came to accept the grim diagnosis. It was a long and harrowing process. As the full implications began to dawn on Wymarc, he staggered to a bench and lowered himself on to it, leaning forward with his elbows on his knees to bury his throbbing head in his hands.

'Think of the shame,' he murmured. 'The dreadful shame.'

'You have my deepest sympathy.'

'Helene! Of all people!'

'There will have to be an inquest, I fear.'

'Everyone will know. Everyone will remember. The whole county will point me out hereafter as the man whose sister took her own life. They will blame *me*.'

'No, my lord.'

'Tongues will wag. Fingers will point.'

'This is not the time to think of yourself,' suggested the doctor softly. 'Save your pity for Helene. She died in fearful circumstances. What made her choose such a painful exit from life? How did such a lovely young girl, with every advantage, come to lose the will to live?'

Wymarc shook his head. 'I do not know.'

'Helene had not been ill, to my knowledge.'

'She was fit and healthy.'

'What of her mind?'

'There was nothing wrong with her mind,' said Wymarc defensively. 'What are you suggesting?'

'Was the girl troubled? Racked by anxiety?'

'Of course not.'

'Had something upset her recently?'

'Helene was very happy,' insisted her brother. 'My wife will tell you the same. Helene was part of a loving family here. She had no cause to be troubled or upset.'

'No broken friendship, perhaps?' said Baldwin, fishing with a delicate line. 'Helene was beautiful. She must have had many admirers. Was there a special friend among them? Someone with whom she may have been involved in a romance?'

'There is no question of that.'

'Are you quite sure, my lord?'

'Completely. I would have known about it.'

'Not necessarily.'

'She was my sister, Baldwin,' the other reminded him. 'She lived under my roof. I know everything that Helene did and said. There was no romance with anyone. I would have forbidden such a thing. She would not have dared even to consider it.'

'I fear that you are mistaken.'

'That is impossible.'

Baldwin took a deep breath and steeled himself.

'You will have to know it sooner or later, my lord.'

'Know what?'

'Helene deceived you.'

'My sister was an obedient girl. She would never do that.'

'The proof is undeniable.'

'What are you talking about?'

'There was a romance of some sort, my lord. I examined her with great care. There is no room for doubt.' He gulped in some more air before delivering the blow. 'Helene was with child. When she swallowed that poison, she did not just take her own life. Mother and baby quit this world together.'

During the brief exchange with him in the courtroom, Ralph Delchard had taken an immediate dislike to Bertrand Gamberell and the man did not improve on acquaintance. When he cornered Ralph in the bailey of Oxford Castle the following morning, Gamberell was almost aggressive.

'What did you say to Robert d'Oilly?' he demanded.

'That is none of your business.'

'I wish to know.'

'You are wasting your breath by even asking,' said Ralph. 'The sheriff and I had a private conversation yesterday. We felt no obligation to include you in it.'

'I am deeply involved here.'

'From what I hear, Bertrand Gamberell is deeply involved with himself. Do not flaunt your vanity in my face for I'll not endure it.'

Ralph had been on his way to the stables when he was accosted by Gamberell. The latter's debonair appearance was at odds with his belligerent manner but he was nothing if not flexible. Realising that he could not harass Ralph to any effect, he tried another approach, producing the dazzling smile which had won him so many friends and conquests among the ladies of the county. Hands on hips, he appraised his companion.

'I like you, my lord,' he decided.

'You have a strange way of showing your affection.'

'Forgive my rash conduct,' said Gamberell easily. 'I have been sorely tried these past few days. First, one of my knights is slain at Woodstock, then my finest horse is stolen.'

'I committed neither of these crimes.'

'That is very true. Indeed, you have gone out of your way to help us solve one of them. That calls for thanks rather than condemnation.' He touched Ralph familiarly on the arm. 'Let us be friends, my lord. I have a strong feeling that we are cut from the same cloth.'

Ralph had an equally strong feeling that they had very little in common but he said nothing. Gamberell was a key figure in the murder inquiry. It would be foolish to spurn his help when he was in a mood to co-operate. Ralph offered him a non-committal smile which the other was quick to misinterpret.

'That is better,' said Gamberell happily. 'We both want the arrest and conviction of this assassin so we may as well work together. All I wish to know is why Ebbi was released.'

'Did you put that question to my lord sheriff?'

'Yes.'

'What did he say?'

'That your evidence had been very persuasive.'

'Then there is an end to it.'

'But I do not know exactly what that evidence was.'

'Suffice it to say that it proved Ebbi's innocence beyond any shadow of doubt. Did you really believe that a skinny old man like that could plot and carry out so cunning a murder?'

'Well, no, my lord,' lied Gamberell. 'To be candid, I always had grave reservations. Ebbi was totally unknown to me.'

'What do you mean?'

'I was the target of that attack. Whoever killed Walter Payne was really striking at me. Ebbi had no motive to do that. I thought at first he might have been hired by someone who had a grudge against me but such a person would surely engage a more reliable assassin.'

'Someone able to kill then elude arrest.'

'Exactly.'

'And to show some ingenuity in the process.'

'Ingenuity?'

Ralph told him about the hiding place in the copse which he and Gervase had discovered at Woodstock. Gamberell was duly astonished and impressed. He was also puzzled.

'Why have you become embroiled in this?' he said. 'You are here simply to decide who owns what land and how much tax should be paid on it. Tiresome work that should keep you immured in the shire hall. Why ride all the way to Woodstock to look into a crime that can surely hold no personal interest for you?'

'But it does, my friend.'

'How?'

'The major dispute which we have come to Oxford to settle concerns, as you well know, three claimants to the same property.'

'Milo, Wymarc and myself.'

'Is it not strange that exactly the same men are involved in a horse race during which a murder is committed? That is too much of a coincidence to ignore.'

'There was a fourth party involved, my lord. Ordgar.'

'His name only thickens the stew. Much of the land which Milo Crispin now holds was once in Ordgar's possession. You, too, have appropriated some of Ordgar's former manors. Can you see now why I am so curious about this whole matter?' said Ralph, eyeing him shrewdly. 'Four people engaged in a tenurial battle also take part in another kind of race.'

'And I was the loser!' sighed Gamberell.

'Suspicion must therefore fall on your three rivals.'

'I accused them to their faces.'

'And how did they respond?'

'Milo was a block of ice and denied the charge. Wymarc screamed his innocence and swore he'd take out an action for slander against me. Needless to say, he did not. Wymarc is all bark and no bite.'

'What of Ordgar?'

'He has neither bark nor bite,' sneered Gamberell. 'And none of the guile needed to plan such a crime. Besides, he expected his colt to win. Why set up a murder which is bound to render the contest void?'

'Apart from these three, do you have any other enemies?'

'Several, my lord.'

Ralph grinned. 'Vengeful husbands, perhaps?'

'Who knows? My concern is that the man is apprehended quickly. He has already killed one of my men and stolen my horse. The next outrage may be a direct attack on me.'

'I think that unlikely.'

'Why?'

'To begin with, you have no proof that the assassin and the horse thief are one and the same man.'

'He *feels* like the same man.'

'Not to me.'

'He is hell-bent on hurting me, my lord.'

'Then ask yourself this,' said Ralph, watching a horse as it was led out of the stables. 'Would someone who is ready to kill your man in broad daylight be content merely to take your stallion? He would be much more likely to slaughter the animal and send him back to you in pieces.'

Gamberell saw the logic in his argument and nodded. But the new perspective on the crimes brought him no comfort.

'It seems that I now have two enemies instead of one.'

Ralph shook his head. 'I am not entirely persuaded that you have any who would go to such lengths.'

'I must have. An assassin killed my man.'

'Then we should be looking at Walter Payne's enemies. It will be a blow to your self-esteem but you may have to accept the fact that Bertrand Gamberell is in no way involved in this murder.'

'I am bound to be. Walter was one of my knights.'

'He was the intended victim.'

'As a means of getting at me.'

'No,' said Ralph, feeling his way through the argument. 'As a means of getting at Walter Payne. The race was seen by the killer as both an opportunity and a decoy.'

'Decoy?'

'It made you look in the wrong direction. Our assassin is more guileful than I thought. He has led you by the nose. All this time, you have wondered who is striving to get at Bertrand Gamberell instead of asking yourself who had a motive to kill Walter Payne.'

'Nobody.'

'We all have enemies of some sort.'

Gamberell was perplexed. He was so convinced that he had been the indirect target of the murder that he could not easily accommodate a theory about the crime which relegated him to a peripheral role. He felt obscurely cheated.

Ralph pursued his new line of thought relentlessly.

'Your stallion, I hear, was previously invincible.'

'Hyperion won all three races.'

'And who was in the saddle each time?'

'Walter Payne.'

'So he was your preferred rider?'

'My best horseman. And the only person, apart from myself, who could handle such a fiery animal as Hyperion.'

'The assassin knew that he would be in the race that day,' said Ralph. 'All that careful planning would not be wasted.'

'Everyone *liked* Walter.'

'Everyone but the killer.'

'Walter Payne was a good man. Loyal to a fault.'

'Had he always been in your service?'

'No,' said Gamberell. 'He came to me a couple of years ago. Before that, he was in the employ of Geoffrey, Bishop of Coutances. Walter fought under the bishop's banner many a time and talked fondly of those years. That is why his death is such a tragedy. Walter was looking forward to the banquet with real excitement.'

'Banquet? Here at the castle?'

'Yes, my lord. On Saturday. The honoured guest is none other than Bishop Geoffrey himself. I promised to take Walter along with me as my guest so that he could be reunited with his old master. Fate can be so treacherous.'

Ralph said nothing. His mind was racing with Hyperion.

Having come to church to pray, Gervase Bret stayed to listen to the choir rehearsal. He sat at the rear of the nave as their voices soared up to heaven under the direction of Arnulf the Chaplain. The eight members of the choir looked vaguely incongruous when they first arrived but their voices blended perfectly. Gervase was enchanted. He found himself singing the Kyrie eleison with them.

The door opened and a figure slipped quietly into the church. Gervase guessed who he was. When Bristeva sang her solo, the newcomer's face was a study in pride and pleasure. Gervase waited until the rehearsal was over before intruding on the old man's joy.

'You are Bristeva's father, I believe,' he said.

'That is so. My name is Ordgar.'

'The chaplain talked about you. He has a high opinion of your daughter. Having heard her sing, I share that opinion.'

'Thank you.'

Gervase introduced himself and the two fell easily into conversation. The old man watched his daughter with a smile but there was a wealth of sadness in his eyes.

'Bristeva has a gift,' observed Gervase.

'It comes from her mother. She, too, could sing.'

'But not in any church choir, I suspect.'

'No, sir. That would have been out of the question.'

'Arnulf has wrought many changes here.'

'He is a good man,' said Ordgar readily. 'We did not have to come to him. He went out into the town and beyond, looking for choristers and making no distinctions. He would take anyone who was willing to learn.'

'It was a wise policy. Bristeva is proof of that.'

'I refused to let her come at first,' admitted Ordgar. 'This is a garrison. I know how crude soldiers can be. I did not want my daughter exposed to ribald comments and worse.'

'What changed your mind?'

'Arnulf the Chaplain. He promised me faithfully that no harm would come to the girl and none has. Arnulf has shielded her from any unpleasantness. Here in the church, she and the others are perfectly safe.'

'It has been a delight to listen to them,' said Gervase. 'And I look to hear more of Bristeva when she sings at the banquet on Saturday.'

'If indeed she does so.'

'But it is all arranged. The chaplain has already chosen the two songs which she is to sing. You have heard her, Ordgar. Your daughter is more than ready for such a test.'

'It is not my daughter who is the problem, sir,' sighed the old man. 'It is my son, Amalric.'

'Your son?'

'I have tried to overrule him but he is too headstrong. Amalric hates the idea of his sister performing in front of revellers at a banquet in a Norman castle. He has sworn to me that somehow or other he will stop Bristeva from singing here on Saturday night.'

Chapter Ten

His horse was saddled and his men ready to depart from the castle with him but he first had to take his leave of his wife. Golde had come down into the bailey to wave Ralph Delchard off. He strode swiftly across to her to collect a farewell kiss.

'I thought you might have gone by now,' she said.

'Bertrand Gamberell detained me.'

'I have heard that name a lot in the last day or two.'

'So have I, alas!'

'He is very popular with all the ladies in the castle.'

'Yes,' said Ralph, 'and he knows how to trade on his popularity. A backstairs man, if ever I saw one. A smiling, soft-voiced predator of the bedchamber. A sly, dangerous, devious satyr with the fiendish good looks to seduce a holy nun and turn her into a rampant harlot. No woman is safe while Bertrand is on the loose.'

'Are you warning me?' she teased.

'Only if you feel in need of a warning,' he said with a grin. 'And I doubt that. No, you would be more than a match for Bertrand Gamberell. You are too strong and self-possessed to fall for his tricks. He finds his victims among the weak and unprotected. You are neither.'

'I am still interested to meet this man.'

'You will, Golde. He will be back in time. He is leading the hunt for his missing horse again. A black stallion named Hyperion. One stallion is searching for another.' He stole a second kiss. 'But I must away.'

'Where are you going?'

157

'To Wallingford.'

'As far as that?'

'I want to speak with Milo Crispin,' explained Ralph. 'He was another witness of the race at Woodstock. He may furnish me with details which others forgot or were too distracted to notice. Milo is a shrewd man. I met him briefly yesterday but we had no time for conversation.'

'My lady Edith adores him.'

'She would. He is her son-in-law.'

'She says that he is a cool and capable man.'

'I saw something of his coolness in the courtroom,' said Ralph. 'It is certainly not shared by Bertrand Gamberell. Still less by Milo's father-in-law. Robert d'Oilly is a peppery sheriff when he is crossed. I am glad that I am not one of his underlings. A man with such a vile temper can be vicious.'

'We both saw evidence of that.'

The two of them looked involuntarily at the dungeons.

'No more brooding on that,' said Ralph, trying to depart on a more cheery note. 'What will you do while I am gone?'

'Pine for your return.'

He laughed. 'I'm sure you have other plans.'

'I do, Ralph,' she said. 'There are still many decisions to be made about the banquet. My lady Edith wants me to help her. Last evening, we went down to the kitchen and discussed the fare to be served. Today, we finalise the entertainment.'

'You are entertainment enough for me, my love.'

'I am talking about public performance,' she scolded. 'It is going to be the most wondrous feast. Almost everybody of consequence in the shire will be there. I am glad that our stay in Oxford has been extended so that we will be here for the occasion. My lord Maurice deserves our thanks for that.'

'If for nothing else!' said Ralph seriously. 'Maurice Pagnal has much to answer for, I fear.'

'My lady Edith tried to sound me out about him.'

'What did you tell her?'

'Nothing whatsoever.'

'Good. Her husband obviously set her on to you.'

'Surely not. She was simply being curious.'

'He ordered her to question you, to see if she could find out from you what I would not divulge to him. Say nothing, Golde. Trust nobody.'

'Would he really use his own wife as a spy?' she said, mildly shocked by the notion. 'Would he drag her down to that level?'

Ralph glanced around to make sure they were not overheard.

'Robert d'Oilly would stop at nothing,' he said bluntly. 'And that includes having a man murdered during a horse race at Woodstock. I am almost coming to believe that our host may be the one who instigated this crime. What better way to cover his own tracks than to lead the inquiry into a murder which he himself set up?'

Bristeva was so full of girlish excitement that her father did not have the heart to mention the cloud on the horizon. On the ride back to their home, he let her talk about the rehearsal at the church and rhapsodise about Arnulf the Chaplain.

'He is the kindest man in creation, father.'

'A true Christian.'

'Some of the boys snigger at him,' she said, 'but they don't know him as well as I do. And they are jealous because he has chosen me to take over from Helene.' She giggled with delight. 'They were so angry when Father Arnulf told them that I was going to sing at the banquet in front of the Bishop of Coutances. Father Arnulf said such wonderful things about me. I know it is a sin to be vain but I could not help enjoying his praise. Out of the whole choir, I am the only one who will go to the banquet.'

'It is a signal honour, Bristeva.'

'I am so looking forward to it!'

'Yes,' he said with forced enthusiasm. 'So am I.'

Ordgar was only half listening to his daughter. His mind was grappling with the problem of what to do about his son.

Amalric had been quite adamant. Having thought it over, the boy had decided to do all he could to prevent his sister from taking part in what could be the most important night of her life so far. Bristeva's joy was very fragile. It would be shattered beyond repair if her chance to sing at the banquet was taken away from her. Ordgar mused on the perils of fatherhood. There seemed to be no easy way to reconcile his children. They were locked in conflict. The happiness of one directly depended on the unhappiness of the other.

They were close to home when Bristeva raised the issue herself. She knew that deep disapproval awaited her.

'Will you speak to Amalric for me, please?' she said.

'I will try.'

'Make him understand how much this means to me.'

'Yes, Bristeva.'

'And talk to Edric as well. In some ways, he is worse.'

'They see things rather differently from us.'

'Why?'

'When you are older, I will explain.'

'I cannot believe that I am doing anything wrong.'

'You are not, Bristeva.'

Amalric was working in the field when they rode up. He shot them a hostile glance then turned away without even offering them a greeting. Bristling at the insult, Ordgar vowed to confront him at once and compel his obedience. They dismounted and Bristeva went running into the house, eager to scavenge in the kitchen for food. Her father waited until she was out of sight then swung round and marched purposefully towards the field. He was soon overhauled.

'One moment!' called Edric the Cripple, hobbling after him on his crutch. 'We need to talk.'

'The accounts will have to wait, Edric.'

'This is nothing to do with the accounts.'

'I must speak to Amalric first.'

'Let me save you the trouble, Ordgar.'

'What do you mean?'

'Stand still and I will tell you.'

The old man came to a halt and Edric moved in close.

'I know what you are going to say to your son.'

Ordgar was forceful. 'I will say the same to you, Edric. Leave Bristeva alone. I will not have the girl baited by either of you. She has had precious little enough to smile about since her mother died. Now that something good has finally happened to her, I will not let you and Amalric ruin it. It is not kind. It is not fair.'

'I know,' admitted Edric shamefacedly. 'I am sorry for pouring cold water on her happiness. It was a terrible thing to do. Why should I spoil the girl's pleasure? I have reasons of my own to loathe Oxford Castle and all that it stands for but it means something else to Bristeva. I see that now.'

'Do you?'

'Yes. Mine is one story, hers another.'

'It is such a relief to hear you say that!' exclaimed the other, embracing him warmly. 'In all the years we have known each other, this is the one thing on which we have disagreed.'

'Not any more.'

'Do I have your word on that?'

'I will not censure Bristeva again,' vowed Edric. 'From now on, I will hold my tongue in her presence.'

'This pleases me more than I can tell you. I want amity in my home. I am so grateful, Edric. If only my son would come to his senses in the same way.'

'It will take more time to persuade Amalric.'

'He is threatening to cause mayhem on Saturday.'

'Leave him to me,' advised the other. 'Challenge him now and you will only stir up his anger. The boy needs a day or so to calm down properly. I'll choose the right moment to reason with him.'

Ordgar was touched. 'Would you do that for me?'

'For you and for Bristeva.'

'I want my children to be reconciled, Edric.'

'They will be.'

'What will you say to him?'

'I am not sure yet. But I will find the words.'

'You always do.'

Ordgar knew that the steward had far more influence with his son than he did. Edric the Cripple was like a second father to him. His values were the ones that Amalric admired, his life was the one which the boy wanted to emulate. There was a time when Ordgar had resented his son's obvious preference but he was now resigned to it, and saw how it could actually work to his advantage. At a stroke, Edric had relieved him of the task of reprimanding his son and guaranteed that Bristeva's role as a performer at the banquet at the castle was no longer under threat.

The two men headed back towards the house.

'We will go without him,' decided Ordgar.

'Without him?'

'On Saturday night. To the banquet. Amalric and I were invited to join the feast so that we could listen to Bristeva sing. It would put too much of a strain on him. He can be so impulsive. He might do something wild.'

'Not if I curb him strongly enough.'

'Amalric is not easily curbed,' sighed Ordgar. 'Besides, you will not be at the banquet. Suppose he loses control? Suppose my son starts an affray? He would bring shame down on the whole family.' He flung a glance over his shoulder. 'It will be safer to leave Amalric here.'

'But he has been invited, Ordgar.'

'That is true.'

'How many times will he be asked to sit at the sheriff's table and revel in his company?'

'Never again, probably.'

'Then why take this one opportunity from him?' said Edric. 'It is not every day that the Bishop of Coutances visits Oxford. Let your son see the great man in the flesh. He will not like him but that is no reason to deny him the right to meet him.'

'I hate to deny my son anything but I have to lean towards caution here. Amalric can be hot-blooded. We both know that. How can I enjoy the performance of my daughter if I am afraid that my son may suddenly disrupt the banquet?'

'There is one obvious solution.'

'Is there?'

'Take me to the castle with you,' volunteered Edric. 'I will undertake to stifle Amalric. He might defy you, Ordgar, but he would not dare to disobey me.'

Ordgar was surprised. 'Can you be serious?'

'I would never make such an offer lightly.'

'After all that has happened? You would be prepared to attend a banquet at Oxford Castle in the presence of Robert d'Oilly and the Bishop of Coutances?'

'Yes, Ordgar.'

'Here is a change indeed!'

'It is long overdue,' admitted Edric. 'Even hatred mellows with time. I am coming round to your view. When I was in Warwickshire earlier this week, I gave much thought to the problem. Bitterness destroys. It eats you up from the inside. I will not spend the rest of my days fighting a battle that was decided many years ago.'

'These words are music to me, Edric.'

'Take me with you to the castle on Saturday.'

'I will.'

'Amalric will cause no upset. I give you my promise.'

Brother Columbanus faded so completely into the background that they almost forgot he was there. With the work of the tribunal suspended, the monk's official duties ceased until further notice and he exploited his unexpected freedom. Gervase Bret was coming in through the castle gates when he met Columbanus. He was pleased to see the beaming countenance of his friend once more.

'Well met!' he said. 'We have missed you.'

'I have deliberately made myself scarce, Gervase.'

'Why?'

'Because I do not wish to get in your way.'

'We enjoy your company, Brother Columbanus.'

'And I delight in yours,' said the other genially, 'but therein lies the danger. When I break bread with you, I also have the urge to sup ale and that is a temptation I must suppress in every way.'

'A monk is allowed to drink ale in moderation.'

'Yes, Gervase. But what is moderation? If I drink one cup of ale, I tell myself that a second cup is a moderate amount. After that, a third is irresistible. By the time I am reaching for a fourth, all thought of moderation has left me. You see my dilemma?' He gave a merry chuckle. 'I am a weak vessel.'

'Recognition of your weakness is a strength in itself.'

'That is my solace. Since I cannot always resist the temptation, I will henceforth avoid it altogether. That is why I have been absent from the table.'

'Where have you been taking meals?'

'Here and there, Gervase,' said Columbanus. 'Here and there. The canons of St Frideswide's fed me last night and gave me spiritual nourishment as well. I am on my way there now to draw on their fellowship.'

'Then I will not hold you up.'

'When will I be needed again?'

'Not until Canon Hubert arrives.'

'And when will that be?'

'A day or two at least,' reckoned Gervase. 'Probably more. We rode from Winchester on swift horses. Canon Hubert will only travel on his donkey and that sets a much slower pace. He may not arrive until Sunday.'

Columbanus brightened. 'After the banquet, then?'

'Yes. Does that make a difference to you?'

'No, no, Gervase. Not in the slightest.'

He let out another chuckle, patted his companion on the arm, then walked jauntily out through the gates. Gervase was both amused and puzzled by his behaviour. Columbanus was a jovial Christian who freely owned up to human fallibility but his joviality was edged with contrition. Gervase wondered why.

He stood aside as six riders trotted across the bailey and clattered out through the gates. The soldiers were patently in a hurry. Arnulf the Chaplain provided the explanation.

'They are on their way to Woodstock,' he said, walking over to meet Gervase. 'To begin the hunt all over again. My lord sheriff was not pleased to release Ebbi. He truly believed that he had the killer of Walter Payne locked up in a cell.'

'The assassin is still at liberty.'

'And so is Ebbi now. Thanks to you and my lord Ralph.'

'We could not let an innocent man die.'

'He suffered great indignities while he was here,' said Arnulf. 'By rights, he is owed some compensation.'

'What hope is there of that?'

'None, I fear.'

'My lord sheriff will never be accused of compassion.'

'He gave you a fair hearing, Gervase,' countered the other, keen to defend his master. 'My lord sheriff had the grace to admit that he was misled. When you presented your evidence and let Leofrun bear witness, he accepted that Ebbi had been wrongfully imprisoned and ordered his release at once.'

'That is not quite what happened,' said Gervase, recalling the sheriff's intense reluctance, 'but the result is what counts. Ebbi was set free. Leofrun will medicine his wounds.' He pursed his lips as he gazed up at the keep. 'What alarms me is the speed with which the legal process moved. Is the law always administered with such celerity in Oxford? A man is killed, a suspect is arrested, a trial is ordered. I have never known such summary justice. Why did my lord sheriff feel the need to act so swiftly?'

'He abhors delay of any kind.'

'Delay can mean the difference between life and death. Had we not been here, Ebbi would have been tried, convicted and executed for a murder that he did not commit.'

'Nobody regrets that possibility more than I.'

'It is almost as if Robert d'Oilly had a private reason to rush this trial. Do you know of such a reason?'

Arnulf shook his head and Gervase let the matter drop.

'I heard the choir practice earlier on,' he said.

'We saw you at the rear of the nave.'

'A small congregation but an appreciative one.'

165

'Thank you.'

'Bristeva was in fine voice.'

'Yes,' sighed Arnulf, 'but whether that fine voice will be heard at the banquet on Saturday is open to question. Her father gave me disturbing news.'

'I spoke with Ordgar myself.'

'Then you will know the problem we face. Bristeva is eager to sing for us but Amalric, her brother, is just as eager to stop her. I offered to talk to the boy myself but Ordgar felt that it was his duty to do that. He did, however, agree with my other suggestion.'

'What was that, Arnulf?'

'On the eve of the banquet, Bristeva will sleep here at the castle. It will give us more time to rehearse together, and if she is away from home she will not be subject to Amalric's sneers. It grieves me that I have to protect a girl from her own brother but there is no other way.' He gave a wry smile. 'My choir is afflicted by unhelpful siblings.'

'So it seems.'

'First Helene. And now Bristeva.'

'Both have met with opposition from their brothers.'

'My lord Wymarc was a more formidable proposition. He took Helene away from me. That is not going to happen to Bristeva,' Arnulf vowed. 'I will fight to keep her. She is my Helene now.'

Hours of pleading had left Wymarc's voice hoarse. Ignoring the pain in his throat, he summoned up all of his remaining energy for a final assault on Baldwin the Doctor.

'I beg you, man! Please help me!'

'I wish that I could, my lord, believe me.'

'Save me from certain scandal and disgrace.'

'The law must take its course,' said Baldwin.

'Only if the true facts of the case are disclosed.'

'As they must be.'

'No, Baldwin!' hissed the other. 'You are Helene's doctor. Give out that she was taken ill and died before you could reach her. We will say that she has been sickening for days, which, in a sense, is true. Nobody will question your word and the hideous truth will be kept within these four walls.'

'That is not possible, my lord.'

'Why not?'

'Honesty compels me to reveal all. It is my duty.'

'Do you not have a duty to me? As your friend?' Wymarc clutched at his purse. 'I would not expect you to do this service for nothing. Name your price. It will be paid.'

'No amount of money can make me do what you ask.'

'Please!'

'It is wrong, my lord.'

Wymarc let out a gasp of despair and turned away to sink down on a stool. Baldwin crossed to stand beside him, fighting off his own fatigue and reminding himself of the solemn obligations laid upon his profession. Though he had some sympathy for Wymarc, he could not even consider what the latter was trying to persuade him to do.

'Understand my position,' he said reasonably. 'I am a doctor. I have a code of ethics. If I suppress the truth, I am committing a terrible crime. The consequences would be quite horrendous.'

'Only if the crime came to light.'

'It is bound to, my lord.'

'Is it? Who else knows besides you and me?'

'Your wife knows that Helene is dead. So do your servants.'

'We will tell them she died of natural causes.'

'Is it natural to barricade yourself into a bedchamber? Is that the action of someone who is desperately ill?' Baldwin shook his head. 'No, my lord. Nobody would believe that story. A healthy young woman will not expire so suddenly. Your wife and servants know that full well.'

'I'll force them to keep their mouths shut!'

'How long would such enforcement last?'

'Indefinitely!'

'You would not be able to stand guard over them twenty-four

hours a day,' argued Baldwin. 'It would only need one person to let slip an inadvertent remark and the whole fraud would be exposed. In any case,' he added, 'there are two people whom even you are not able to gag.'

'Who are they?'

'One of them stands before you, my lord. I simply will not countenance such a gross deception. And then there is Helene's chosen accomplice.'

'Accomplice?'

'Your sister did not concoct that poison herself. It was supplied to her by someone with skill enough to make such a lethal preparation. When that person hears of Helene's death, the cause will be self-evident.'

'Such a person would not dare to come forth.'

'Do not be so sure, my lord.'

'In providing a fatal poison, he will have assisted in the crime of suicide and be liable to arrest. It is in his interests to remain silent about his role.'

'But think of the power they would wield.'

'Power?'

'Over you, my lord,' said Baldwin. 'The cunning apothecary who sold Helene that bottle of death will wish to make even more profit from the transaction. He would be in a position to lay information against you that would bring the sheriff and his men galloping out here to investigate. An unsigned letter is all that it would take.' He covered a yawn with his hand. 'In brief, you would be open to blackmail.'

'I'd part with every penny I have to keep this secret buried!' howled Wymarc, jumping to his feet and punching a fist into the palm of his other hand. 'I'd give *anything*, Baldwin.'

'It will not come to that.'

Baldwin spoke with untypical firmness and Wymarc's hopes crumbled. The doctor would not conceal the truth. Helene's suicide would become common knowledge and her brother would be left behind to bear the brunt of the infamy. Her pregnancy would subject him to further humiliation and he could already hear the crude speculation that would arise.

Wymarc had failed his sister abysmally and his failure would now be published.

Grateful to be allowed to leave, the doctor paused at the door to offer some parting advice to the grieving brother.

'There is someone we have forgotten, my lord,' he said.

'Who is that?'

'The man who fathered the child. If, as it seems, Helene took her young life to escape the shame of bearing a child out of wedlock, then the man must take some responsibility.'

'He will,' vowed Wymarc. 'He will.'

'Seek him out. That is my counsel.'

'It will be done, Baldwin.'

'Do you have any idea who he might be?'

Wymarc did not hear him. His mind was seven miles away in Oxford Castle, watching a handsome man on a black stallion, preening himself as he waited to talk to Helene.

Milo Crispin was less than pleased to see his uninvited guests riding into Wallingford Castle but neither his expression nor his manner hinted at annoyance. Ralph Delchard and his men were given a courteous welcome and offered refreshment after their journey from Oxford. While his six knights were taken off to be fed in the kitchen, Ralph himself was conducted to the hall where he accepted a cup of wine and picked at a bowl of fruit set out on the table in front of them.

They soon dispensed with conversational niceties.

'You have come to talk about Woodstock,' guessed Milo.

'Yes,' admitted Ralph. 'I want to hear from all four of you who were involved in that race.'

'Why?'

'Because it will enable me to build up a complete picture of what actually occurred.'

'I see that, but why should you bother to do so?'

'Why not?'

'It is the sheriff's duty to solve the crime.'

'I am giving him a helping hand.'

'Even though he has not requested it?'

'With respect to your father-in-law, he needs all the help that he can get,' said Ralph, selecting an apple. 'If I had not seen fit to aid him in this investigation, a blameless man would have been sent to his death for the crime. Is that what you would have preferred?'

'Not at all.'

'Then why do you object to my involvement here?'

'It is not so much an objection as a polite enquiry,' said Milo smoothly. 'When you set out from Winchester, I imagine that you had more than enough work to occupy you in Oxford.'

'We did. Satchels full of it.'

'Yet you somehow find the time to ride around the county and talk about a horse race. It does seem strange to me.'

Ralph grinned. 'I have always been eccentric.'

'I hope these eccentricities will not get in the way when you sit in judgement on me at the shire court.'

Ralph's grin broadened. Milo Crispin was a more appealing man than either Wymarc or Bertrand Gamberell. The one had fawned and flattered while the other postured irritatingly. Milo had poise and self-control. Nobody could intimidate him. He would never try to curry favour with a royal commissioner. Milo Crispin and Ralph Delchard occupied the same baronial rank. In every sense, they met on equal terms.

'Did you know Walter Payne?' asked Ralph.

'Yes.'

'Very well?'

'As well as I wished to do,' said Milo. 'He was a fine horseman but he was not the sort of knight I would ever keep in my retinue.'

'Why not?'

'He was too boorish. And too wayward.'

'Bertrand Gamberell called him a good man.'

'Do not trust his definition of goodness.'

'He said that Walter was exceptionally loyal.'

'But loyal to what?' said Milo evenly. 'Loyal to the Gamberell code of boasting and bullying. Those knights of his are drunken oafs. My own men have clashed with them often enough to get their measure. Walter Payne was among the worst of them. Always trespassing on my land and harassing my tenants for sport.'

'Bertrand painted a rather different portrait.'

'He would.'

'You hated this Walter Payne, then?'

'Let us say that I did not shed a tear at his funeral.'

'Did you have a motive to kill him?'

'Several.'

'Were you the assassin's paymaster?'

'No.'

'How can I be sure of that?'

'Because I would never have assigned the removal of Walter Payne to anyone else. I prefer to settle my own scores.'

Ralph chewed on a piece of apple and regarded him with fresh interest. Milo's composure was extraordinary.

'Thank you,' said Ralph.

'For what?'

'Giving me straight answers.'

'It saves time.'

'I would be grateful if you could pass on that advice to your father-in-law. He has been less forthcoming.' He rose from the table and wandered idly to the window, gazing down into the courtyard. 'I rode through Wallingford once before,' he continued. 'Some twenty years ago when we were still trying to acquaint the Saxons with the concept of defeat. They took time to accept it, especially in this area. King Edward kept a garrison of his housecarls here. I seem to remember that they gave us stiff resistance for a while.'

'They were doughty warriors.'

'Just like those who fought against us at Hastings.' He swung round. 'But I did not come to reminisce. I am here to find the man who killed Walter Payne and you have already helped me in that search.'

'Have I?'

'By eliminating yourself as a suspect.'

Milo was firm. 'My horse took part in that race in order to

win. No other business drew me to Woodstock that day. My sole aim was to beat Hyperion in a fair contest.'

'Hyperion has been a thorn in your flesh.'

'My hope was to pluck it out.'

'Who stole the horse from Bertrand?'

'I have no idea.'

'Then it was not you, I take it?'

'No,' said Milo patiently. 'I am a busy man, my lord. You have ridden across my land and seen how much responsibility all those acres place upon me. I simply do not have the time to hire an assassin or to steal a horse. Nor would I demean myself by sinking to such depths.'

Ralph walked back to the table and stood close to him.

'Who did kill Walter Payne?'

'Someone who despised the man enough.'

'Was the assassin really striking at Bertrand Gamberell?'

'No.'

'That was my feeling.'

'Why go to such trouble to kill a servant when the same guile would enable you to kill his master? Bertrand was not the target. Walter Payne was the intended victim. His murder was carefully planned.'

'Who contrived it?'

'That is for you to find out.'

'I would be grateful for some more help.'

'All that I can offer is a wild guess.'

'There will be nothing wild about anything you say, my lord. I am certain of that. You are one of the most deliberate men I have ever met. Now, sir. What is this guess?'

Milo kept him waiting. Getting to his feet, he crossed to the door and opened it to indicate that the discussion was being terminated. His tone was neutral.

'Ride north again,' he advised.

'Why?'

'The man you are looking for had a grudge against Walter Payne because he was riding Hyperion. Why kill him during a race if not to disable him from winning yet again? Who knows, my lord? With another rider in the saddle, Hyperion might not be quite so invincible.'

'Give me a name.'

'I could easily be wrong.'

'You know the parties involved far better than I.'

'Then talk to the man who lost most heavily in the previous races,' said Milo calmly. 'Talk to the one who took his defeat most to heart. Talk to the one whose younger sister was plagued by the attentions of Walter Payne. Talk to the one who would do anything to preserve the girl's virginity. Talk to someone with real cause to fear Walter Payne.'

'Who is that?'

'Wymarc.'

Exhausted, dishevelled, unshaven and half asleep, Wymarc was slumped in a chair in his parlour. His wife flitted around him like a demented butterfly, anxious not to upset him yet eager to say something which might comfort him and relieve her own mind. She did not yet understand the enormity of what had happened in an upstairs room. A tragedy which had crushed her husband's spirit and reduced him to an inert mass was still making her twitch violently and grasp feverishly at non-existent solutions to their plight.

'The doctor may have made a mistake,' she said nervously. 'It was late when he arrived. Baldwin was weary and over-wrought. His diagnosis was wrong. It has to be wrong. Helene would never do such a thing. It is unthinkable. Helene was a good girl. We brought her up with true Christian precepts. She could not do this to herself.' A shockwave made her whole body shake. 'Or to us. Helene would never hurt us. She loved us. She had to love us. We were her family. Helene was part of a loving family.' Her voice trailed to a whisper. 'These things do not happen in . . . loving families.'

There was a long pause as she gathered her strength for a second burst of self-delusion. Wymarc was motionless. When there was a loud banging on the door, he did not even blink. A servant answered the door and the visitor was admitted.

Arnulf the Chaplain darted across to her at once.

'I came as soon as I got your summons!' he said.

'We prayed that you would.'

'Tell me everything. Can this hideous news be true?'

'Ask my husband,' she said, indicating Wymarc. 'He spoke with the doctor. He knows the details.'

Arnulf had not even noticed Wymarc when he first arrived in the room. He now went over to the crumpled figure and saw the deep distress he was suffering. The chaplain put out a gentle hand to touch his bowed head.

'It is Arnulf,' he said softly. 'You sent for me, my lord. And I have come. I am here for you.'

Wymarc slowly raised his head and looked at him with no sign of recognition. It was a full minute before he realised that it was the chaplain who was standing in front of him. A sudden fit of anguish coursed through Wymarc and he flung himself on his knees, gibbering pathetically and clutching desperately at Arnulf.

'Help us!' he implored. 'In the name of God, help us!'

Chapter Eleven

Rumour swept through the castle like wildfire. What first reached the privileged ears of the sheriff was soon in the mouths of his underlings. Hardly a soldier or servant in the place had not picked up and passed on the sensational gossip. Even the guests caught wind of it. The story took on new shape and force each time it was told. A paucity of facts did not hamper its narrators in any way. It merely permitted greater invention. Endlessly embellished, the tale was soon vaulting over the high walls of the fortress into Oxford itself to be used as common coinage in the market before being dispersed breathlessly throughout the whole community.

It was Gervase Bret who gave the sad tidings to Brother Columbanus. Shaken to the marrow, the monk crossed himself by reflex and offered up a silent prayer. The shining face was now a wrinkled map of concern.

'This is dreadful intelligence!' he wailed.

'It has shocked everyone, Brother Columbanus.'

'How certain are you of the facts?'

'I had them from Arnulf the Chaplain,' said Gervase. 'He was sent for by the family because he knows the girl so well.' He winced slightly before correcting himself. '*Did* know her.'

'What age would this Helene be?'

'But fourteen.'

'God in heaven! A child! A mere child!'

'Her life over before it had really started.'

'By choice, Gervase,' mourned the other. 'Her life is over

by choice. That is the tragedy here. The girl chose to do this terrible thing. With a whole bright future stretching out in front of her, Helene went down this irrevocable path. Why?'

'She did not see her future as altogether bright,' said Gervase sadly. 'If the rumours are to be believed, she had some cause for pessimism.'

'What was it?'

'She may have been with child.'

Columbanus goggled. 'Spare her that, please!' he gasped. 'To take her own life is a black enough sin in itself. Do not let us hear that she also committed infanticide. The very thought unseats my brain, Gervase. To kill an innocent babe in the womb? Helene would have to be deranged to do that.'

'Or driven to despair.'

'Did the chaplain confirm this gruesome detail?'

'He confided simply that suicide was confirmed,' said Gervase. 'The rest I have gathered from a dozen or more tongues and less credence can be placed in it. What is beyond dispute is that, some time yesterday, my lord Wymarc's sister ended her days on this earth.'

'With a virulent poison, you say?'

'That is what I was told.'

Brother Columbanus took refuge once more in prayer. He had been returning to the church of St George's-in-the-Castle when he was intercepted by Gervase. If anyone had to break such heart-rending news to him, he was glad that it had been his young friend. With a careful use of words, Gervase had softened the impact of his report. Elsewhere in the town, the storytellers were doing the very opposite, garnishing the bare facts with spicy details to give them more flavour and pungency.

The monk reached into his memory for guidance.

'I call to mind the words of St Augustine of Hippo,' he said. 'He rightly argues that Christians have no authority to commit suicide in any circumstances.'

'I know, Brother Columbanus. I have read *De Civitate Dei*.'

'An inspiring text. Inscribed upon my soul.'

'Canon Hubert often quoted it to us.'

'Were he here now, he would doubtless remind us of St Augustine's argument that it is significant that nowhere in any of the sacred canonical books can be found any injunction or permission to commit suicide either to attain immortality or to avoid or escape any evil.' His eyebrows soared. 'The sixth commandment is clear: "Thou shalt not kill." We must not kill another person but, equally, we are forbidden to kill ourselves. That is God's law.' He gave a shudder. 'And if the murder of an unborn child is involved here . . .'

'We are not certain of that,' Gervase reminded him, 'and it might be safer not to speculate until we have more facts.'

'Quite so.'

'The poor girl deserves our utmost compassion.'

'Perhaps,' said Columbanus. 'But if our worst fears are realised, we must not shrink from censuring Helene. Sin is sin and it must be proclaimed as such. Suicide is a brazen act of blasphemy.'

'My sympathy goes out to my lord Wymarc and his wife.'

'Is Arnulf with them now?'

'Yes, Brother Columbanus.'

'He is a sound man.'

'And a good friend to Helene.'

'He will be as shocked by this as her family,' said the monk sorrowfully. 'But he will cope with this awful blow. Arnulf is an ordained priest. Trained to bear the weight of other people's grief and help them through their tribulation.' And no tribulation could be worse than this.' He nodded confidently. 'Arnulf will know what to do.'

The house was in turmoil. When Arnulf arrived, that turmoil seemed to converge on him from all directions until he felt like an axle at the centre of a wheel that was spinning helplessly out of control. It took him over an hour to slow down the wheel and to impose a degree of calm on the abode. Wymarc made the chief claim on his attention, shifting between a morbid fear and a whining self-pity, hoping that somehow the chaplain could exonerate him from any blame whatsoever.

'It was not my fault, Arnulf.'

'We must all take some share of the responsibility.'

'But I was guiltless with Helene. You saw that.'

The chaplain nodded. 'You always did your best.'

'What will happen to me?'

'My thoughts lie with Helene at this moment, my lord.'

'Mine, too,' he said quickly. 'She dominates my mind.'

There was a long pause. Arnulf sounded tentative.

'Did she say anything to you before this tragedy?'

'Nothing at all.'

'She gave no hint of the distress she was in?'

'None.'

'There must have been some small clue, my lord.'

'She would not speak to us at all,' said Wymarc. 'She locked herself away in her room and refused even to eat. Now we realise why. If only I had known!'

Arnulf nodded sadly. 'Try to rest,' he counselled.

'How can I?'

'It has been a night of terror for you. No man could live through that ordeal without a heavy toll being taken on his mind and body.' He eased him back in his chair. 'Rest, my lord. Close your eyes and yield yourself up. Replenish your strength for the difficult time that lies ahead. I am here now. I will take care of everything. Share your load.'

Having placated Wymarc to the point where the latter drifted harmlessly off to sleep, Arnulf set to work on the rest of the household. The arrival of the chaplain had allowed the wife to be seized by the fit of hysteria she had kept at bay while her husband was in need of her support. Now that Wymarc had been reassured, she made her bid for consolation, weeping copiously and wringing her hands, giving full vent to her emotions.

Arnulf combined sympathy with firm action. Taking the woman by the wrists, he shook her hard until she was jerked out of her lachrymose display and stared at him open-mouthed.

'This is no way to behave, my lady,' he said.

'Helene is dead and by her own hand!'

'Then it is for the living to show her some respect.'

'She will go down into the deepest pit of Hell.'

'Put such thoughts aside.'

'Helene killed herself,' wailed the other. 'And lost all hope of entering into the Kingdom of Heaven. That is the Church's teaching, is it not? Suicide is a sure road to damnation.'

'God will take pity on Helene.'

'After what she has done?'

'Have faith, my lady. Do not despair.'

The chaplain spent even more time with her than with her husband, but she was eventually calmed enough to be left alone while he moved among the servants. Faces blank with horror, they snatched at every crumb of comfort he offered them. A suicide was not a merely personal calamity. It touched everyone in the household with its clammy fingers. Arnulf probed the servants to see if any of them had guessed at Helene's plight and foreseen the catastrophe. No suspicions of any kind had existed. The servants had been taken completely by surprise. Helene had confided in nobody. She kept sorrow penned up inside her until it burst out uncontrollably.

When a grisly tranquillity settled on the house, Arnulf found a moment to steal quietly upstairs to her bedchamber. He let himself in and recoiled at once from the nauseous smell that was easily winning the battle against the sweet herbs strewn around the floor. Helene lay on the bed beneath a shroud. The sheets were still stained by the posthumous effusions from her body.

Arnulf moved up to the side of the bed and lifted the shroud to take a look at her face. His stomach turned. What he remembered was the beautiful young girl with soft skin, who looked and sang like an angel in his choir at the church. Helene was no angel now. Rigor mortis had set in, freezing her expression of agony and robbing her of all grace and charm. It was a cruel transformation.

Falling to his knees beside her, Arnulf prayed with his hands clasped tight together. When he rose, he bent over the corpse to make the sign of the cross on her forehead as if baptising her afresh. He pulled the shroud over her face again and went out. As he descended the stairs in a daze, he could hear the haunting sound of a fourteen-year-old girl singing joyously in an empty church.

On the journey back to Oxford, they made a detour in order to pay a second unheralded visit. Ordgar was in the house when he heard Ralph Delchard and his men ride up. The old man came out to give them a wary greeting. Over by the stables, Amalric reached instinctively for a wooden hayfork, fearing that the soldiers had come to take possession of his colt, but he put the improvised weapon aside when he realised that they were not Milo Crispin's men.

Ralph dismounted to be taken into the house by Ordgar. It was a typical Saxon dwelling, long and low in design, divided into a series of bays and with a sunken floor that was covered with rushes. The thatched roof harboured spiders, mice and other denizens. Light was frugal. After the timbered splendour of Wallingford Castle, the place seemed small and dismal. Ralph did not care for the faint smell of damp. He lowered himself on to the stool to which he was politely waved.

'Do you know who I am?' he said.

'Yes, my lord. I was at the castle when you walked into the courtroom and stopped the trial. You saved a man's life.'

'Ebbi was innocent.'

'But unable to prove his innocence without your help.'

'I am glad I got there in time,' said Ralph. 'We went to a lot of trouble to establish that he could not possibly have been the assassin. We wanted our evidence heard. The poor man was arrested and charged on insufficient grounds.'

'My lord sheriff felt he had grounds enough.'

'What do you mean?'

'You know the law as well as I,' said Ordgar without bitterness. 'When a Norman soldier is slain, the murderer is always presumed to be a Saxon. If he is not caught or turned in, the district surrounding the place where the crime occurred is amerced for a substantial fine. We have lived with that law for a long time now.' He hunched his shoulders. 'My lord sheriff wanted a Saxon killer. His soldiers found one.'

'It was not as simple as that,' said Ralph. 'The law of which you speak was brought in as a protective measure after the Conquest. England was not easily subdued.'

'Did you expect it to be, my lord?'

'Not at all. People are entitled to defend what they believe is theirs. Until it is taken away from them. That is when it is time to sue for peace.'

'Peace without honour.'

'Peace with land to work. Peace with food in your belly.'

'Imposed from above.' He gave a philosophical smile. 'But you are right, my lord. Peace is better than war. Even a lesser existence is better than death. I accept that.'

'Many did not, Ordgar,' said Ralph. 'Rebellions, ambushes, brutal assassinations. On and on they went. The law was enacted to protect us from those Saxons who still thought they ruled this island. And they do not,' he reminded his host. 'The killing which has brought me here today is of a very different order.'

'Is it, my lord?'

'Walter Payne was murdered to pay off an old grudge.'

'By whom?'

'I do not know yet.'

'Supposing that you never find out?' asked Ordgar. 'If my lord sheriff also fails to track down the assassin, he will invoke the law of which we just talked. A Saxon hand will be presumed to have thrown that dagger. A murder fine will be levied on those who dwell near Woodstock.'

'It will not come to that. I'll catch the villain.'

'How?'

'With your help, Ordgar.'

The old man gave a weary smile and sat on the bench opposite him. Ralph studied him in the gloom. His assessment of Ordgar was favourable. The latter had a quiet pride which even the indignities forced upon him had not extinguished. He showed respect but not fear. There was a pleasing absence of rancour in him.

'Let us talk about the race,' suggested Ralph.

'If you wish, my lord.'

'I have spoken with Wymarc, Milo Crispin and Bertrand Gamberell. They gave me varying accounts of what took place at Woodstock that day. I wanted to hear your version.'

'I doubt that I will have anything new to add.'

'Describe the race.'

Ordgar collected his thoughts then gave his version of events. He spoke slowly, honestly and with a pervading regret. When the old man stopped, Ralph had the first question ready.

'How did your colt win the race?'

'Fairly, my lord.'

'Hyperion lost his rider.'

'Even with a man in the saddle, he would have lost.'

'Why?'

'Cempan is better.'

'Better bred? Better trained? Better ridden?'

'All three.'

'Who deserves the credit for that?'

'Edric the Cripple and my son,' explained the other. 'Edric is my steward but his knowledge of horses is second to none. He raised and trained Cempan. He also taught my son how to ride him properly.'

'A cripple riding a horse?'

'He was not always disabled. Edric was once a warrior, a housecarl in the service of King Edward. He lost his leg in combat. I gave him a place here.'

'He must be grateful to you, Ordgar. Not many men would employ a crippled soldier to oversee their land.'

'Edric has repaid me a thousandfold.'

'How did you prepare for the race?'

'Prepare?'

'Cempan did not win by chance,' decided Ralph. 'You

were up against the fastest horse in the county and Hyperion
had already raced on that course three times. You were at
a complete disadvantage.'
A sly grin. 'Not quite, my lord.'
'Let me guess. You took the colt to Woodstock beforehand.
You let him get the feel of the course.'
'We did more than that,' admitted the other. 'Edric and I
watched an earlier race. We saw how Hyperion ran and how
his rider handled him. That taught us much.'
'Sensible preparations.'
'My son, Amalric, then rode Cempan over the course. It has
many undulations. They are deceptive and can knock a horse
out of his stride. Edric showed him how to take a line that
would miss the worst of the slopes and dips. They trained for
hours in the twilight.' A full smile came. 'We borrowed money
from many people, my lord. We had to be sure to win.'
'Your victory was obviously deserved.'
'But not upheld.'
'Something puzzles me,' said Ralph. 'Edric the Cripple had
an important role in your success yet you never mentioned him
during your account of the race.'
'He was not there.'
'Not there? After all that effort he put in, he was not there
to see the results?'
'Edric was invited to the wedding of his kinsman. He was
away in Warwick for three or four days. He offered to miss the
wedding in order to watch the race but I urged him to go.'
'Would not his presence have helped your son?'
'Yes, my lord. But there was another consideration.'
'What was that?'
Ordgar became uneasy. 'Edric finds it hard to accept the
changes that have come about. You talked earlier of those
who refused to surrender. Edric is one of them. Something
of the warrior still burns inside him.' He blurted out the truth.
'To be candid, I was glad that he was not at the race because
he might have said something out of turn.'
'A Saxon hothead upsetting a trio of Norman lords.'

'There are times when the loss of his leg rankles. It makes him lash out wildly and not always wisely. Besides,' said Ordgar, 'we won the race without him. If not the prize.'

'Was your stake returned?'

'No, my lord.'

'Held over until the race is run again?'

'Not exactly.'

'Then what is the situation?'

'I do not wish to speak ill of my lord Milo,' began the other cautiously, 'but he has been vindictive. He is very eager to win the race against Hyperion. Because our colt is the only horse likely to do that, he wants to buy him from us.'

'You would be mad to sell him.'

'We may be given no choice in the matter.'

'Milo would *force* you to sell?'

'He offered to exchange our stake money for Cempan.'

Ralph was shocked. 'I thought better of him.'

'Needless to say, I refused such a corrupt bargain but I fear that he will come for Cempan one day.'

'Only when the race is run again and that cannot happen until Hyperion is found. Bertrand Gamberell has shed more tears over that animal than over Walter Payne. You would think that it was Hyperion who was killed at Woodstock.'

'His reputation was, my lord. By us.'

Ralph tried to catch him unawares with a blunt question.

'Who murdered Walter Payne?'

'I do not know, my lord.'

'Would you tell me, if you did?'

Ordgar took much longer to find an answer this time.

'Perhaps.'

Edric the Cripple was riding across the fields towards the house when he saw them depart. As their horses cantered back to Oxford, they left a cloud of dust in their wake. Edric went straight to the stables and dismounted. He found the boy lifting a saddle on to Cempan and gave a sigh of relief.

'I thought they had come to take him away,' he said.

'So did I,' confided Amalric. 'But they only wished to talk to father. They were complete strangers to me. I will have to ask him who they were.'

'What mood were they in when they left?'

'Friendly.'

'Normans are never friendly. Unless they are trying to trick something out of you. What were they after?'

'I do not know, Edric. Only one of them went into the house with father. When they came out together, they were smiling.'

'Ordgar is too easily taken in.'

'You know what he always says,' the other reminded him as he tightened the girth. 'Better to work with them than against them.'

'Look where it got him with Milo Crispin!'

The chestnut colt whinnied. Cempan was keen to be ridden out. Edric patted the animal's neck affectionately. Amalric adjusted the stirrups. The boy seemed relaxed and happy. The steward decided to broach an important topic with him.

'We need to talk about Bristeva,' he began.

'Why?'

'I think we have both been unkind to her, Amalric.'

'What does it matter? She is only a girl.'

'She's your sister. You should love her.'

'I do,' said the other defensively. 'But she can be very silly at times and I've no patience with her. Neither have you, Edric. You're sharper with Bristeva than I am.'

'It was wrong of me.'

'Wrong?'

'To speak so harshly about this choir of hers.'

'She talks about nothing else. It vexes me.'

'You talk about nothing but Cempan,' the other pointed out, 'and Bristeva must be equally vexed, but does she rail at you? Does she mock the horse the way you mock her choir?'

Amalric was surprised by the steward's change of tone.

'Has father been speaking to you about me?' he guessed.

'We exchanged words.'

185

'Did he order you to keep me on the bit?'

'No!' said Edric hotly. 'He would never order me to do anything. I am my own man. You should know that.' He took a moment to calm down. 'I offered to sound you out in order to save you from being excluded.'

'From what?'

'The banquet at the castle. Ordgar is afraid to take you. He fears that you will somehow prevent Bristeva from singing.'

'I will!'

'Why?'

'You are the last person who should need to ask that,' said the boy with feeling. 'Think of the people she would be entertaining at the banquet. Robert d'Oilly. Milo Crispin. Bertrand Gamberell. And many others.'

'Geoffrey, Bishop of Coutances among them,' said Edric.

'Him, especially. Look who those men are. Remember what they have done to us. I'm not going to let my sister perform in that hall for their benefit. Just imagine, Edric. She will be singing to please Milo Crispin – the man who is trying to steal Cempan from us! I *have* to stop her.'

'No, Amalric.'

'Why not?'

'Because I say so.'

The dark menace in his eyes made the boy's anger dissolve at once. Amalric was suddenly afraid and confused. Edric the Cripple had always encouraged him to resent and to subvert. Now he was insisting on Amalric's good behaviour and backing up that insistence with a naked threat. The boy was unsettled.

Edric chuckled and punched him playfully on the arm.

'Let us stay friends, Amalric.'

'Yes. We will.'

'Forget your sister,' advised the other. 'Her ambition is clear. Tell me this. What would *you* most like to do?'

'Win a second race against Hyperion.'

'Are you sure that Cempan will beat him?'

'Certain!'

'Then you will have your wish.'

'How can that be?' asked Amalric. 'Milo Crispin will take him from us so that Cempan runs for him. I will not be allowed to ride in that race at all.'

'Then we must arrange another one.'

'Another?'

'Two horses. Head to head. Cempan against Hyperion.'

'But that is impossible!'

'Is it?'

Edric grinned and the truth slowly dawned on the boy. The two of them were soon shaking with a silent laughter that bonded them together.

Robert d'Oilly was in a bad temper and even the presence of his wife did not calm him down this time. Edith and Golde were in the hall at the castle, making a provisional seating plan for the banquet, when the sheriff stormed in through the door. His steward and two of his soldiers were close behind him and their grim expressions showed that they had already felt the lash of their master's tongue.

Edith's greeting died on her lips as she saw his face.

'What ails you, my lord?' she asked.

'Everything!'

'Has something happened?'

'It never stops happening, Edith!' he complained. 'There are times when the office of sheriff is too great a burden for any one man. I am the agent of the Crown in Oxfordshire. I collect taxes. I administer justice. I raise and lead any militia that is needed. In short, I receive the King's writ in this county and execute his instructions.'

'And you do so with great efficiency,' agreed Edith.

'When I am not troubled by other matters.'

'What do you mean?'

'This week has been a nightmare for me, Edith,' he said in exasperation. 'Gamberell's man is murdered. The wrong suspect is arrested and tried. When we search afresh for the killer, the trail has gone cold. A black stallion is stolen and we find no trace of that either. Wymarc's sister commits suicide. I have another crisis on my hands. What else will descend out of the skies to plague me?'

Edith traded a worried glance with Golde before speaking.

'This may not be the ideal moment to mention the banquet,' she said sweetly, 'but it may provide the rest that you so surely deserve.'

'It only increases my problems.'

'How so, my lord?' asked Golde.

'We will take care of all the arrangements,' added Edith.

'Yes,' he said, 'but you cannot take care of the murder, the theft of Gamberell's horse and this turmoil in Wymarc's family. How can I enjoy a banquet when all this is hanging over me? What opinion will the Bishop of Coutances form of me if he sees me so fretful and oppressed?'

'The bishop knows your qualities well enough.'

'I need to impress him, Edith.'

'You will, my lord. No question of that.'

'The banquet will be sumptuous,' promised Golde. 'Your wife will see to that. It will be fit for the King himself.'

'But what about Oxford itself?' he growled, beyond all reassurance. 'When the bishop rides in with his entourage, he will expect a town that is firmly under control. Instead of that, he will find himself in a madhouse that is buzzing with tales of murder, theft and suicide. I wanted everything in its place when he arrived here. That is why I brought the trial of the prisoner forward. I wanted to clear some of the stink out of the way so that it would not offend the bishop's nostrils. But now,' he said, 'he will hardly be able to breathe for the stench.'

Edith let her husband rant on for a few more minutes before signalling discreetly to Golde. The two women slipped out of the hall. When they closed the door behind them, they could still hear the sheriff in full flow.

'Take no notice of that,' said Edith smoothly. 'Robert sometimes has to let his feelings show through. He is a most able sheriff and keeps a firm grip on the shire.'

'I have seen that for myself, my lady.'

'Oxford is fortunate to have such a man.'

'And he is fortunate to have such a wife,' said Golde with admiration. 'I do not know how you preserved your calm in there. If Ralph rounded on me like that, I could never be as poised and supportive as you were.'

'How would you respond, Golde?'

'I'm not sure. I'd be tempted to box his ears, I expect.'

Edith laughed. 'That might be the best remedy of all.'

They moved out of earshot of the continued protests.

'I did feel a twinge of guilt, though,' said Golde.

'Guilt?'

'Your husband *is* overburdened. We are part of his load.'

'Nonsense!'

'The strain would be eased if we were not here.'

'The opposite is true,' said Edith with a smile. 'You have helped to ease the strain on us. It has been a joy to have such interesting guests at the castle. You have reminded us how to relax and enjoy good company again. There has been a separate blessing for me. The preparations for the banquet have been half the trouble with you beside me.'

'I have been glad to help.'

'Then no more of this foolish talk about being a burden.'

Golde nodded and was about to go off for a walk in the bailey in search of fresh air. Listening to the sheriff's moans had left her jangled. Then she remembered something.

'My lady?'

'Yes?'

'Is it true what they say? About this poor girl?'

'Helene?'

'Yes. Was she with child?'

Edith sighed. 'I believe so!'

'Then the situation is more terrible than I imagined.'

'It does not bear thinking about.'

'What on earth could drive someone to that pitch of desperation?' Edith shook her head. 'You knew the girl, I believe. Was

189

there anything in her character which could have given the slightest hint of this?'

'Nothing,' said the other. 'Nothing whatsoever. Helene was a charming creature. She sang both in the choir and during any banquets we held here. I spoke with her often and found her honest, respectful and conscientious. She was the last person in the world I would have expected to take her own life.'

'The decision was forced upon her, my lady.'

'So it appears.'

'Someone's attentions may have been forced upon her as well,' said Golde. 'Most people will rush to condemn the girl but there is another culprit.'

'The father.'

'Yes, my lady. Who is he?'

Bertrand Gamberell took his horse at a brisk trot through the crowd in the High Street, buffeting anyone who got in his way and treating anyone who dared to complain to a burst of vituperation. The six knights who trailed behind him in single file were equally inconsiderate. A long, hard, fruitless day in the saddle had deprived them all of even the most basic courtesies. Several bruised shoulders and outraged faces were left behind them. They did not care.

When he led his men through the castle gates, Gamberell was in determined mood. Dismounting in the bailey, he marched towards the keep and was gratified to see that Robert d'Oilly was in residence. The sheriff was standing with Gervase Bret on the flight of stone steps that were set in the mound. The fact that they were engaged in private conversation did not hold back the impetuous Gamberell. He barged straight in.

'I demand more assistance, my lord sheriff!' he said.

Robert d'Oilly turned a jaundiced eye upon the interloper.

'I never respond to demands,' he said.

'We have been searching for Hyperion all day.'

'Without success, by the look of you.'

'It is your duty to help me.'

'A troop of men has been combing the countryside.'

'I need more.'

'You have all that I can spare,' said the sheriff. 'Now, please excuse me. Master Bret and I have a more important topic to discuss.'

'Nothing is more important to me than Hyperion,' returned Gamberell. 'You do not seem to appreciate what a remarkable animal he is. He has been stolen. That is a crime.'

'I have sent men out in search of the criminal.'

'Not enough of them.'

'The theft of a horse is not a priority, Bertrand.'

'It is for me.'

'Have you forgotten the murder of your knight?' scolded d'Oilly. 'The killer is my main target. I would much rather catch an assassin than a mere horse thief. That is where I have assigned most of my men. To the murder hunt.'

'I want Hyperion back!'

'Excuse me, my lord,' said Gervase, intervening to prevent the violent row that was about to break out. 'You have clearly not heard the sad tidings. My lord sheriff and I were talking about the tragedy when you stole upon us.'

'The only tragedy I know is the theft of my horse.'

'And the murder of Walter Payne,' said the sheriff.

'Yes. That, too, of course.'

'Let me add a third misfortune,' said Gervase politely. 'You are, I am sure, familiar with my lord Wymarc's family.'

'I have met his cold fish of a wife, if that is what you mean. Mean, maggoty, thin-faced lady who twitches all over you. What about her?'

'I am referring to his sister.'

'Helene?' A confiding chuckle. 'Now she is a different proposition altogether. A truly gorgeous young creature. I have waited outside the church for her more than once, I can tell you. Helene is a girl to be cultivated.'

'Not any more, my lord.'

'What do you mean?'

'Helene is dead.'

Gamberell gaped at him then turned to the sheriff. The latter gave a nod of confirmation. Gamberell reeled.

'Dead? Helene? She was so full of life.'

'It was not a natural death, my lord.'

A gasp of incredulity. 'Someone killed her?'

'Helene took her own life,' said Gervase softly, 'and that of the child she was carrying.'

Bertrand Gamberell was rocked. He looked from Gervase to the sheriff and back again. Then, without another word, he ran down the steps and across the bailey. He was soon spurring his horse out through the gates of the castle as if the hounds of hell were on his tail.

Chapter Twelve

Bristeva was singing quietly and sewing assiduously when she caught a glimpse of the visitor through the window. She gave a little cry of excitement. Abandoning her chore at once, she set it aside and went scurrying out to greet Arnulf the Chaplain. He looked pained and fatigued but he managed a welcoming smile for her. She held the reins of his horse while he dismounted.

'How are you, Bristeva?' he said.

'Very well, thank you.'

'Have you been practising that song I gave you?'

'I was singing it to myself as I was at my sewing.'

'Good.' He glanced around. 'Is your father here?'

'In the lower field.'

'I want to speak to him.'

'Let me fetch him for you,' she volunteered.

'No need.'

'I will run all the way.'

'You stay here. I will find him myself.' He looked at her for a moment and brushed her cheek with the back of his hand. 'Go back to your sewing and practise that song, Bristeva. It must be perfect. On Saturday, you will sing before a bishop.'

'I know.'

'Do not let me down.'

'I would never do that, Father Arnulf.'

'Is that a promise?'

'I give you my word of honour!'

He was touched by her earnest commitment. Waving a farewell, he started off on the long walk to the lower field. Bristeva ran back into the house and took up a position in the window from which she could keep him in view. Watching the man who had given a meaning to her life, she gathered up her sewing and sang with more pleasure than ever.

When the chaplain came up, Ordgar was supervising two of his men as they tried to repair a broken plough. Still in their yoke, the oxen bellowed mutinously. At the sight of Arnulf, the old man left the cottagers to struggle on alone with their work. He and his visitor walked a short distance away so that they could converse in privacy.

'What brings you out here, Father Arnulf?' said Ordgar.

'Sorry news.'

'Not about Bristeva, I hope?'

'Indirectly.'

Ordgar was alarmed. 'Her place at the banquet is not in jeopardy, is it? My daughter has set her heart on singing at the castle. It would destroy her if that chance were somehow snatched away from her.'

'That is why I came to see you.'

'What has happened?'

A considered pause. 'Let us walk back to the house.'

They fell in beside each other and trudged up the field.

'I came straight here from my lord Wymarc's home,' said Arnulf. 'An appalling tragedy has befallen the family.'

'Someone has died?'

'It is worse than that, Ordgar.'

'Worse? How can that be?'

'His sister, Helene. Suicide.'

The old man was struck dumb. He had weathered many losses and ordeals in his long life, and witnessed much crime and brutality, but here was something quite outside his experience. The very notion of suicide made him shudder. The fact that it involved a girl, who was younger than his own daughter, gave the blow greater impact. He looked up at the distant house.

'Have you told Bristeva?'

'No.'

'She liked Helene. They were friends.'

'That is why she must not know yet, Ordgar,' said Arnulf. 'It would upset her too much. Bristeva would never be able to sing at the banquet with this on her mind. I came to beg you to keep this from her until afterwards.'

'That will not be easy.'

'But very necessary. You do see that?'

Ordgar thought it through. 'Why, yes. You are right. Tell her now and she would be distraught. I am stunned myself in spite of all my years. A suicide? Dear God! By what means?'

'Poison.'

'What provoked such an act?'

'We do not yet know.'

'Did her brother have no explanation?'

'My lord Wymarc is too distressed to talk about it. I offered what comfort I could in the household but there is a limit to what anyone can do.'

'Taking her own life! This is dire news.'

'It is all around the town by now and will soon spread out to the countryside. I wanted you to hear the truth from me and not some butchered account of it from the local gossips.'

'That was very considerate.'

'Bristeva must be protected from this.'

'She will be, Father Arnulf. Trust me.'

'I do. It is your son and your steward who worry me. Sooner or later, they will surely hear the rumours. I would hate to think of one of them blurting it out to Bristeva.'

'They will not.'

'Should I speak to them?'

'It is my office. I'll not shirk it.' A long sigh escaped him. 'There is no love lost between myself and my lord Wymarc but I do pity him. And his wife. They have a terrible burden to bear from now on.'

'The guilt will never leave them.'

'Nor the ignominy. Suicide. It is against Nature.'

'Helene must have been pushed to extremes.'

'How? By whom?'

'That will emerge in time,' said Arnulf. 'My immediate concern is to safeguard Bristeva's performance at the banquet. It may be a long time before another chance like this presents itself.'

'I understand that.'

'Keep her close, Ordgar. Tell her nothing. Bring her early to the castle tomorrow.'

'I will.'

'Bristeva will sleep there overnight,' said Arnulf. 'I will ensure that nothing of this tragedy disturbs her. She will be kept in ignorance.' He gave a wry smile. 'Bristeva is almost a woman yet we must keep her a child. And children must be shielded from such horrors. When it is time to tell her, I will frame it as gently as I can.'

'I would prefer that she heard it from you,' said Ordgar. 'My tongue would surely blunder. You would choose the right words and Bristeva has such great admiration for you.'

'I will wait until the banquet is out of the way first. At least, she will not be robbed of that joy. Bristeva will stand in the hall where Helene last stood to sing for the company.'

The old man came to a sudden halt as a thought intruded.

'I talked to Helene once.'

'Did you?'

'When I came to pick up Bristeva from a choir rehearsal. My daughter introduced me to her. Helene was a good girl. I remember how polite she was. Even to me.'

'Helene always showed respect.'

'She said how much she loved to sing,' recalled Ordgar. 'She was so grateful to you for making that possible. At home, she was enjoined to hold her peace and attend to her work, but in church she was allowed to be herself.'

'It would have been a crime to suppress that talent.'

'Yet that is what happened when she was forced to leave the choir by her brother. My lord Wymarc was the one who suppressed that wonderful voice of hers.' He looked up questioningly. 'Could that be her motive? Despair at being taken away from you and the choir?'

'No, Ordgar. I think not.'

'Helene was like Bristeva. She lived to sing.'

'Leaving us no doubt hurt her,' said Arnulf, wincing at the memory. 'It certainly caused us pain. But that would not be enough to incite her to such a dreadful act. There are other reasons behind this and I suspect that they are nothing to do with the choir.'

The two men set off again, walking in step towards the house. When they got close enough, they could see Bristeva waving enthusiastically to them from the window. Ordgar felt a pang of remorse when he saw her. Her joy depended wholly on her innocence. Arnulf nursed his own recriminations. He would have to hide an ugly truth from someone with a right to know it.

Unaware of the calamity which had struck down her predecessor, Bristeva was singing at the top of her voice.

Ralph Delchard was overcome by a deep sadness. For a while he was quite dazed. When his head cleared, he grabbed Gervase Bret by the shoulders and sought corroboration.

'Is this true?' he gasped.

'Unhappily, it is.'

'Suicide? An unborn child?'

'This is what I have been told,' said Gervase. 'Arnulf went out to the house in answer to a summons. Before he left, he confirmed to me that Helene had taken her own life.'

'But this other horror? The baby?'

'I had it from our host. The doctor gave a full report to my lord sheriff. The facts are no longer in doubt.'

Ralph released him and walked away a few paces to grapple with the frightful intelligence. They were alone together in the hall. A meal was set out on the table and others would soon join them. Gervase had been keen to forewarn his friend about the news which would surely dominate the conversation. He was surprised by Ralph's reaction. Close acquaintance with the savagery of war had left Ralph largely impervious to the shocks and setbacks which troubled others. Since he usually treated the Church with a cheerful irreverence, he could hardly be expressing the disgust of a true Christian at the dreadful implications of the act of suicide.

Walking back to him, Ralph gave an apologetic shrug.

'Forgive me, Gervase. This news unnerved me.'

'But you did not know Helene.'

'She is a girl,' said Ralph quietly. 'That is enough. A young girl and a mother-to-be. Two lives cut hideously short. There is no comparison with my situation, I know, but I was hurled back into it for a moment. I thought of Elinor, my first wife, my first love. It was a happy marriage, Gervase, but it lacked the one thing which we both dreamed about. Children. Time went past but Elinor simply would not conceive. The doctor told me that Nature might be showing kindness.'

'Where is the kindness is keeping a woman barren?'

'That is what I said to him. He pointed out that Elinor was not strong. She had a delicate constitution and was prone to minor ailments. Childbirth held danger for her.' He bit his lip as the memory took a tighter hold. 'Then, out of the blue, against all expectation, Elinor conceived our child. We were overjoyed, Gervase. What two people in our predicament would not be? We spurned the doctor's warnings. God had blessed our union and that was paramount. You know the rest.'

'Your wife and child did not survive the delivery.'

'Elinor must have known,' insisted Ralph. 'In her heart, she must have known the appalling risk that she was taking. But she was so determined to give me the son I longed for that she bravely accepted that risk. Can you understand what I am saying?'

'I think so, Ralph.'

'Childbirth was a form of suicide for her.'

'That is not true.'

'It seemed so at the time.'

'Then you must rid yourself of that thought,' said Gervase seriously. 'Elinor could not have foreseen what would happen. No woman would sacrifice her own life and leave her husband with a stillborn child. In any case, your experience is very different from the situation we find here. Your child was conceived with love within the bounds of holy wedlock. Helene's was patently not.'

'I know that, Gervase, and I am sorry to talk of my own sorrow when my sympathy should be given elsewhere. But the news caught me unawares. A mother and child lying dead. It brought back a vivid picture I have tried to wipe from my mind.' He straightened his back. 'No more of me. Let us think of the girl and what brought her to such an ignoble end.'

Gervase looked up as servants brought in more food and wine to set out on the table. He waited until they left.

'There will be time enough to talk of this with the others,' he said. 'While we are still alone, I am anxious to hear your news. How did you find Milo Crispin?'

'His blood is ice-cold, Gervase. When he makes water, it probably congeals in the air. I never met such a master of self-possession.'

'What did you learn from him?'

'A great deal,' said Ralph. 'He did not prevaricate.'

He gave his companion a brief account of all that had passed between him and Milo Crispin, adding salient details which his men had picked up while talking with members of the garrison at Wallingford Castle. Gervase was particularly interested in the news that Walter Payne had pursued Helene with lecherous intent. He was bound to wonder if the soldier might be the father of her child.

'Milo did, indeed, give you straight answers.'

'So I thought at the time,' admitted Ralph. 'But that was before I talked to Ordgar. He made me look at Milo from a slightly different angle. Some of those straight answers began to seem as crooked as the hind leg of a donkey.'

'What do you mean?'

'The best way to divert attention from yourself is to accuse another. That is why he pointed a finger at Wymarc. Walter Payne clearly pestered Helene in a way that angered her brother, but would that anger be enough to provoke Wymarc to such extreme action? No, Gervase. Perhaps we should go back to the race itself again and search for motives behind that.'

'You think that Milo Crispin was involved in the murder?'

'Examine the facts,' said Ralph. 'He knew and hated Walter Payne. It must have been galling for him to see the man astride Hyperion as the stallion outpaced his own horses every time. Milo's urge to win that race was overpowering.'

'Then why disrupt it by instigating a murder?'

'In order to weaken his rival. Bertrand Gamberell is not a man who can ignore a challenge. Milo would have set up another race with a larger purse. Hyperion is fast but every horse needs a good rider in the saddle.'

'Walter Payne.'

'Renowned for his horsemanship.'

'Even without him, Hyperion might still win.'

'Not if he came up against Cempan, the chestnut colt.'

'That is Ordgar's horse.'

'Milo intends to buy it from him. By force.'

Gervase assimilated the new information very quickly.

'My lord Milo is determined to win,' he said. 'By fair means or foul. This contest is much more than a race between horses. It is a battle between deadly rivals.'

'Milo expects to be the victor.'

'Why?'

'He is a more ruthless soldier. He takes no prisoners.'

The clash of steel reverberated around the courtyard of Wallingford Castle. Wearing helm and hauberk, Miles Crispin used both hands to wield his sword with vicious force. The savagery of the attack made his opponent back away, unable to do anything but parry the blows with his own weapon and wish that he had not been chosen to fight the duel. Intense pressure finally told. The man lost his footing and fell backwards to the ground. Milo was on him at once, standing astride his prey, his swordpoint aimed at the man's throat.

'Fight harder next time,' he ordered.

'You were too strong for me, my lord.'

'That is why we practise. To build your strength.'

'I will work more diligently in future.'

Milo offered a hand to pull him up. The defeated soldier was glad that his humiliation was over. Milo kept his own skills in good repair and few in the garrison could provide a real test for his swordplay. A dozen or more soldiers had watched the display. Milo was about to address them when a call from the guard on the rampart made him turn.

A lone rider was approaching the castle. When he heard who it was, Milo ordered the gate to be opened. It was not long before Bertrand Gamberell brought his horse into the courtyard at a canter. He reined the animal in. Milo saw that the horse was lathered up and its rider was panting for breath. Handing his sword and helm to a servant, he went to greet his eager visitor.

'You seem in a great hurry to get here, Bertrand.'

'I was.'

'How far have you ridden?'

'From Oxford.'

'Alone?'

'I wanted no company.'

'Why not?'

'I will tell you in a more private place, Milo.'

The castellan nodded and led him towards the keep. He was already speculating on the possible reasons that had brought his visitor there in such haste. Bertrand Gamberell had more cause to stay away from Wallingford Castle than to come to it. Milo conducted him to the hall and poured him a glass of wine. When he had taken a long sip, Gamberell began to regain a touch of his more usual nonchalance.

'I was minded to call upon you, Milo,' he said.

'You have never felt that need before.'

201

'We are rivals, I know, and we are in dispute over those
hides of land, but that does not mean we have to stand apart
and glower at each other.'

'This show of friendship is very alarming.'

'Do not be so cynical.'

'What has happened?'

'I have come to see you, that is all.'

'Like a man running from the devil,' noted Milo coldly.
'What are you afraid of, Bertrand? Who is after you?'

Gamberell took a longer sip of his wine before speaking. The
swaggering confidence was now tempered with prudence.

'In the heat of the moment, all of us can be guilty of rash
action. There are times when it is sensible to keep out of the
reach of such reckless behaviour until tempers cool and wiser
counsels prevail.'

'Can this be Bertrand Gamberell I am hearing?'

'Do not mock me.'

'All I am doing is to marvel at the transformation,' said Milo
with light sarcasm. 'You are the last man in the world entitled
to preach a sermon against impetuous action. Who has been
more reckless than you? By heaven, you will turn pacifist next
and tell me that soldiering is a sinful trade.' He fixed his visitor
with a glare. 'Get to the truth, man.'

'Wymarc's young sister is dead.'

'Helene?'

'By her own hand.'

'Can this be so?' asked the other, shocked. 'Suicide?'

'I heard it from a most reliable source.'

'Then it is grim news and will cause Wymarc untold pain
and damage. He was Helene's guardian. This is bound to reflect
adversely on him.' His voice hardened. 'But you did not gallop
all the way here simply to bring these tidings to me. There is
more, I think. Tell me.'

Gamberell drained the cup before setting it on the table.

'Helene was with child.'

'So that is it. The father wants a place to hide.'

'No, Milo!'

'We all saw you, chasing after that girl.'

'Helene was merely a friend.'

'Like all the others.'

'You are jumping to the wrong conclusion.'

'Am I?' said Milo levelly. 'Helene would not be the first pretty girl you have led astray. Wymarc only took her away from the choir because of the interest you showed in her. Evidently, he acted too late.'

'That is not how it stands, Milo.'

'Now I see why you rode here with such speed. To escape the wrath of a vengeful brother. This is the one place where Wymarc would never think to find you. Wallingford Castle is to be your church, is it?' He gave a hollow laugh. 'You have come in search of sanctuary.'

The commotion in the bailey was so loud and unrelenting that Robert d'Oilly was forced to leave his guests at the table while he went to investigate. When the sheriff came striding angrily down from the keep, Wymarc was still circling the bailey on his destrier with a dozen men-at-arms, waving his sword in the air, yelling at the guards who tried to stop him, then making his cry ring around the whole castle.

'Bertrand Gamberell! Where are you?'

'He is not here!' boomed the sheriff.

'Where are you hiding him?'

'Nowhere.'

Wymarc brought his horse to a halt in front of d'Oilly.

'How dare you ride in here like this with your men at your back!' demanded the sheriff, pulsing with fury. 'If I did not know the cause of your high temper, I would have you thrown into my dungeons for disturbing the peace.'

'I did not mean to offend you, my lord sheriff.'

'Well, you have done so. Be warned. Any more of this riotous behaviour and you will spend the night in chains. You and every man with you.'

Wymarc glanced around. Half the soldiers in the garrison

now surrounded him and his knights. Hopelessly outnumbered, he needed to show a less aggressive attitude.

'I received word that Gamberell was here,' he explained.

'He came and went.'

'And where did he go?'

'That is irrelevant.'

'To his manor, I think. We'll seize him there.'

'You'll not lay a hand upon him!' decreed the other. 'I uphold the law in this county. I'll have no bloodshed. You will leave Bertrand Gamberell alone.'

'I demand revenge.'

'You will get it by legal means.'

'Did he entice my sister by legal means?' howled Wymarc. 'I'll not wait for any inquest. I know what I must do. Avenge my sister and make sure that Gamberell will never do this to another woman.'

The sheriff gave a signal and the ring of soldiers closed in on the mounted knights. Two of the castle guard grabbed Wymarc and pulled him firmly from the saddle to stand before Robert d'Oilly.

'Do I have to teach you respect?' said the sheriff.

'You know my situation,' pleaded Wymarc. 'My sister lies dead. Poisoned by her own hand. Show some understanding.'

'That is what I am doing. I deeply regret what has happened. It is a tragedy. But it does not entitle you to elect yourself Sheriff of Oxfordshire and claim the power of life and death over another man. Calm down, man. Instead of charging around my courtyard here, you should be comforting your wife at home.'

'What comfort can either of us have until that foul seducer pays for his crime?'

'Find proof of his guilt before you condemn him.'

'Helene is the proof, my lord sheriff,' wailed the other. 'Her corpse is an indictment of Bertrand Gamberell.'

'How do you know?'

'He pursued her. I saw him.'

'And did you also see him take his pleasure with her?'

'I would have killed him if I had!'

'Then you would have been accountable to me.' His tone softened and he put a hand on Wymarc's shoulder. 'Your blood is too hot, man. Let it cool. It may be – who knows? – that Bertrand Gamberell is involved here.'

'I feel it in my bones!'

'He still has the right to defend himself. And I will ensure that he enjoys that right. Do you hear me?'

Wymarc nodded, his ire slowly ebbing away. The sheriff saw Arnulf walking towards them in concern. The chaplain did not need to be told what had brought Wymarc there. He was keen to add soothing words to a tense situation.

'Come, my lord,' he said, taking Wymarc by the elbow. 'Come with me into church. Let us talk. Let us pray. That is where consolation lies and not with the sword. Come.'

Wymarc allowed himself to be led meekly away.

Relieved when the tumult in the bailey ceased, the guests sat over their meal and quietly discussed the issue which had produced such clamour down below. Ralph, Gervase and Golde were enjoying the company of Edith once more. Brother Columbanus had joined them to offer his strong views on the topic which preoccupied them. Refusing to touch the ale, he instead permitted himself a cup of wine and it deepened the glow in his cheeks at once.

'I come back to St Augustine of Hippo.'

'Again!' murmured Ralph.

'Yes, my lord. Are you familiar with *De Civitate Dei*?'

'I read from it daily,' said the other with light irony.

'Then you will recall what St Augustine says.'

'That is why I do not need you to remind me.'

'Others may be less familiar with the work,' said the monk, distributing a smile around the table. 'St Augustine talks at length about suicide being caused by fear of punishment or disgrace. One passage is lodged in my mind.'

'Let it stay there!' said Ralph solemnly.

'It concerns Judas. Listen to the argument. "We rightly

205

abominate the act of Judas, and the judgement of truth is that when he hanged himself he did not atone for the guilt of his detestable betrayal, but rather increased it, since he despaired of God's mercy and in a fit of self-destructive remorse left himself no chance of saving repentance." I translate freely here, of course. St Augustine's prose has greater resonance.'

Ralph rolled his eyes at Golde. 'Thank heaven that *he* is not at this table!'

'Let us hear Brother Columbanus,' returned Golde gently.

'Do you see what this means?' continued the monk. 'When Judas killed himself, he killed a criminal, and yet he ended his life guilty not only of Christ's death, but also of his own; one crime led to another. Suicide is always a crime.'

'A very persuasive argument,' said Edith solemnly.

'Who could fault it?' added Golde.

Columbanus nudged Ralph. 'Do you follow it, my lord?'

'Yes,' said the other. 'Helene hanged herself on an elder because she felt guilty about being given thirty pieces of silver for singing in the choir!'

'That remark is profane.'

'Then do not provoke me. Judas is not relevant here. What equivalent crime did this girl commit? None! In her case, one crime does not lead to another.'

'One sin led to another,' said Columbanus. 'It was her guilt over the sin of fornication that led her to the grosser sin of suicide.'

'How do you know?' asked Gervase.

'All the evidence points that way.'

'What if the girl's chastity was violated?' asked Edith. 'It is difficult to believe that she was a willing sinner.'

'Exactly, my lady,' said Gervase. 'On this point, too, St Augustine can offer us some guidance.'

'Not you as well, Gervase!' moaned Ralph.

'He reminds us of Lucretia's suicide.'

'That noble Roman matron,' said Columbanus.

'When she was ravished by the son of King Tarquin, she

revealed the crime to her husband then destroyed herself. Lucretia was unable to endure the shame and indignity. Yet she was only the victim of the crime here. She was praised for what she did,' observed Gervase. 'It was felt that two persons were involved but only one committed adultery.'

'That is not the Christian attitude,' said Columbanus. 'What was admired in ancient Rome should not be condoned today in Woodstock. If a Christian woman is violated, she should not take vengeance on herself for another's crime. In the sight of God, she has the glory of her chastity still within her. The testimony of her conscience should be her guide. There is no excuse to add the crime of self-slaughter to that of lust. St Augustine makes that clear.'

'And so have you,' said Ralph, hoping to silence him.

'Heart and head are in conflict in this matter,' said Edith with a wan smile. 'My heart reaches out to the poor girl but my head inclines to Christian precept. Suicide is a crime. It is a denial of God's ordinance.'

'Quite so, my lady,' agreed Columbanus, helping himself to a second cup of wine. 'There is no equivocation here.'

'We still do not know the true facts of the case,' said Golde. 'Until then, our suppositions may be unjust to Helene.'

'A valid point, my love,' said Ralph.

'And one on which to conclude the debate,' added Gervase. 'Well said!'

There was a long pause as they addressed themselves to their meal. Columbanus discovered that his second cup of wine had somehow disappeared so he ventured to pour himself a third. St Augustine jogged his memory once more and he was about to mention the example of Cato's suicide. The sudden return of Robert d'Oilly put paid to that.

'Saints preserve us!' said the sheriff as he came back into the hall. 'As if I didn't have enough to contend with already!'

'What was the problem?' asked Ralph.

'Wymarc.'

'Roused to anger?'

'Determined to geld the man who lay with his sister. I had

to subdue him before he added another crime to my list. This week beggars description,' he complained. 'Everything but fire, flood and famine have afflicted me.'

'Only indirectly, my lord sheriff,' said Gervase.

'When a crime is committed, *I* bear its full weight.'

'I would have thought the victim did that.'

'Robert has endured much this week,' said Edith, coming to his support with a consoling smile. 'You have been sorely oppressed and you have our utmost sympathy. We have all admired the way that you have dealt with each new crisis.'

'Thank you, Edith.'

'I could not have done it,' said Ralph ambiguously.

'With respect,' returned d'Oilly, 'I doubt if you would ever be given the shrievalty of any county.'

Ralph chuckled. 'I am relieved to hear it.'

'It is so strange,' mused Columbanus. 'A case of an oak growing from a harmless little acorn.'

'Do I hear St Augustine again?' grumbled Ralph.

'No, my lord,' said the monk amiably. 'The acorn in question is the race which took place at Woodstock on the day of our arrival. A small event to any but those engaged in it. Yet out of that race has come murder, wrongful arrest, theft, violence and – indirectly – suicide. Could it be, for instance, that Walter Payne was the father of her child and that Helene killed herself out of grief at the death of her lover? That would not excuse what she did but it might help explain it. So many crimes have been committed here and behind them lie others yet to be discovered.' The third cup of wine was supplanted by a fourth. 'A great oak tree of wickedness, spreading its branches everywhere until it blocks out the light. And it all began with a horse race.'

They rode silently through the night. Edric the Cripple led the way on his mare and Amalric rode behind him on the chestnut colt. Moonlight was kind to them, shedding enough illumination to show them their path but leaving ample shadows to hide them from any curious eyes. Amalric was baffled. He thought he knew the area well but he was being taken over land that was totally unfamiliar.

When they reached their destination, Edric held up a hand.

'Where are we?' asked Amalric.

'Close to my stable.'

'How did you find your way?'

'I know every inch of this shire.'

'Who owns this land?'

Edric grinned. 'Bertrand Gamberell.'

'Hyperion is hidden on his own property?'

'Right under his nose.'

'No wonder he could not find him.'

'Stay here.'

Edric left him under a tree and went the remainder of the way on his own. The boy watched with fascination. He could hear running water nearby. On the bank was an abandoned mill, once a home and a source of livelihood until the river capriciously altered its course and turned a surging tributary into a sluggish stream. Edric rode round the building in a wide circle to make sure that it was safe to approach. Satisfied that all was well, he dismounted and, pulling his horse after him, hopped on his one leg through the door.

There was a long delay and Amalric feared that something untoward had occurred inside. Had the steward been ambushed? Injured in some way? Or had one of the horses been hurt by accident? The boy wanted to investigate but a sixth sense told him to stay well clear. His patience was eventually rewarded. When Edric next appeared, he was riding Hyperion.

'Does he mind being locked up in there?' said Amalric.

'Yes. But he is well fed.'

'What about exercise?'

'This is not the first night I have been here.'

'You have ridden Hyperion before?'

'I had to keep him in training.'

'Where do we go now?'

209

'To the course.'

Flushed with exhilaration, Amalric followed him on a tortuous route across the fields. The boy's ambition was about to be fulfilled. His own horse and his skill as a rider would be pitted against Hyperion. With Edric in the saddle, the black stallion would have a rider every bit as good as Walter Payne. It would be a fair race.

When they reached the course, Edric took him over it so that he could inspect it with care. A mile long over open ground, it posed no problems apart from the slight upward gradient over the final furlongs. A clump of bushes marked the finishing post. They trotted back to the designated starting place, eager to compete, each resolved to win. The horses pranced with nervous energy, wanting the race as much as the riders and relishing the headlong dash through the moonlight.

Edric brought Hyperion's head round to face the course. The clump of bushes could be seen in distant silhouette on the rising slope. Amalric adjusted his position in the saddle and gave Cempan a pat of encouragement.

'How will we start?' he asked.

'When you are ready,' said Edric, 'just go.'

'What about you?'

'I will be alongside you all the way.'

It was a confident prediction but it fell short of the truth. When Cempan surged forward, Hyperion went after him like a dog after a rabbit, running him down inside the first furlong and passing him comfortably to lead by a couple of lengths. Amalric used his heels to urge more speed out of the colt and it gradually closed the gap on its rival.

In spite of his handicap, Edric was riding like a master, pacing his horse superbly and coaxing the best out of the black stallion. But Amalric had more fire in his veins and a greater need of victory. He pushed Cempan to the limit. By the halfway point they were level and he flashed a smile at Edric before easing past him. It was the colt who now had a lead and he never relinquished it. Hyperion came back at him over the last furlong and Cempan was tiring badly as they ascended the slope, but Amalric was still able to goad his mount on.

He flashed past the clump of bushes a clear winner and was close to ecstasy as he slowed his horse to walking pace. Edric brought the black stallion alongside him and patted the boy on the back.

'Well done!' he said. 'Now we know.'

Chapter Thirteen

Golde knew that he was not asleep. She could hear his breath in the darkness. It came in short gasps rather than in the long, deep, measured way that always accompanied his slumber. Ralph Delchard was disturbed about something and it was keeping him awake in the dead of night. She rolled slowly over in the bed to face him.

'What is it?' she whispered.

He came out of his reverie to nuzzle against her.

'Nothing, my love. Go back to sleep.'

'Your mind is troubling you.'

'I will doze off in a minute.'

'You are upset.'

'I am fine, Golde.'

'Tell me why.'

'I did not mean to keep you awake.'

'I want to know, Ralph.'

She reinforced her wish with a playful bite on his chest. He kissed her on the forehead and hugged her to him, rolling on to his back so that she was pulled directly on top of him. He caressed her haunches before kissing her again.

'I still want to know,' she persisted.

'It is so trivial.'

'Let me judge for myself.'

'Very well,' he said as a wave of fatigue hit him. 'I was thinking about what Brother Columbanus said.'

'At the table this evening?'

'Yes. Even a fool says a wise thing sometimes.'

213

'Brother Columbanus is no fool.'

'True, my love. He may yet turn out to be the shrewdest man among us. Especially when drink is taken for it seems to sharpen his wits.' He gave a chuckle. 'I just hope we will not have another outburst of penitence from him in the morning.'

'He talked about St Augustine.'

'He never *stopped* talking about St Augustine,' sighed Ralph. 'Then Gervase started quoting St Augustine at me as well. I am grateful that Canon Hubert was not there or I would have been assailed from three directions at once. No,' he said, relaxing again, 'Columbanus said one thing which had nothing to do with St Augustine of Hippo.'

'Remind me.'

'It was that remark about an acorn and an oak.'

'I thought it rather apposite.'

'Yes, Golde. It was. So apposite and so obvious that it had just never occurred to me. I have been lying here trying to work out why. My brain is addled.'

'Go back to that acorn.'

'It was planted that day in Woodstock,' said Ralph. 'When Walter Payne was killed, an oak stirred out of the ground. In a short time, it has grown to monstrous proportions.'

'Frightening to watch.'

'Yet all coming from that same acorn,' he said. 'All branches of the same huge tree. Brother Columbanus put it so eloquently. Every crime is linked to the others.'

'Even this suicide?'

'Yes.'

'How?'

'I do not know but there has to be a connection. Our merry monk may seem unworldly, but he made a very sound suggestion. Suppose that Walter Payne really was the girl's lover? That would give Wymarc a strong motive to arrange his death. And it would account for the fact that Helene was so overcome with grief, she took her own life.'

'We have no proof that she was overwhelmed by grief.

Helene may have been prompted by fear. Or by self-disgust. Or by something else. I do not see this connection you talk about.'

'No more do I, my love. But I know it is there. That is why Brother Columbanus was helpful for once. He has set me looking in the right direction.'

'I do not understand.'

'They are here, Golde.'

'Who are?'

'The men behind it all,' he argued. 'The one who killed Walter Payne or arranged his murder. The one who stole the black stallion. The one who seduced that poor creature and drove her to suicide. The one who is provoking violence between Wymarc and Gamberell. The one who is so keen to win a horse race that he will take another's colt away by force.'

'How many men are you talking about?'

'One, two, perhaps more,' he said. 'But this much I know. I have met them, Golde. Talked with them all. Wymarc, Ordgar, Milo Crispin, Bertrand Gamberell and Robert d'Oilly.'

She was surprised. 'You include the sheriff?'

'He is waist-deep in this morass.'

'But it is his task to solve the crimes,' she reasoned. 'You heard his complaints this evening. He is finding the cares of office very burdensome.'

'Those cares are more than outweighed by the rewards.'

'What do you mean?'

'Look around you, Golde,' he urged. 'This castle is one of the finest and strongest in England. Only a rich man could afford to build it. Robert d'Oilly holds ten manors in Oxfordshire and collects rent from his subtenants on twenty-one others. And do you not remember your walk through the town with Arnulf?'

'Only too well.'

'What struck you most?'

'The number of derelict houses.'

'How did they get in that condition?'

215

'I do not know.'

'Then let me tell you. The sheriff has forty-two inhabited houses in Oxford but only sixteen of them pay tax and tribute. The other inhabitants are too poor. Robert d'Oilly has a further eight dwellings which are derelict because the families who lived in them have been forced out.' He eased her on to her side. 'This sheriff of ours, who finds the cares of office so burdensome, has bled this town dry. To build his castle and construct his bridge, he levied taxes on every household in Oxford.'

He checked himself and gave her an apologetic kiss.

'But what sort of conversation is this for a man and wife to have in their bedchamber?' he said softly. 'I am sorry, my love. These arguments should be heard in daylight.'

'Go on,' she encouraged him. 'I am interested.'

A yawn threatened. 'We need our sleep.'

'Not until you explain your charge.'

'It is no charge, Golde. I am thinking aloud.'

'You truly believe that the sheriff is involved?'

'If a shire is corrupt, its sheriff must take much of the blame. Maurice Pagnal was probably bribed by the sworn brother of our host. I too was probed to see if I would yield to influence. Oxford is rotten to the core.' He stroked her hair. 'None of this may make the sheriff an accessory to murder. But the speed with which he sought to prosecute an innocent man keeps his name on my list.' He grinned in the dark. 'Here endeth the lesson.'

'I have had quieter nights,' she said.

'My fault. I will make amends.'

'I am fully awake now.'

'That is why I will administer a sleeping draught.'

'Sleeping draught?'

'Yes, my love,' he said, rolling gently on top of her. 'We will take it together then slumber in each other's arms.'

Golde smiled lazily and pulled him to her.

Dawn found them riding side by side over the last mile to

Oxford. A fine drizzle was carried on the breeze. Ordgar brooded anxiously but Bristeva was in a cheerful mood. As her pony trotted along the track, she watched the distant town grow slowly in size on the horizon.

'I cannot wait to get there,' she said excitedly.

'It will not be long now, Bristeva.'

'Just think, father. I am to sleep at the castle tonight.'

'You must be on your best behaviour.'

'In my wildest dreams, I never thought to have such an honour,' she said, eyes still on the town. 'To be a guest at Oxford Castle then to sing at a banquet. These things do not happen to someone like me.'

'They did,' said Ordgar wistfully. 'In the old days, my family were accustomed to have such privileges heaped upon them. We were always invited to banquets. We mixed with the greatest in the land. Your father was a thegn, Bristeva, and you must never forget it. You are the daughter of nobility.'

'I know.'

'Then think yourself entitled to these honours.'

The pride in his voice made her heart leap and she put out a hand to squeeze his arm. Ordgar was a pragmatic man. He adapted with dignity to changes he could not resist but his memories of former glory remained undimmed.

'I saw Amalric before we left,' she recalled. 'He was in the stable with Cempan when I went for my pony.'

'Did he speak to you?' he asked with slight alarm.

'Only to bid me farewell.'

'He said nothing else?'

'Nothing, father. That is what surprised me. Amalric knew where I was going this morning yet he did not even tease me about it. I thought he would berate me again.'

'I am delighted to hear that he did not.'

'Did you speak sternly to him?'

'Amalric was warned.'

'Thank you for that,' she said. 'I feared that he might try to stop me riding to Oxford today. He and Edric have been so cruel in their comments.'

217

'That is all past, Bristeva.'

'I do hope so.'

'Neither of them will tax you again.'

'I am pleased to know that, father.' A frown surfaced. 'Amalric seemed in a happy mood today.'

'Happy?'

'I have never seen him like that before.'

'He has little to be happy about at the moment.'

'Unlike me.'

'Yes,' he agreed. 'Unlike you.'

Conscious of the dark secret he was hiding from her, Ordgar was finding it difficult to keep up a conversation with his daughter. Her joy came in such sharp contrast to his own sadness. Ordgar was pleased that she would sing at the banquet but he regretted the circumstances in which her performance would take place. In shielding her from the knowledge of Helene's suicide, he felt that he was being both kind and cruel to her. He was fearful how Bristeva would react when she realised that he had conspired with Arnulf to keep her ignorant of the tragedy. He and the chaplain were partners in betrayal.

'Do all that you are told,' he instructed.

'I will, father.'

'None of this would have happened without Father Arnulf. We are indebted to him and you must show your gratitude by your obedience to him.'

'I always do.'

'Listen to nobody else but him, Bristeva.'

'Why do you say that?'

'No reason.'

The drizzle thickened and they increased their pace. As Oxford came ever nearer, the girl's excitement knew no bounds.

'I am to sing before my lord sheriff and his lady,' she said, luxuriating in the thought. 'The Bishop of Coutances will be there with his train. And Father Arnulf tells me that royal commissioners are staying at the castle. Everyone will hear me,' she said with a giggle. 'I will be famous!'

'Enjoy the moment.'

'I will, I will.'

'You deserve it Bristeva.'

'I do. I worked so hard in the choir. And now I've been chosen to take over from Helene.' A thought nudged her. 'Do you think she will be there?'

'Who?'

'Helene. Her brother will surely be invited.'

'That is true.'

'Will he bring her along with him?'

Ordgar had to force the words out between his lips.

'No,' he said awkwardly. 'Helene will not be there.'

Wymarc had spent so long before the altar on his knees that his whole body was aching. His thighs were on fire, his calves were assaulted by cramp and his shoulders felt as if a great weight was pressing down on them. When he struggled to his feet, he tried to rub some of the stiffness out of his neck. Discomfort had brought its rewards. Wymarc had prayed for help and a measure of consolation had come. His earlier rage had been drained out of him to leave him calm and reflective. He was even ready to take some share of the blame for the desperate action of his sister. An hour of humility had taught him many things about himself as well as about Helene.

When he left the church of St George's-in-the-Castle, he saw a young man walking towards him across the bailey but he paid no heed to him. Gervase Bret, however, took an instant interest in him. Guessing at his identity, he quickened his stride to intercept the visitor as the latter untethered his horse.

'My lord Wymarc?' enquired Gervase.

'Who are you?'

'My name is Gervase Bret,' said the other politely. 'I believe that you have met my colleague, Ralph Delchard. We sit in commission together.'

'Ah, yes. I remember. He rode out to Woodstock and I showed him the exact place where the murder occurred.' A sour note intruded. 'When my back was turned, he sneaked on to my land without permission and searched for evidence.'

'I was his accomplice in that search,' admitted Gervase, 'but I am not ashamed to own it. Our investigation resulted in the release of an innocent man. Would you have preferred your slave, Ebbi, to have died for a crime he did not commit?'

'No, I would not.'

'Then our trespass was justified.'

'Why did you not come to me first? I would not have forbidden you entry. I could have helped you in your search.'

'I am hopeful that you may be able to do that now, my lord,' said Gervase. 'This is not an appropriate time to raise the matter, I know. I offer you my sincerest condolences.'

'Thank you,' mumbled Wymarc.

'I can appreciate the enormous strain you must feel.'

'It is crushing me, Master Bret.'

'The chaplain has spoken to me of your distress.'

'Arnulf has been wonderful. Both at my house and here in the castle when my fury got the better of me. The man is blessed. He gentled me.' He glanced over his shoulder. 'That is why I came to his church this morning. To give thanks and to seek further guidance.'

'I trust that you found that guidance.'

'What is this help you spoke of?'

'The murder remains unsolved,' said Gervase, 'and the sheriff fears the killer may have fled far from here.'

'That is my fear as well.'

'It is not ours, my lord. We believe that he is a local man. Only someone who knew the area well could plot that killing and plan his escape so cunningly. And who else would know Walter Payne but those in the vicinity?'

'True.'

'How well did you know the fellow?'

'Only by sight and reputation.'

'Reputation?'

'His skill as a horseman was well known,' said Wymarc,

'and I saw far too much evidence of it myself. But the fellow also had a reputation for wild behaviour.'

'My lord Ralph mentioned that.'

'Walter Payne and his friends went on drunken rampages from time to time. They would pick fights, cause damage to property and even assault womenfolk.'

'Did nobody complain?'

'Nobody whose protest carried any strength,' said Wymarc. 'Bertrand Gamberell would simply laugh and refuse to discipline his men. They were entitled to their pleasures, he would say.' His jaw tightened. 'Bertrand sets great store by pleasure.'

'How did Walter Payne come into his service?'

'They are birds of a feather.'

'My lord Bertrand is not known for drunken behaviour.'

'He spreads his destruction by more subtle means.'

A spark of anger came into his eye but it soon died. The conversations with Arnulf and the early morning visit to the church had quelled his urge for vengeance.

'This Walter Payne,' continued Gervase, probing tenderly. 'You had no personal grudge against him, then?'

'Indeed I did! He cost me a small fortune. Every time he rode Hyperion to victory, he made a fresh hole in my purse. I would not have thrown the dagger that killed him but neither will I mourn his death.'

'Who *would* have thrown it, my lord?'

'How do I know?'

'You might be able to suggest names.'

'Of whom?'

'Those harassed by Walter Payne and his fellows,' said Gervase. 'One of your manors is contiguous with my lord Bertrand's land. Were any of your subtenants the victims of their wild misconduct?'

'Occasionally.'

'Who bore the brunt of his roistering?'

'None of my people,' said Wymarc. 'Walter Payne let them off lightly. Most of his prey were on Milo's land. He ran riot across it a number of times. Milo's subtenants were always protesting about Walter Payne.'

'Did those subtenants include Ordgar?'

'Probably. Why?'

'I ask out of idle curiosity, my lord,' said Gervase. 'Nothing more. Thank you for giving me your time. I will intrude on your grief no longer. Farewell.'

As Wymarc rode out of the castle, a pensive Gervase watched him leave. A chance meeting had yielded much of value. Instead of going into the church, Gervase went off to report to Ralph.

The room was small, bare and featureless with only the most meagre portion of light coming through the tiny arched window. The stone walls and floor gave off a chill that was not relieved by the single flickering candle in the alcove. A mattress lay in one corner with a stool beside it. On the wall above the mattress was a wooden crucifix.

Bristeva was thrilled with her accommodation.

'This will be very suitable,' she said gratefully.

Arnulf was apologetic. 'It is a mean chamber, I fear.'

'Not at all.'

'I sought to find you an apartment in the keep,' he said. 'But all are reserved for the guests. When the bishop arrives with his train, the castle will be filled to bursting. You will have to make do with this humbler lodging next to the church.'

'I will be quite content here.'

'Good.'

'I am comforted to know that you are nearby.'

'Yes,' said Arnulf, pointing a hand at one wall. 'I am in the adjoining chamber and Brother Columbanus is further down the passage.'

'Brother Columbanus?'

'He travels with some important visitors who have come to Oxford and serves them in the office of a scribe. You will like him, Bristeva. In spite of his cowl, he is a jolly man.'

'I am always a little afraid of monks,' she confided.

'Why?'

'I do not know. Their holiness frightens me.'

Arnulf smiled. 'Does my holiness frighten you as well?'

'Oh, no!'

'I am relieved to hear it.'

'You are different, Father Arnulf.'

'Thank you.'

He gazed at her with fondness and reached out to adjust the edge of her wimple. Singing at the banquet would be a supreme test for her but he had every faith in Bristeva.

'I need to ask a special favour of you,' he said.

'It is granted before it is even asked.'

'Talk to nobody inside the castle.'

She was confused. 'Not even you, Father Arnulf?'

'Nobody except me,' he clarified. 'Whenever I can I will stay close by you, but there will be times when you are alone. Keep to this chamber. Too much scurrilous gossip floats around a castle and I do not want your young ears corrupted by it. Give me your word, Bristeva,' he said, taking her gently by the elbows. 'Do not speak to anybody.'

'Not even Brother Columbanus?'

'I was forgetting him.'

'You said a moment ago that I would like him.'

'Why, yes. I did,' he recalled. 'And he would certainly cause you no harm. Let me speak to him first. Brother Columbanus might help to stave off boredom for you.'

'I could never be bored when I am here with you.'

Arnulf smiled and took his hands away from her.

'Is your father looking forward to the banquet?' he said.

'Very much.'

'The hall will be crowded with guests.'

'I hope I am not too nervous.'

'You will have no problems.'

'But there will be so many distinguished guests there,' she said. 'I have never performed in front of such a large gathering before. Was Helene ever nervous?'

'No, Bristeva.'

223

'Did she ever let you down?'

'Never.'

'I asked father if Helene might be at the banquet but he seemed to think she would not be. Is that right?'

He nodded ruminatively. 'My lord Wymarc confirmed it. He was here even before you this morning, Bristeva.'

'What did he say.'

'Helene is indisposed. She will not be coming.'

'I am disappointed to hear that.'

'We all are.' He became brisk. 'Now that I have shown you where you will sleep, let me take you to the hall where you will sing. We need to rehearse in there while we may. There will be little opportunity once the guests arrive.'

'I'm ready,' she said.

'Thus far, you have only sung in the church. Your voice will sound very different in the hall. You need to get used to that difference. Come, Bristeva,' he said, taking her out into the passage. 'We will make a start. When we have earned a rest from our rehearsal, I will bring you back here to introduce you to Brother Columbanus.' He remembered something. 'If we can actually find him, that is.'

Brother Columbanus opened a preliminary eye in the firm conviction that he would find himself in his chamber. He expected to see a finger of light poking in through the little window and pointing reverentially at the crucifix on the wall above his head. But he saw nothing. No wall, no window and no crucifix. He was in the pitch dark. Could it still be the middle of the night? A second eye joined the first in a vain attempt at probing the gloom. Where was he?

When he shifted his bulk, he felt something hard and uncomfortable beneath him. He was not lying on his mattress. Instead, he seemed to be propped up against a wall in a room that was thick with dust and devoid of any furniture. How had he got there? Columbanus racked his brain to tease out every detail of the meal in the hall. He recalled the vigorous debate about suicide and the words of St Augustine came back to him with reassuring exactness. Beyond that, however, all he could remember was that the food had been delicious.

Had he eaten to excess? Had he so disgraced himself that he had been cast into outer darkness? Or had he wandered off into some remote part of the castle and simply got lost? Brother Columbanus was totally perplexed. He was about to offer up a prayer for guidance when he felt something in his lap. He reached down to discover that he was holding a flagon of wine. It was still half full. Its contents swished around delightfully. He put the flagon to his lips.

Columbanus was soon fast asleep again in the undercroft beneath the church. He no longer cared how he had got there. The wine was as sweet this morning as it had been the previous night. There was another bonus. St Augustine was waiting in his dreams to welcome him once more.

Ralph Delchard was intrigued to hear what Gervase had gleaned.

'Wymarc came here?' he said, raising an eyebrow.

'He felt the need for spiritual comfort.'

'Then why not go to the nearest church? Why ride all the way into Oxford before dawn?'

'Arnulf is here. Wymarc holds the chaplain in high regard.'

'So does the sheriff,' noted Ralph. 'When Wymarc and his men rode in here last night, our host was able to shout them down but it was Arnulf who really subdued the vengeful lord. This chaplain is a useful man to have around the castle.'

'Much more than useful, Ralph. He is invaluable.'

'And blessed with astonishing tolerance.'

'Tolerance?'

'Yes, Gervase. What other man of God would put up with such a bellicose master as Robert d'Oilly?'

'Arnulf will hear no criticism of the sheriff. He is blind to the man's faults.'

Ralph pointed to the river which ran below them.

'Can one look at the Thames and be blind to the water?'

They shared a wry laugh. They had left the castle to walk

down to Grandpont for a combination of exercise and privacy. Resting against the parapet of the stone bridge which Robert d'Oilly had built over the river, they were enjoying a quiet moment together. The drizzle had stopped now and sunshine was giving the water a bright sheen. Accustomed to spending their days in musty shire halls, Ralph and Gervase were grateful for the enforced respite though still wounded by the disclosures which had prompted it.

'Do you think that Canon Hubert will come?' said Gervase.

'We will know soon enough. The messenger we dispatched to Winchester should return later today. However ill Hubert is, he will not desert us in our hour of need.' He gave a snort of disgust. 'As for Maurice Pagnal, he will have the King's displeasure visited upon him. I look to find him behind bars when we return.'

'He took me in completely.'

'I, too, was fooled, Gervase.'

'But for Brother Timothy of Westminster, we might never have uncovered the deceit. Islip would have been awarded to Roger d'Ivry's wife, Maurice would have pocketed his bribe and we would have been none the wiser.' Gervase gave a rueful sigh. 'Brother Timothy was our salvation.'

'Alas, yes. I hate to be beholden to a monk.'

'Would you rather sit alongside a corrupt judge?'

'You know the answer to that.'

Gervase watched a kingfisher skim over the river.

'What is our next move to be, Ralph?'

'We do not make one. Golde agrees with me.'

'About what?'

'Biding our time, Gervase,' he said. 'We have spoken to the four men whose horses ran in that race. Wymarc, Ordgar, Milo Crispin and Bertrand Gamberell. And let us not forget that three of them are involved in another kind of contest – the dispute over that property near Wallingford. Four men with good reason to hate each other. I have come to believe that one of them has outwitted us.'

'How?'

'In the same way as Maurice. By being too plausible. By telling us exactly what we wished to hear at the time we needed to hear it. Maurice Pagnal stood right in front of us yet we could not discern his villainy. One of those four men has done precisely the same. And I would add a fifth name.'

'Robert d'Oilly?'

'He is involved in everything in this town,' said Ralph. 'We may yet find that the murder has some connection with him. Five names, Gervase. Which one would you choose?'

'I am not sure. But I would eliminate one already.'

'Who is that?'

'Bertrand Gamberell.'

'Why?'

'He would never set up the murder of his own man.'

'Stranger things have happened in this shire.'

'It meant that he lost the race,' said Gervase, 'and that went hard with him. Besides, what motive would he have?'

'He and Walter Payne may have fallen out. Over the girl, perhaps. We know that Gamberell lusted after her as well. If he learned that his own man had seduced Helene in his stead, he would have been enraged.'

'Then he would have taken revenge in private and not in such a public way. Walter Payne's involvement with Helene is only speculation. Even if there had been a relationship between them, Payne would have made certain that his master never found out about it.' Gervase pursed his lips in thought. 'No, Ralph,' he decided. 'I do not believe that Gamberell fell out with his rider. He was too anguished by the killing.'

'Gamberell made a lot of noise about it, that is true. But he also led the search for the assassin in the copse. That was the perfect way to turn suspicion away from himself.' He scratched his head. 'I know that it seems unlikely but we must keep his name on the list.'

'If you insist.'

'For the rest, we wait until tomorrow.'

'Tomorrow?'

'The banquet, Gervase,' he explained. 'All of our five men

227

will probably be there. The only possible absentee is Wymarc and even he may find it politic to be in Oxford to lick the episcopal arse of Geoffrey of Coutances.' He rubbed his hands together. 'Our man is among them somewhere.'

'All we have to do is to pick him out.'

'Yes. It is that simple.'

Gervase laughed. 'If only it were!'

Bertrand Gamberell returned home that morning at a sedate trot. He had spent an uneasy night at Wallingford Castle but it had been a sensible precaution. Wymarc's fury would have spent itself in a fruitless search, he decided, and the coast would now be clear. When he reached his own land, he felt no watching eyes upon him and feared no ambush. Wymarc and his men were not lying in wait to wreak vengeance. The danger was past.

The fact was confirmed by his steward when Gamberell strode into his home. There had been no angry callers during his absence. His whereabouts had not been sought.

'Has nobody at all been here?' he said.

'Not until this morning, my lord,' replied the steward.

'Someone from Wymarc, by chance?'

'The messenger would not name his master.'

'What letter did he bring?'

'It is here, my lord.'

The steward handed it over then withdrew to the other side of the parlour so that Gamberell could read the missive in private. Breaking the seal, the latter unfolded the parchment and read the two evocative lines penned there. The letter was in the code which he had taught her to use and its meaning would be beyond anyone else. It made Gamberell grin with pleasure. She had written with a flowing hand which showed character and urgency. He longed to have those same fingers practising their calligraphy on him again.

Her timing was perfect. After the storm he had just weathered, he felt the need of safe harbour in which to lie gloriously at anchor for a few hours. His last visit had been marred by

228

the theft of Hyperion but that was not her fault. She had given him all that he wanted and was now offering more. Gamberell could not refuse her. The generous body would be a partial recompense for the loss of his stallion. After reading the letter once again to savour its promise, he folded it and stuffed it into his belt.

He had forgotten that his steward was there. In the background, the man coughed discreetly to attract attention. His master looked sharply across at him.

'Yes?'

'Will there be a reply, my lord?'

'I will deliver it in person.'

Edric the Cripple was working at the accounts when he heard the boy come into the house. Amalric's jaunty tread showed that he was still nursing happy memories of his midnight race against Hyperion. It also suggested that the gossip from Oxford had not yet worked its way through to him. Edric had been into the town that morning and found that its interest in the suicide of a young girl had in no way faded.

When Amalric came into the bay where the steward sat at a table, he was grinning broadly. Victory had been dear to him. A sudden yawn proved that it had not been without cost.

'A boy of your age should get more sleep,' said Edric.

'Who needs sleep when they can ride a horse?'

'I do, Amalric. But my bones are older than yours.'

'Shall we race again tonight?'

'No!'

'You can ride Cempan this time.'

'The issue has been decided. Ours is the better horse.'

'That was never in doubt.'

'No,' agreed Edric. 'But we enjoyed good fortune last night. Nobody saw us. Nobody interrupted our contest. We might not be so lucky a second time. It is foolish to take any more unnecessary risks. That is why I will return Hyperion.'

'Return him?' gasped Amalric.

'After dark.'

'But that would be madness,' argued the boy. 'You stole him in order to prevent another race taking place and thus stop my lord Milo from seizing Cempan. If you restore the black stallion to his master, the race will surely be set up.'

'Not for some while at least.'

'How do you know?'

'Because they would not run without my lord Wymarc's horses in the contest to swell the purse. They are not like us, Amalric. Cempan against Hyperion. They will want more horses in the race.'

'My lord Wymarc will provide them willingly.'

'Not for a while,' said Edric, closing the account book. 'His grief would not allow it.'

'Grief?'

'His young sister has died.'

He passed on the news. When he heard the details, Amalric was visibly shaken. Helene had been in the same choir as his own sister and close to Bristeva's age. He thought for a moment how they would feel if the tragedy had befallen her and not Wymarc's sister. The fear and the shame would be truly overwhelming.

'You are right, Edric,' he conceded at length. 'It will be a long time before this race is held again. But I would still be sorry to see Hyperion released.'

'He has served his purpose in both ways.'

'Both ways?'

'Yes,' explained Edric. 'By stealing him, I saved Cempan from being stolen. But I also found a hiding place for us if that need does arise. If Hyperion can be stabled in that mill without being discovered then so can Cempan.'

The boy rallied. 'I never thought of that!'

'Bear it in mind. The decision may fall to you.'

'What do you mean?'

'You will see, Amalric,' he said, putting a hand on the boy's shoulder to haul himself upright. 'But let us take it one step at a time. First, I will return Hyperion.'

'Where will you take him?'

'To the place from which I stole him.'

'And where was that, Edric?'

'A house where Bertrand Gamberell had no right to be,' said the other. 'He dotes on that black stallion but he may not be so pleased to get him back from that particular house.'

Edric the Cripple shook with malicious glee.

Chapter Fourteen

Arnulf the Chaplain was confronted by an unforeseen problem. It was impossible for him to spend all his time with Bristeva and yet he was afraid to leave her entirely alone lest she somehow hear the loud whispers concerning Helene's suicide which were still blowing about the castle like a stiff breeze. The one person to whom he could entrust her was the discreet and kindly Brother Columbanus but the affable monk had completely vanished. Nobody had seen him and Arnulf's own hurried search through the fortress had proved futile. It was a worrying situation.

Bristeva was anxious not to be a nuisance to him.

'I will stay in my chamber,' she volunteered.

'It is so cold and cheerless.'

'I do not mind, Father Arnulf. I can practise my songs. When I am singing, I do not really care where I am.'

'I promised your father I would look after you,' said the chaplain, 'and that does not mean abandoning you for the whole afternoon. But my lord sheriff has summoned me and I am not able to ignore his call. His needs are paramount.'

'Go to him. Let me stay here.'

He heaved a sigh. 'I may have no choice, Bristeva.'

'I could always sit in the church,' she offered.

'No, no. You are safer here.'

'Nobody will talk to me in there.'

'I would rather not take that risk,' he said quickly. 'Besides, you need to rest and you will not do that with people coming to and from the church. Stay here. And do not stir from this chamber.'

'I will not go anywhere.'

'Close the door after me.'

'Yes, Father Arnulf.'

'I will return as soon as possible.'

'Do not worry about me. I am used to being alone.'

Bristeva smiled bravely and he gave her arm a delicate squeeze. When he went out, she closed the door behind him. He waited long enough to hear her begin the first song before moving along the passage to peer into Columbanus's chamber in the vain hope that the monk may have returned. The room was still empty. As he headed for the bailey, Arnulf's lips were pursed in anxiety.

He was halfway up the steps to the keep when Golde emerged from the door to the tower and descended towards him. Her smile flowered immediately. He gave an answering nod of greeting to her.

'I am so glad to meet you like this,' she said.

'Are you, my lady?'

'Yes. You can solve the mystery that is puzzling me.'

'Mystery?'

'That beautiful voice I heard in the hall earlier on,' she explained. 'I was walking past when the divine sound came wafting out. My curiosity was roused at once but I did not dare to interrupt.'

'I am grateful that you did not. We were practising.'

'With your little songbird from the choir?'

'Yes, my lady. Bristeva.'

'Her voice is as clear as a bell.'

'I have taught her how to project it.'

'Then you have taught her well, Father Arnulf,' said Golde with enthusiasm. 'Girls are not usually allowed to develop their talents. We are expected to sit quietly and speak only when spoken to. That is how my father brought me up. Had I been a boy, my world would have been much larger.'

'Unhappily, that is so.'

'I can imagine the resistance you met when you first introduced girls into your choir.'

'More derision than resistance,' he recalled. 'We still have much censure to withstand from those who cling blindly to tradition.'

'It was a courageous thing to do. I hope that you feel vindicated now.'

'I do, my lady.'

'If Bristeva is an example of your choristers, you should be very proud. She was a joy to listen to in the hall. How many other Saxon girls would have such a wonderful chance as this? The girl must worship you.'

'She trusts me. That is far more important.'

'Is there any chance of my meeting her?'

'You will see her at the banquet tomorrow.'

'I wanted to talk to her properly,' said Golde, 'to find out more about her, perhaps even to help her. A castle as big as this must be an intimidating place for a young girl. It unsettles me and I have been here for days. Bristeva must be quite overawed by it.'

'She is, my lady.'

'The sight of all these soldiers will only increase her discomfort. She might welcome some female company. Where is the girl now?'

Arnulf did not hesitate. He had a deep admiration for Golde. She was a gentle, considerate, kind-hearted woman who would be a far more suitable companion for Bristeva than a Benedictine monk. Golde would offer a maternal warmth which would help to reassure the girl.

'Bristeva is in her chamber, my lady,' he said.

'May I go to her?'

'There is something you must understand before you do that. Bristeva knows nothing of Helene's tragedy. It would shatter her if she did. I have to guard her from the truth until after the banquet. You do appreciate that?'

'She will hear nothing from me,' promised Golde.

It was settled.

* * *

The church of St George's-in-the-Castle was not simply a place of worship. It was an integral part of the fortifications. Its square tower served both as a belfry and as a key part of the castle's defences, providing as it did a high point from which the town could be kept under surveillance and an almost impregnable base from which arrows, rocks and other missiles could be discharged by unseen soldiers at any attackers below. As he strolled towards the church, Gervase Bret glanced up at the massive stone structure and noted with sadness how religion was forced to go hand in hand with military might.

When he had said his prayers at the altar rail, he moved to a bench and sat for an hour or more in the dank interior, lost in thought. Meditation was impossible in any other part of the castle, where the sound of many voices and much activity blended with the movement of men and horses to produce a mild chaos which lasted throughout each day. Alone in the church, Gervase felt refreshingly isolated from the worst of the din outside. It was only when the bell tolled that he abandoned his contemplation.

Edith was walking towards the church as Gervase emerged into the sunlight. He blinked to adjust his eyes to the glare.

'You are a devout parishioner,' she said with approval.

'Only because I have time on my hands, my lady. When we came to Oxford, we expected to spend every daylight hour in the shire hall. It is highly unusual for our work to be suspended in this way.'

'When will it resume?'

'When Canon Hubert arrives,' he said. 'The messenger brought word back from Winchester this afternoon. In spite of his ailments, Canon Hubert has consented to answer our call but he is not able to set out until today.'

'Will he reach us in time for the banquet?' she asked. 'He would be most welcome to take his place at the table.'

'Nothing would please him more, my lady. However, I have grave doubts. Canon Hubert travels slowly. My guess is that we will see him some time on Sunday morning.'

'I regret that his journey is necessary.'

'So do we.'

'My lord Maurice seemed like an upright man.'

'He took great pains to appear so.'

'Robert liked him and my husband is a sound judge of character. He was shocked by the revelations.'

'Yes, my lady,' said Gervase guardedly.

'I see that you do not believe me.'

'What makes you think that?'

'I am not blind,' she said. 'You and my lord Ralph show my husband the respect that is due but you both harbour doubts about him. Why deny it? I've seen it in your eyes. I do not censure you for it. In your position, I would probably think the same. But you are wrong.'

'Are we?'

'Robert is a good man and a loving husband. It has not been easy to keep the peace in a county as unruly as this.'

'My lord sheriff seems to have succeeded very well.'

'Only because of his dedication. Take that into account before you pass judgement on him.'

'We pass no judgement, my lady.'

'You have not seen him at his best,' she said defensively. She studied him with interest for a moment. 'Golde tells me that you are betrothed.'

'That is true.'

'Her name is Alys, I understand.'

'Yes, my lady.'

'She is fortunate in her choice.'

'Alys does not always think so,' he admitted with a smile. 'We long to be together, but as soon as I return to Winchester we are dispatched on some new investigation. She vexes during my absence.'

'A sure sign of love.'

'It is mutual.'

'Her good fortune does not only lie in having such a handsome and able young man as her future husband,' said Edith wistfully. 'It resides in her freedom to choose you in the first place.' There was a long pause. 'I did not have that freedom of choice.'

'You do not have to explain that, my lady.'

'I think I do,' she continued. 'I know what all of you must think when you see me with my husband. We must look ill matched in some ways. Robert can be brutal but only when that brutality is essential. I have learned to live with that.'

Gervase was embarrassed. 'This is a matter between you and your husband. You do not have to justify yourself to me, my lady. What I see is a gracious and loyal wife.'

'But I had to learn that grace and loyalty. My situation was so different from yours. You and Alys have a love match. In my case,' she confessed, 'respect and duty came first. Love grew slowly out of them. It took some years. My husband has true nobility and I am honoured to share my life with him.'

Gervase was touched. Anxious to defend her husband, Edith was confiding details of her courtship. She was not merely a marital decoration on the arm of the sheriff of Oxfordshire. She was a concerned and faithful partner who had seen all of Robert d'Oilly's finer qualities and – while aware of his defects – had come to love him as a result.

'It is my lord sheriff who is fortunate,' he observed.

'Thank you. But I will not hold you up,' she said. 'I came in search of Brother Columbanus.'

'He is not in the church, my lady.'

'I supposed him to be in his chamber nearby.'

'You may find him there,' he said, stepping aside to let her past. 'But I doubt it. We have all been looking for Brother Columbanus. He is a Benedictine magician. He seems to have disappeared into thin air.'

When he came fully awake, Brother Columbanus put the empty flagon aside and started to make a more detailed survey of his surroundings. He felt warm, happy and strangely guiltless. As he groped around in the darkness, his hand touched nothing but bare earth. It was when he tried to rise that he had some indication of where he was. His tonsured head collided so hard with a wooden beam that he was momentarily dazed. The impact sobered him at once.

The low ceiling and the earthen floor told him that he must be in the undercroft and his brain was now functioning well enough for him to work out how he had got there. On his return from the hall the previous night, he had evidently been too inebriated to find his chamber and had strayed into the undercroft by mistake. He was reassured to learn that he was still on consecrated ground.

Taking care to avoid a second collision, he scrambled around in the gloom until he finally located the door. He was soon rejoining the world of the castle, padding across the bailey and dusting off his cowl with a vigorous palm. Ralph Delchard was talking to some of his men near the stables. He looked up as the monk approached.

'There you are, Brother Columbanus!' he said.

'Did you want me, my lord?'

'We have all wanted you. Where have you been?'

'With the canons of St Frideswide's,' said Columbanus.

The cheerful lie did not even prick his conscience.

It was early evening and Golde was still engrossed in her conversation with Bristeva. She found the girl delightful and an immediate friendship had formed. Bristeva reminded her so much of herself at that age that it was uncanny. On her side, the girl was thrilled to have such interest taken in her and she revelled in the rare pleasure of talking to the wife of a Norman baron in her own tongue. They were in Bristeva's chamber close by the church. Neither of them even noticed how cramped and uncomfortable it was.

'Are you looking forward to the banquet?' asked Golde.

'I have thought about nothing else for days.'

'Your songs will be a joy to hear.'

'I hope so, my lady,' said the girl. 'Father Arnulf has rehearsed me so carefully. For his sake, I wish to do well.'

'Will your family be there to hear you?'

'Yes, they have been invited.'

'You will make them feel very proud.'

'I will try, my lady. My father will love me whatever I do. It is Amalric who will need persuading.'

'Amalric?'

'My brother. He does not want me to sing here.'

'Why not?'

As soon as she asked it, Golde answered her own question and the girl's blush confirmed that the answer was correct. If Bristeva had to defy her brother in order to sing, it must take some of the pleasure out of the occasion for her. The girl remembered a compensation and her smile returned.

'Father Arnulf told me that the guests would be very appreciative if I sang well enough,' she said.

'I am sure they will.'

'They sometimes gave Helene money for her performance. It would be wonderful if they did that for me. Not that I would keep it for myself,' she stressed with a serious frown. 'I would give it to Father Arnulf for the alms box.'

'But you will have earned the reward, Bristeva.'

'Only because of him.'

'That is a very noble gesture to make.'

'It is the least I can do to show my thanks.' The frown vanished. 'Do you know how many will be there tomorrow?'

'As many as a hundred, I am told.'

'All coming to hear me!'

'There will be other entertainment, Bristeva,' Golde reminded her with an indulgent smile, 'but they will not compare with you, of course. You will have us all at your feet.'

'My only disappointment is that she will not be there.'

'She?'

'Helene.'

'Ah, yes.'

'I would so love her to watch me taking her place,' said Bristeva, 'but they say she is unlikely to come.'

Golde felt the pain of holding back the truth from her.

'I'm sure that you will not notice her absence in such a large gathering,' she said soothingly. 'It will be late before the banquet ends. Will you ride home through the night with your father and brother?'

'No, my lady. Father Arnulf wants me to spend a second night here so that I will be able to join the rest of the choir for Matins on Sunday.'

'That will save you two journeys.'

'Yes.' Bristeva was quizzical. 'May I ask you something?'

'Please do.'

'How did you meet your husband?' Golde laughed in surprise and the girl was immediately contrite. 'Oh, dear! I did not mean to pry,' she said quickly. 'Please do not take offence. I should not have asked. It is no business of mine.'

'You took me unawares, Bristeva, that is all.'

'Forget what I said.'

'No,' said Golde pleasantly. 'I will give you an honest answer. I have nothing to hide. I met my husband by chance when he came to visit my home town.'

'And where was that?'

'Hereford.'

'Edric used to live in Hereford.'

'Edric?'

'My father's steward,' she said. 'He never talks about it to me but Amalric told me that he was once in the service of the Earl of Hereford.'

'Some time ago, then. The county has no earl now.'

'The name I remember is Earl Roger.'

Golde nodded. 'Roger of Breteuil. He disgraced himself, Bristeva. He joined with two other earls in a revolt against the King. The revolt was put down and Earl Roger was sent to prison. We have had no earl in Hereford since.'

'According to my brother, Edric will say very little about his time there.'

'That is understandable if he was Earl Roger's man.'

'I think there is another reason, my lady.'

'What is that?'

'Our steward is known as Edric the Cripple,' said the other.

'Hereford has unhappy memories for him. That is where he lost his leg.'

Towing his own horse on a lead-rein, Edric the Cripple gave himself the pleasure of riding Hyperion for the last time. The moon was hidden behind the clouds. He hugged the trees for additional cover. When he got close to the house, he tethered his own horse to a bush and eased Hyperion forward at a walking pace. A dog began to bark but the clank of a chain showed that he was not at large. Edric waited until the barking stopped then nudged the black stallion on.

It was over in a matter of minutes. When he closed the stable door, Edric looked up at the house where a contented man slept unwittingly with a wayward wife. Edric smirked. He took pleasure in being able to destroy their marital harmony. He used his crutch to hop away through the shadows. Hyperion was no longer his problem. The stallion would cause worries for somebody else now. Mounting his own horse, he was soon making his way back home at a steady trot.

When the dog barked again, Edric was miles away.

She was still in her night attire. Sitting on a chair in the bedchamber, she combed her hair with languid strokes and imagined the pleasure of having her lover's fingers running through her tresses. He had liberated her as a woman. After years in a stale bed with an older man, she had finally found someone who could ignite her passion until it crackled with delight and burned itself out in an explosion of pure ecstasy. She knew that he would come to her again. Her letter had been sent in the code which he had given her. Meaningless to anyone else, it held a promise of utter bliss for them.

She cocked an ear to listen for the departing hoofbeats. Her husband would be away in Oxford for the whole day. Having left a bored and unsatisfied wife, he would return to a woman whose every desire had been fulfilled by her lover. The beauty of it was that her husband would observe no difference. He had long ago stopped looking at her with any interest. She was completely safe. He would never know.

When the hoofbeats did not come, she crossed to the window to investigate. They should have left by now. Her lover would be concealed nearby, waiting in the trees for her husband and his reeve to ride past him on the road to Oxford. Until that happened, he would not come near the house. She grew fretful. What was causing the delay?

The door burst open and her husband stormed in.

'Why is his black stallion in my stables?' he demanded.

'Whose stallion?' she asked.

The blow sent her reeling to the floor.

'Bertrand Gamberell. Everyone in the county knows that horse of his.'

Arnulf the Chaplain was heartened to see so many communicants in church that morning. He did not flatter himself that they came in response to his own efforts to build a congregation. Shock and uncertainty had brought many of them there. The suicide of a girl in Woodstock had stirred them deeply and reminded them of the need to keep their spiritual lives in repair. They came in search of guidance and reassurance. They wanted to be told how Christians ought properly to view the tragedy and to be reaffirmed in a faith which Helene had so conspicuously betrayed. Arnulf was tolerant of their shortcomings. He put bread on their tongues and held the chalice to their lips without discrimination.

When the service was over, he went quickly back to the chamber where Bristeva was lodged. He tapped on the door but there was no reply. Inching the door ajar, he saw that the girl was still fast asleep. Bristeva lay on her back. He was struck by how beautiful she looked with her hair loose and her face brushed by the light from the window. It was a peaceful slumber. The girl was completely at ease in the strange surroundings and he knew that Golde was partly responsible for that. She had helped Bristeva to relax and settle in.

Arnulf was about to step into the room when he heard a

shuffling noise behind him. Brother Columbanus had come out of his own chamber and now stood behind him. Over the chaplain's shoulder, he looked down at Bristeva.

'She is an angel at rest,' he said.

'Bristeva worked hard yesterday. It tired her.'

'Then let her sleep on.'

'I will.'

'This is a big day for her, Arnulf. Do not bring her into it until she is ready to come. Let her awake in her own time.'

'You are right, Brother Columbanus.'

He stepped back and closed the door gently behind him.

Bertrand Gamberell began to wonder if there had been a mistake. Having waited in his hiding place for the best part of an hour, he could still see no sign of a departing husband. Had the woman sent him the wrong message? Or had there been a change of plan? He felt certain that she would have sent a second message if there was any serious problem, and he could not believe that she had dragged him all the way there in order to humiliate him by keeping him at bay. Was it possible that her husband had left even before he arrived?

Gamberell wondered if he should approach the house. A cautious reconnaissance would establish if its master was still at home. He decided against the idea. If she was already alone, she would surely have found a means to signal to him. All that he could do was to sit and wait. It was a small price to pay for the delights which lay ahead.

Relief eventually came. He heard the distant clack of hooves on the road and two horsemen appeared from the direction of the house. Gamberell walked up the slope once again to make sure that they would not turn back. From his lofty perch, he saw the pair of them riding at a steady canter. Husband and reeve were clearly in a hurry to get to Oxford. Gamberell slapped his thigh and retrieved his own mount. He rode down to the house.

Recalling his last visit, he skirted the stables and instead concealed his horse in some thickets, looking around to make sure that he was unobserved. He did not want the same embarrassment again. When he was certain that nobody had seen where the animal was hidden, he crept back towards the house. From the edge of the stables, he could see the window of her bedchamber. She was there. A simple gesture from her hand was enough. Gamberell broke into a gentle run.

He let himself in by the rear door which had been left open for him then headed for the staircase. Surging up the steps, he went straight to her door and knocked on it with a proprietorial firmness. Before she could answer, he flung it open and stepped in to claim her. The woman was standing against the wall beside the bed. Gamberell beamed at her. In a moment he would saunter across and take her in his arms.

Then he saw the bruise on her temple and the blood that trickled from her mouth. He took a worried step towards her.

'What happened?' he asked.

The door slammed shut behind him. Gamberell swung round to find himself staring at her enraged husband. Two other men stood with him, each armed with a wooden stave. Gamberell recovered his poise with remarkable speed.

'I can explain all this,' he said cheerfully.

'Do,' said the husband coldly. 'Afterwards.'

Before the secret lover could even move, he was felled by a blow from a stave. Both men belaboured him without mercy. The woman screamed at the top of her voice and begged them to stop but the husband urged them on.

Bertrand Gamberell writhed in pain.

Ralph Delchard remained sceptical about what he had heard.

'This is her husband's work,' he decided.

'I think not,' said Gervase.

'He told her to plead on his behalf.'

'That is unlikely, Ralph.'

'I agree,' said Golde. 'He may have asked her to sound me out because he assumed I would be an easier target. But he could hardly expect such an approach to work with Gervase.'

The three of them were sitting over the remains of breakfast in the hall. Having risen late, they were enjoying a leisurely start to the day. Gervase had told them of his conversation outside the church with Edith.

'That is the other thing,' he argued. 'It was a chance encounter.'

'Was it?' wondered Ralph. 'Perhaps she saw you go into the church and lurked outside in readiness.'

'For a whole hour?'

'That is a ridiculous idea,' said Golde. 'Besides, my lady Edith said nothing about her husband which is going to alter Gervase's mind. It sounds to me as if she were merely trying to answer the question we have all posed. Why did she marry Robert d'Oilly?'

'A death wish!' declared Ralph.

'Expediency,' she said.

'My lady Edith was at pains to suggest there was more to it than that,' remembered Gervase. 'To her, he is not the ogre he may appear to others.'

'Appear!' repeated Ralph with a snort. '*Appear*, Gervase? He is. When a man taxes you out of your home, or beats you senseless, he does not appear to be an ogre. He *is* one.' He gave a mirthless laugh. 'Speak to Ebbi. Ask him if Robert d'Oilly appeared to be cruel when he struck Ebbi down.'

'Let us not bring that up again, Ralph,' said Golde.

'Let us not forget it either.'

'I was pleased that my lady Edith spoke to me the way that she did,' said Gervase. 'She was not trying to excuse or offer extenuation. She wanted me simply to understand her position.'

'We do,' concluded Ralph. 'She is married to an ogre.'

'Who happens to be our host,' reminded Golde.

'An hospitable ogre, then.'

The three of them laughed and rose from the table. Tension evaporated. They strolled across to the door. Ralph turned back and waved an expansive arm.

'This place will be full to the ceiling tonight,' he warned. 'And the noise in here will be deafening.'

'Until Bristeva sings,' noted Golde.

'Is that the young Saxon girl you mentioned?'

'Yes, Ralph.'

'She is Arnulf's prize chorister,' said Gervase.

'I can see why,' said Golde. 'I heard her practising in here yesterday. She is a charming girl and deserves her chance to shine. Her father will be here to support her.'

'We have met Ordgar,' said Ralph.

'Have you met his steward? Edric the Cripple?'

'No, my love. But Ordgar talked at length about him.'

'Did he say how the man lost his leg?'

'In combat.'

'Do you know where?'

'We have not yet managed to find it,' he said with sarcasm. 'We have searched everywhere for that missing leg.'

Gervase grinned. 'Ignore him, Golde.'

'It was such an odd coincidence,' she said.

'Coincidence?' said Gervase.

'Yes,' she continued. 'Edric was once in Hereford. At a time when I lived there myself. He was in the service of Roger of Breteuil, once the Earl of Hereford.'

Ralph looked startled. He shot a glance at Gervase.

'Is that not a coincidence?' she said.

'Yes,' agreed Ralph. 'It certainly is.'

Robert d'Oilly posted men on the northern road to Oxford so that he could have advance warning of the bishop's approach. Geoffrey of Coutances was an important visitor who needed to be welcomed in style and looked after with the utmost care. When he left Oxford, the bishop would ride south to Winchester where he would doubtless give a full account to the King of his time with the sheriff. It was vital that that account was wholly complimentary.

Edith had helped to supervise the banquet itself. He had no qualms about that. It would be a splendid occasion. Once the bishop and his entourage were feasting in the hall, they would notice none of the problems which were besetting the town, and they would ride away with pleasant memories and a high opinion of Robert d'Oilly's cordiality. All that the sheriff had to do was to greet his distinguished visitor with the pomp and pageantry that he would expect.

The preparations were thorough. Guards were doubled on the ramparts. Banners were trailed over the walls. A flag was hoisted up each pole. Every man in the garrison was on parade in the bailey, lined up in readiness to impress the newcomers. Oxford Castle exuded a sense of order, alertness and power.

In her finest attire, Edith stood beside her husband.

'How long will they be, Robert?'

'A matter of minutes.'

'It will be good to see the bishop again.'

'I could wish the circumstances were more propitious,' he said. 'He will be riding into a castle that is besieged with all kinds of difficulties.'

'Rise above them,' she said, squeezing his arm.

'I will try, Edith.'

A warning cry from the top of the church tower told him that the travellers were at hand, their cavalcade swinging right at the crossroads to make the short journey westwards to the castle. The sheriff signalled to his captains and orders were shouted. The ranks straightened. The rows of helms glinted in the sunlight. The flags fluttered in the wind. It was a fitting tribute to the arrival of one of the wealthiest, most celebrated and most ostentatious of Norman prelates.

Ralph, Gervase and Golde watched from windows in the keep. Brother Columbanus took up his position in the bailey. Arnulf the Chaplain brought Bristeva out from the church so that she could witness the magnificence of the bishop's train. Ostlers and servants made sure that they did not miss the moment of arrival. The whole castle quivered in anticipation.

Through the castle gates came the leading horse, ridden by a soldier who bore the banner of Geoffrey, Bishop of Coutances. Six more knights came next in pairs, followed by the august person of the bishop himself on a white horse, flanked by four outriders and trailed by two monks, two priests and ten more armoured knights in a winding procession. They clattered into the bailey like members of a conquering army and the bishop acknowledged the assembly with a condescending wave.

Bristeva's mouth went dry and her heart pounded. She had never seen anything like it. The sight of Robert d'Oilly always impressed her, but Geoffrey, Bishop of Coutances made him seem small and insignificant. Erect in the saddle of his white charger, and wearing a scarlet robe that was trimmed with ermine, he was a huge, hunched, red-faced man who exuded an extraordinary amalgam of power and religiosity. Bristeva was so overwhelmed by him that her legs began to tremble and she feared that she would never be able to sing in front of someone so terrifyingly eminent. She leaned against Arnulf for support and he put a steadying hand on her shoulder.

Robert d'Oilly stepped forward to welcome the bishop with a short, flowery but reverential speech and Edith added her own greeting with a low curtsey. Geoffrey remained in the saddle to preserve his authority and to run a satisfied eye around the bailey. He liked to feel expected. His voice was deep and commanding.

'It is good to be in Oxford again, Robert.'

'You are always most welcome here, your grace.'

'It has been a tedious journey from Warwickshire.'

'We will help you to shake off the dust.'

'I hear that you have commissioners in the town.'

'That is so.'

'I served in that office myself when the first circuits were drawn up,' boasted Geoffrey. 'This second team only looks under the stones that we lifted for them. I will be glad to meet them and give them the benefit of my advice.'

'They await your company.'

'What else awaits me, Robert?'

'A banquet in your honour, your grace.'

'I like the sound of this.'

'You will feast royally at my table.'

Geoffrey was content. He took his horse in a wide circle to inspect the parade which had been laid on for his benefit and then he signalled to one of the soldiers. The man ran forward to help him dismount, offering his shoulder for support to the episcopal hand as the bulky frame was heaved out of the saddle. Even on foot, the Bishop of Coutances still towered over most of those around him.

'How do I find Oxford?' he asked.

'In good order,' lied the sheriff manfully. 'You find it well governed and well maintained.'

'We heard rumours of trouble as we rode south.'

'They were only rumours, your grace.'

'I knew that they were,' said Geoffrey with a grin. 'Robert d'Oilly would never allow anything to upset the even tenor of his county.' He turned to Edith. 'Would he?'

'No, your grace,' she said.

'Oxford is an example to every town in the realm.'

'I strive to make it so,' said d'Oilly.

'You succeed, Robert,' confirmed the bishop, gazing around once more. 'This castle is a symbol of your governance. I am truly glad to be within its comforting walls.'

'Your peace will not be disturbed here, your grace.'

It was an unfortunate prediction. No sooner had it left the sheriff's mouth than it was contradicted in the most striking way. Another visitor came trotting in through the castle gates but with far less ceremony. Hyperion, the black stallion, scattered the other horses as he came to the centre of the bailey and halted in front of the bishop.

Tied across his saddle, covered in bruises and dripping with blood, was the naked body of Bertrand Gamberell.

Chapter Fifteen

An hour later, the gruesome sight still vibrated in the memory of all who witnessed it. Hyperion had been stabled, his cargo lifted off, the bishop and his entourage bestowed in their lodgings, the bailey cleared, the garrison returned to its quarters, the servants and ostlers restored to their duties, the watching faces removed from the windows and the whole scene of pageantry wiped away as if it had never existed. Yet it remained as fresh and vivid as ever in the mind.

Even viewed from a distance, it had been horrific.

'It was hideous!' recalled Gervase.

'I still shake at the very thought of it,' said Golde.

'Hardly the best welcome for a bishop,' said Ralph drily.

'Can my lord Bertrand still be alive?' she asked.

'Apparently, my love. The doctor is still with him. I managed to grab a brief word with the sheriff but he would not let me into the room to see the patient.'

'Would you want to see him in that state?'

'I'd want to ask him how he came by his injuries.'

'He seemed to have been beaten close to death,' said Gervase. 'Who could hate him enough to do that?'

'There is one obvious suspect,' said Ralph.

'Who is that?'

'My lord Wymarc.'

'No,' said Gervase thoughtfully. 'I doubt if this is his work. When the fury was really on him, he came after Bertrand Gamberell but not to batter him like that. He would have killed him outright.'

'Death might have been more merciful, Gervase.'
Golde shuddered. 'No mercy was shown to him today.'
'There is another thing,' said Gervase. 'If my lord Wymarc
had delivered this beating, he would hardly have sent his victim
back to the sheriff with his signature all over him. That would
render him liable to instant arrest.'
'True,' agreed Ralph.
'When I spoke with him, my lord Wymarc was more
preoccupied with grief than with revenge. This deed must
be laid at someone else's door.'
'It is one step short of murder,' observed Golde.
'A dire warning, my love.'
'Of what?'
'We shall see. But one crime has been solved.'
'What is that?'
'The theft of Hyperion. It is no accident that Bertrand
Gamberell came in stark naked on his black stallion. There
was a message in that. Whoever assaulted him must also have
stolen his horse.'
'It looks that way,' said Gervase.
'What other explanation is there?'
'I do not know, Ralph, but the timing seems strange. Why
steal a man's horse, keep it hidden for days and only then set
upon him? It does not feel right.'
'Neither does poor Bertrand!'
They were in the apartment shared by Ralph and Golde. In
their separate ways, each was disturbed by what they had seen.
Golde was horrified, Gervase filled with compassion for the
victim and Ralph obsessed with finding out the exact nature
of his injuries in the belief that they themselves might be
clues which would lead to the assailant. None of them was
even thinking about the banquet they were due to attend that
evening. Bertrand Gamberell had deprived every guest in the
castle of his appetite.
'We can cross one name off our list,' said Gervase.
'Yes,' consented Ralph. 'Bertrand is not our man. He is
a victim himself. He was always an outsider on the list but

had to be considered. That still leaves us four names to play with, Gervase. Can one of them really be responsible for all the crimes committed here?'

Gervase was pensive. Doubts crowded in upon him.

'I am not so certain,' he said at length.

'Why?'

'This latest incident breaks the pattern.'

'What pattern?'

'All the other events fit together.'

'This is linked to them somehow.'

'No, Ralph. I think not.'

'It must be.'

'The man who killed Walter Payne was not the one who attacked Bertrand Gamberell. Why murder a knight yet only hand out a beating to his master?'

'Only!' exclaimed Golde. 'Did you *see* him?'

'It was a savage assault,' said Gervase, 'and that is what makes it so different. The assassin was quick and decisive in his work. That beating took time and deliberation.'

'Not to mention strength,' added Ralph. 'Bertrand is in his prime. It would not have been easy to overpower him.'

'He may have been taken unawares.'

'And set upon by more than one assailant.'

'Please do not go on about it,' implored Golde. 'I keep seeing that horse trotting into the castle with a bleeding carcass across its back. It was horrendous!'

'We did not mean to distress you, my love,' said Ralph. 'Nothing can be done until we hear from Bertrand himself. He will name his attackers.'

Covered by a sheet, Bertrand Gamberell lay on a bed while the doctor bent over him. The patient was still unconscious. His body had been washed clean and the flow of blood stemmed with heavy bandaging but there were limits to the physician's skill. He could do nothing to hide the revolting ugliness of a face which had been smashed to a pulp. The nose was broken, the eyes blackened, the

lips swollen dramatically. The chin was one huge glowing bruise.

Baldwin the Doctor stood back with a sigh of sympathy.

'That is all I can do for him, my lord sheriff.'

'Will he survive?'

'Yes. But only because he is young and strong. Most men
would have died from such a beating.'

Robert d'Oilly smouldered. 'The villain who did this will
rot in my dungeon!' he vowed. 'I will never forgive him for
the way he humiliated me in front of the bishop. Bertrand's
wounds demand a heavy punishment for the rogue but I have
my own wounds to salve as well!'

As he washed his hands, Baldwin was tentative.

'There is one person who must, alas, be suspect here.'

'I know,' said the other grimly, 'and I have already sent
men to arrest Wymarc. If this is his work, he will regret it for
the rest of his days.'

'He was deeply upset by his sister's suicide.'

'That is no excuse.'

'It may be part of the explanation, my lord sheriff.'

'I want no explanations. I seek revenge!'

Robert d'Oilly paced the little chamber like a caged
lion. Planned with so much care and arranged with such
precision, the lavish welcome for the Bishop of Coutances
had been turned into a spectacle of sheer horror, and the
sheriff knew that the King would hear of the outrage in due
course. It would be one more stain on a shrievalty which
had already been blackened enough that week. Reputation
was everything to d'Oilly. He was eager to retrieve his lost
respect.

When the patient stirred, the sheriff darted across.

'Bertrand!' he hissed. 'Can you hear me, Bertrand?'

'Do not harass him,' advised the doctor.

'I need to speak to him.'

'He may not recover for hours yet.'

'Can you not administer something to revive him?'

'I have given him a healing elixer.'

'I want him awake now.' The sheriff took the patient by the shoulder and shook him. 'Bertrand! Talk to me, man!'

Baldwin protested feebly but his words went unheard. The sheriff could wait no longer. His urgency eventually brought a response. Gamberell groaned with pain as he was jostled. His lids half opened, his eyes mere slits in dark sockets.

'Who did this to you, Bertrand?' asked d'Oilly.

'Leave him be, my lord sheriff,' whispered the doctor.

'Who did this?'

Bertrand Gamberell looked up at the face hovering over him. Searing pain shot through him and he convulsed in agony.

'Who was it?' pressed the sheriff.

Gamberell saw the two men with staves in his mistress's bedchamber. He felt the first vicious blows all over again. He could still hear the woman's screams and her husband's loud exhortations. The ordeal returned.

'Who was he, Bertrand?'

'I do not know,' he said.

Then he lapsed back into unconsciousness.

Ordgar adjusted the brooch on his mantle then reached for his small, pointed cap and pulled it over the silver locks. He was in his finest garb for the banquet at the castle. Bristeva would see her father consorting with the most important men in the county. Proud of her, he wanted his daughter to take an equal pride in him.

When Ordgar came out of the house, Amalric was waiting for him. Seated astride Cempan, he wore a knee-length outer tunic of linen with a decorated hem and gartered trousers. Like his father's, the brooch on his mantle was fastened on his right shoulder. Ordgar saw the dagger in his belt.

'You will not need that,' he said sharply.

'It is for defence, father,' said the boy. 'We ride home at night. It would be folly to travel without a weapon.'

'I will keep it for you.'

He held out a hand. Amalric resisted at first but his father was determined. Only when the boy had surrendered his dagger did Ordgar climb into the saddle of his own horse.

'Before we leave, a word of warning.'

'Edric has already told me,' said Amalric sulkily.

'Do nothing to disgrace this family.'

'It is Bristeva who is doing that.'

'Amalric!'

The boy nodded. 'I will obey,' he sighed.

'I expect more than obedience.'

'Yes, father.'

'Think of your sister for once.'

'That is what Edric said. And I will try.'

'Good,' said Ordgar. 'Let us go. We need to be at the castle well in advance. We will meet Edric there.'

'Will he not ride with us?' said Amalric in surprise.

'No. He went on ahead.'

Edric the Cripple took his horse at walking pace down the hill towards Grandpont. Most of the traffic was going in the other direction as guests headed towards the castle for the banquet. When Edric went over the bridge, he swung to the right and picked his way slowly along the southern bank of the river. It was a warm evening. A few boats were gently spearheading their way through the water. Ducks paddled aimlessly. Geese honked menacingly in the rushes.

When he reached the castle, Edric nudged his horse into the shallows so that it could stretch its neck to take a drink. The rider's attention was on the stone keep which reared up over him on the opposite bank. Through the open windows, he could hear the noisy preparations for the banquet and smell the mingled aromas which emanated from the kitchen. He could almost feel the excitement that was building inside the hall.

Edric had seen what he wanted. It was time to go.

The attack of nerves came when they were just about to leave her chamber. She was tingling all over.

'I am afraid,' said Bristeva, cheeks ashen with fear.

'You have no need to be,' reassured Arnulf.

'I can hardly speak, let alone sing.'

'You will be fine, Bristeva.'

'No, Father Arnulf. I do not feel well.'

'Everyone is uneasy before an occasion like this.'

'I am not just uneasy,' she said. 'I am frightened. I cannot forget the terrible sight of that man tied to his horse. It scared me, Father Arnulf.'

'It upset us all,' he soothed her. 'It was a dreadful thing to behold. The wounded man deserves our deepest sympathy.'

'Do you know who he is?'

'Yes.'

'Who?'

'It does not matter.'

'But I want to know.'

'The sooner you can put him out of your mind, the better.' Arnulf took her by the shoulders. 'Cheer up, Bristeva. This is a big occasion for you. Will it help if I tell you that the man is recovering? The doctor has tended him. I have seen the patient myself and he revives.' He pulled her to him. 'Now put him aside and think only of the banquet.'

'I cannot sing tonight!'

'Bristeva!'

'I hate to let you down but I have no heart to sing.'

'You are bound to feel nervous.'

'They will not miss me, Father Arnulf. There is plenty of other entertainment. What are two songs in the middle of a feast such as that? Nobody will notice I am not there.'

He stepped back to take her chin in his hand.

'*I* will notice,' he said firmly. 'And your father will notice. And your brother. And my lady Golde. Will you betray us all? I expect more of you.'

'I know,' she said guiltily.

'Then no more of this weakness. We have practised the songs many times. When you stand up in the hall, your fears will drop away. You will sing as beautifully as I have taught you and everyone will applaud. Do you understand?'

She lowered her head and gave a reluctant nod.

'Let me hear you say it, Bristeva.'

257

'I understand,' she whispered.

'Good girl!'

He lifted her chin and placed a delicate kiss on her lips. Bristeva looked up at him with her eyes shining. All her fears and reservations were suddenly receding. Arnulf the Chaplain had favoured her above all the other choristers. She could not let him down. Only by performing well could she retain his interest and his love.

'I am ready,' said a cheery voice behind them. 'Shall we go across to the hall together?'

They stepped instinctively apart and turned to see Brother Columbanus in the doorway. Hands hidden in the sleeves of his cowl, the monk gave them his most benign smile.

'I am hungry,' he said.

Robert d'Oilly strove to dispel the air of gloom which hung over the hall. Ordering the musicians to play, and the cups of wine to be distributed, he strode about to greet each new guest with exaggerated affability. His wife Edith, resplendent in a garment of pale blue silk, was a more poised figure, extending her welcome with a warm smile and a friendly gesture of the hand. Between them, husband and wife slowly managed to lighten the pervading atmosphere.

Ralph Delchard and Gervase Bret watched them in action.

'He is such a daunting host,' commented Ralph.

'Daunting?'

'Yes, Gervase. I do not not know which aspect of Robert d'Oilly is the more unsettling, the violent sheriff or the gushing host. He fairly swooped upon me when I entered, as if I were his sworn brother.'

Gervase smiled. 'You are certainly not that.'

'Look at him now with his son-in-law.'

Milo Crispin had come into the room with his wife, Maud, on his arm. They were a striking couple. Milo was as stately as ever and his wife, in a mantle of olive green over a white gown, had a dignified beauty. When she embraced her mother, the resemblance between them was clear. The sheriff greeted them both effusively as if he had not seen them for several years. Then his manner changed in a flash as he took Milo aside for a moment to whisper in his ear.

'We know what the sheriff is telling him,' noted Ralph.

'But does he need to be told, Ralph?'

'What?'

'Milo Crispin does not seem at all surprised to hear about the beating that Bertrand Gamberell took,' observed Gervase. 'It is the sheriff's face that is grim.'

'Milo has hardly raised an eyebrow, let alone blenched.'

'He will repay careful watching.'

The next guest who came through the door astonished them both. Wymarc looked furtive and self-conscious but he forced a smile when he was greeted by his hosts. The wine that was put into his hand was immediately gulped down.

'He is the last person I expected to see,' said Gervase.

'Yes. And he would rather be anywhere else but here.'

'What brought him?'

'Six of the sheriff's men.'

'By force?'

'Originally,' said Ralph. 'I saw him when he was escorted into the castle earlier. My guess is that our genial host had him arrested on suspicion of assaulting Bertrand Gamberell. He obviously proved his innocence and was released.'

'Released from custody but not from his guilt. He still frets over Helene's suicide. You can see it clearly.'

'Yes, Gervase, but he may have taken consolation from the news about Bertrand. It did not cause a ripple on the surface of Milo's face but I wager that it raised at least a smile of satisfaction on Wymarc's.'

Guests surged through the door in greater numbers and the hall began to fill rapidly. The plaintive sound of rebec and harp were drowned beneath the tidal murmur. Ralph looked around for Golde and saw her talking with Brother Columbanus. When he turned back to Gervase, he saw that they had company. Geoffrey, Bishop of Coutances was bearing down on them.

In a convivial setting, he somehow exuded an even greater sense of power. They were highly aware of his standing with the King. He was one of William's chief advisers and had played a major part in the ecclesiastical reforms which had followed the Conquest. In both Church and State, he was an influential figure. Ralph was acquainted with his military exploits while Gervase remembered him for his judicial role. The bishop's smile was shared evenly between them.

'You are the commissioners, I believe,' he said, sizing each man up at a glance. 'Ralph Delchard and Gervase Bret.'

'That is right, your grace,' said Ralph.

'Three of you set out from Winchester.'

'You are well informed,' noted Gervase.

'I have to be,' boasted Geoffrey. 'My intelligencers are everywhere. Where is the third member of your tribunal? I wish to meet Maurice Pagnal as well.'

'You will have to wait until you reach Winchester,' said Ralph sadly. 'And you may need to crack the whip over your intelligencers, your grace. They obviously failed to tell you that my lord Maurice was dismissed from his office and sent away in disgrace.'

'Why?' demanded Geoffrey, eyes bulging in dismay. 'What was his offence?'

'He succumbed to bribery, your grace,' said Gervase.

'A corrupt judge! Unforgivable!'

'His substitute is even now on his way to Oxford.'

'I am pleased to hear it,' rumbled the bishop. 'Nothing is as vital as the incorruptibility of those in a judicial position. Several years ago,' he recalled, grasping at a memory which could inflate his self-importance, 'I presided over a land dispute between Lanfranc, Archbishop of Canterbury and Odo, Bishop of Bayeux and Earl of Kent. The trial was held at the shire court in Penenden Heath. As a lawyer, Master Bret, you will know the case. It stands as an example of judicial impartiality. The King's archbishop or the King's half-brother? Whom should I have favoured?' He clenched a fist. 'Neither! Had an Emperor and a Pope stood before me, I would have been uninfluenced by their rank. Justice was my only concern.' He pointed to Ralph. 'I will see that Maurice Pagnal does not escape lightly for this.'

'That would please me, your grace,' said Ralph.

'It will be done,' promised Geoffrey, letting a glaucous eye rove around the room. 'I will have much to report to the King about Oxford. It will not be complimentary.'

Robert d'Oilly descended on his chief guest to lead him to his place. The steward was meanwhile directing other guests to their seats in strict hierarchical order. Long tables had been arranged in a giant horseshoe so that the central area was left free for the entertainment. Rushes covered the floor. Herbs sweetened the air. Music played on. Two hundred candles shed a fluctuating brilliance over the scene.

Geoffrey, Bishop of Coutances was in the place of honour in the centre of the main table. Robert d'Oilly sat beside him on his right and Edith was on the bishop's other flank. Ralph sat next to his hostess with Golde, then Gervase, next to him. It was a good position from which to view the whole room, though Ralph wished that he could keep Milo Crispin under closer surveillance. The latter was seated on the sheriff's right hand. Maud was between them, separating her husband from her father. She was an arresting figure even in such a glittering array.

Ralph leaned behind Golde to speak to Gervase.

'They are all here,' he said.

'Yes, Ralph.'

'Milo, Wymarc, Ordgar and the sheriff.'

'Which one should we watch?'

'All four.'

His gaze switched to Ordgar. Occupying a humble position at the foot of a side table, the old Saxon was seated between his son and Edric the Cripple. In an almost exclusively Norman gathering, they looked out of place, and their attire was shabby against the bright tunics of the men around them. Ordgar was neither hurt nor insulted by his position at the feast. He was there to enjoy his daughter's contribution and that put him in a mood of quiet elation.

A fanfare sounded and serving men entered in procession to display some of the dishes that were being served. As they paraded the boar's head, the side of pork, the salmon, the venison, the spiced rabbits and the other delights around the hall, they drew gasps of pleasure from the women and approving thumps on the table from the men. There were six choices for the first course alone. Wine flowed plentifully. Ale was set out before the Saxon contingent. The whole assembly was soon drinking heartily and eating their frumenty.

The one person who was holding back from the wine was Brother Columbanus. Seated opposite Ordgar, he tucked into his food with relish but put a hand over his cup whenever someone tried to pour wine into it. Arnulf the Chaplain watched him from the doorway. He had been sitting with Bristeva in an ante-room, trying to still her anxieties and prepare her mind for the test ahead. He now slipped into the hall to check that everything was in order. Walking up behind the monk, he lifted the man's cup and filled it from a flagon on the table.

'No, no,' protested Columbanus. 'I must not.'

'Join in the revelry, Brother Columbanus,' urged the other. 'You are an honoured guest. No man can come to a banquet such as this and refuse a drink.'

'Will you lead me astray, my friend?'

'I wish merely to see you enjoy yourself.'

When the cup was pressed firmly into his hand, Columbanus relented. He beamed at his neighbours.

'One taste, perhaps.'

Ordgar raised a hand to catch the chaplain's attention.

'How is Bristeva?' he asked.

'Nervous but confident.'

'When will she sing?'

'Not for some while yet.'

'May I speak to her beforehand?'

'It might be better if you did not,' said Arnulf. 'She needs to settle before she can perform in front of such an assembly. I will get back and help her through the tension of this long wait.'

262

He poured more wine for Columbanus then withdrew.

Entertainment soon began. The musicians struck up a lively tune and a dozen dancers came gliding into the room, moving with grace and verve as they weaved intricate patterns in front of the spectators. The applause was long and loud. When the guests looked down at the table again, they saw that a new course had been served. Gloom and despondency had been completely banished. A spirit of joy prevailed.

Tumblers came next, sprinting into the hall and thrilling everyone with their acrobatic feats. They were followed by a man who put a flaming brand into his mouth before blowing fire in the air like a human dragon. The dancers returned for a second display then made way for a magician in a long black robe. His performance imposed a hush on the room. They watched in amazement as he made a bunch of flowers vanish before their eyes, and they gasped in unison when he folded his hands in prayer, then opened them to release a white dove into the air. It flew twice around the room before obeying his whistle and returning to perch on his shoulder.

Bristeva heard the thunderous clapping from the hall. She was in the adjoining room with Arnulf and the delay was telling on her already frayed nerves.

'When do I go in?' she asked.

'You are next, Bristeva.'

'I will never get applause like that.'

'They will love you, Bristeva. So will I.'

He embraced her fondly and she felt a glow of pleasure. Her spirits lifted. 'Is my father there?'

'Yes,' he confirmed, 'and Amalric.'

'I so want to please them.'

'You will please everybody,' he said. 'As long as you remember what I told you. Stand still. Keep your head up. Take a deep breath before you start. Then let your voice fill the hall with sweetness. They will be captivated.'

'Will I be as good as Helene?' she wondered.

263

Arnulf felt his stomach lurch for a moment.

'Every bit as good.'

The steward gave a signal and Arnulf guided her towards the door of the hall. Her moment had come. Bristeva was about to sing the two songs they had rehearsed.

The room was still buzzing with wonder at the performance of the magician. When they saw that he was followed by a young girl, they gave her an encouraging clap. With Arnulf at her side, Bristeva moved to the centre of the hall with a poise and confidence that impressed even her brother. She wore a blue gunna over a white kirtle. A circlet of gold held her wimple in place. Bristeva's face had the bloom of innocence upon it. She compelled a respectful silence.

When he had positioned her, Arnulf withdrew to the side of the hall. She was on her own now. There was no hesitation. Shaking off all her apprehension, Bristeva took a deep breath and sang in a voice that seemed to fly around the room with as much delight as the white dove. The songs were simple but melodious, touching refrains which plucked at the emotions. Arnulf was delighted, Ordgar was thrilled, Amalric gave a grudging approval, Brother Columbanus wept with joy and Geoffrey, Bishop of Coutances was entranced. There were no tricks or clever illusions this time. She did it all with the purity of her voice and the quiet power of her presence.

Bristeva was the real magician. When she finished, the applause was sustained and deafening. She curtseyed in acknowledgement. Almost everybody in the room acclaimed her. Ralph Delchard was one of the exceptions. While others were looking at the girl, his attention was caught by the man with the crutch who was hobbling to stand beside a window at the other end of the hall. Edric the Cripple identified himself by his gait. He took no interest in the girl herself. His gaze was fixed on the guest of honour.

A series of images flashed through Ralph's mind. He thought about the skill of an assassin at Woodstock. The soldiering days of his victim. The round indentations in the ground under the ash. The theft of a spirited black stallion. A housecarl in Wallingford. A revolt in Herefordshire. The loss of a leg amid brutal reprisals.

He moved just in time. When Ralph saw the dagger in Edric's hand, he jumped to his feet and leant over to grab the bishop and pull him sideways in his chair. The dagger was already spinning through the air. It missed the guest of honour by inches and buried itself in the back of the chair.

Pandemonium ensued. Men yelled, women screamed, everyone jumped up in alarm and swirled around the room in a panic. Ralph let go of the bishop and fought his way down the hall to the window but Edric had planned his escape on this occasion as on the last. Having flung himself from the keep, he landed in the middle of the river and was now swimming to the bank with his crutch floating behind him. His horse was tethered to a nearby tree.

Enraged to a new pitch, Robert d'Oilly pointed an accusatory finger at Ordgar and his son, roaring above the tumult in a voice of doom.

'This is a conspiracy! Arrest them!'

Four guards pinioned the two men before they could move.

Bristeva screeched with fear before Arnulf swept her up in his arms and carried her away from the scene of confusion. Ralph darted across to her father to begin an immediate interrogation.

'Where has he gone?' he demanded.

'I do not know, my lord,' said Ordgar, quivering.

'You planned this assassination with him!'

'No, my lord!'

'The pair of you will hang alongside him.'

'Please!' begged Ordgar. 'My son and I are innocent. We knew nothing of this. Bring a Bible and I will swear to it, my lord. We came only to hear my daughter sing.'

'Is she part of the conspiracy as well?'

The old man was distraught. 'Bristeva?'

'Distracting us with her songs while Edric lurked.'

'No, no,' said Ordgar with patent sincerity. 'We are as

shocked as you by what has happened. Edric must pay for his crime. I will do all I can to help you catch him.'

'Then tell me where he will go. At once!'

'I have no idea, my lord. That is the truth. I simply do not know.' He turned to his son. 'And neither does Amalric.'

But a telltale glint had come into the boy's eye.

By the time he escorted her back to her chamber, Arnulf had managed to convince her that her father and brother were not in danger. If they were innocent – as she averred – they would come to no harm. Edric the Cripple would bear all the blame. Bristeva was terrified that some responsibility would attach to her. If she had not sung in the hall, the steward would never have been allowed inside the place. Unwittingly, she had given him the cover he needed. It was horrifying.

Arnulf slipped his arms around her to comfort her and she laid her head on his shoulder as she wept. The room was quiet and secluded. They were far away from the chaos in the hall. His soothing words slowly calmed her down. His warm embrace made her feel loved and protected. Bristeva was gradually lulled into a mood of unquestioning compliance.

'I wanted it to be so different,' he whispered.

'So did I.'

'I wanted you to have your triumph in the hall then return here with me to celebrate it. Just the two of us, Bristeva. You and me. We earned that celebration.'

'We did, Father Arnulf!'

'Do you feel better now?' he said, stroking her back.

'Much better.'

'Do not worry about anything. I will take care of you.'

'Thank you.'

She nestled into his shoulder and did not object when his caresses grew more intimate. When he removed her wimple and dropped it on the mattress, her plait uncoiled down her back. His hand stroked it then he wound it playfully around his fingers. He brushed her head with his lips.

Bristeva was in a complete daze. She was both inebriated

by her success in the hall and stunned by the murderous attack which had followed it. She needed sympathy and reassurance. Father Arnulf was providing it for her. When his hands ran down her back to caress her buttocks, she made no complaint. When he rubbed himself against her thighs, she felt no alarm. It was only when his fingers worked their way up to her breasts that she tried to pull away.

'What are you doing!' she said, blushing deeply.

'Comforting you, Bristeva.'

'You frightened me.'

'Then I will do it more gently this time,' he said, reaching out to take the full breasts in the palms of both hands before squeezing them softly. 'I have wanted to do this for so long, Bristeva. You are beautiful. You asked me if you would be as good as Helene and I told you the truth.' He pulled her hard against him. 'Every bit as good.'

The first kiss took her breath away. Crimson with shame and pulsating with fear, she did not know what to do. Arnulf was her friend and protector. She loved him. Yet he was doing things which made her feel hurt and abused. During the second kiss, he eased her down on the mattress and rolled on top of her. There was no uncertainty now. As soon as she pulled her mouth free, she shrieked aloud. The voice which had delighted with its sweetness now became an hysterical cry.

'Nobody will hear you, Bristeva,' he said. 'Be mine.'

He stopped her mouth with another kiss but it was short-lived. Gervase opened the door and dashed in to haul the chaplain off her. Arnulf was strong but he had nothing like Gervase's anger and determination. While the two men struggled, Brother Columbanus slipped in to help Bristeva up and shepherd her out into the passage. It was he who had alerted Gervase to the danger she was in.

A relay of punches finally subdued Arnulf and he lay gasping on the floor. Gervase stood over him, dishevelled but victorious. He looked at the other with utter disgust.

'Is this where you seduced Helene as well?'

*　　*　　*

Edric the Cripple led his horse into the abandoned mill and tethered him to a wooden spike. The animal took time to settle after the long gallop from Oxford. When he nosed the hay at last, he began to chomp it contentedly. Disappointment gnawed at Edric. His careful plan had failed at the last moment. Walter Payne had been killed but a worse enemy had escaped. The consolation was that Edric had survived to fight another day. He allowed himself a congratulatory chuckle. A man with one leg had outwitted and outrun all of them. It had cost him a ducking in the river but he did not mind. He was safe.

It did not take him long to start the fire. Holding a long, straight twig between his palms, he rotated it quickly until the friction produced a spark and the other twigs ignited. He now had a source of light in his refuge and a means of drying his wet apparel. After feeding the fire, he began to remove his tunic. Nobody would find him there. Before dawn, he would have left the county.

'Edric the Cripple!'

The voice cut through the stillness like an axe.

'Come on out!

Edric peered through the gap between the timbers and saw a solitary man, sitting astride a horse some twenty yards away. There was enough moonlight for him to pick out the sword in his visitor's hand.

'My name is Ralph Delchard!' called the other. 'I am here to arrest you for the murder of Walter Payne and for the attempted murder of Geoffrey, Bishop of Coutances.'

Edric looked around in despair. There was no way out. His horse was tired. If one man had found him, there would be others nearby. Resistance was useless. He might prevail in combat against most opponents but there was something in Ralph's voice and the way that he held himself in the saddle which suggested a fearsome adversary.

'You hid in the ground at Woodstock,' said Ralph. 'You cower in a mill here. Come out and fight in the open like a man, Edric. I am ready for you.'

The challenge awakened the warrior in him but Edric still held back. He foresaw only too clearly the gruesome fate he would meet if he was taken prisoner. It was futile to lie low and hope that Ralph would go away. The fire gave him away. Ralph could see its glow and knew that he was in there.

'I know why,' shouted Ralph, circling the mill on his horse. 'You were a mercenary in the pay of Roger of Breteuil. You fought for him during the revolt of the three earls. But you picked the wrong side, Edric. You lost. The uprising was put down by an army led by Geoffrey, Bishop of Coutances.'

'He is an animal!' howled Edric.

'He was short on mercy that day,' admitted Ralph. 'When he overpowered your army, he ordered his men to cut off the leg of every soldier who raised a weapon against him.'

'I was crippled for life!'

'So was your mind, Edric.' Ralph was working himself closer. 'Walter Payne served under the bishop. He took part in that hideous mutilation. You waited a long time for your revenge on him.'

'It was worth it!'

'Come out now! I will not ask again.'

There was a long silence. Ralph's patience snapped and he nudged his horse forward. He did not get far. The door of the mill opened and Edric's horse came out, slapped on the rump to make him run. The door shut again but not before Ralph had seen a glimpse of the fire. Fed by Edric, it started to crackle and blaze. Ralph's horse shied and backed away. He rode it across to a tree and dismounted before tethering it. When he turned back to the mill, he saw that the fire had taken a real hold. Sword in hand, he ran towards the building until he was stopped by a wall of heat. It sent him reeling.

Coughing in the acrid smoke, he made one last appeal.

'Come out, Edric! This is madness.'

But there was no reply. Edric reserved the right to quit the world in his own way. As the blaze lit up the night sky and the heat pushed Ralph further back, there was a loud cackle of triumph from inside the mill.

Edric the Cripple had eluded them all again. They found the charred remains of his crutch beside the body.

Epilogue

There was a full congregation in the church of St George's-in-the-Castle next morning. The service was taken by Geoffrey, Bishop of Coutances and he preached a sermon of thanksgiving for his narrow escape from death. All those present were acutely aware that the chaplain who normally presided at the altar was now lying in one of the dungeons to face a charge of attempted rape. Arnulf had readily confessed to the paternity of Helene's child and was tortured with contrition. When the service came to an end, the bishop felt that he had not so much officiated in the church as conducted an exorcism. A resident devil had been put to flight.

Thoroughly chastened, the congregation trickled out of the building and dispersed throughout the castle. Ralph Delchard was among the last to leave. Golde was beside him. Gervase Bret and Brother Columbanus soon joined them. The monk came over to congratulate Ralph.

'You were justly praised in the sermon,' he said.

'Yes,' said Ralph drily. 'I have always wanted to lay rough hands on a bishop, but when I finally get the chance he ends up thanking me from the pulpit.'

'You saved his life,' reminded Golde.

'No, my love. Edric's crutch did that.'

'His crutch?'

'Yes. When Gervase and I searched the copse at Woodstock, we puzzled over these circular indentations in the ground. A staff? An implement of some kind? I could not work it out. Then I saw Edric the Cripple at the banquet.'

271

'With his crutch.'

'And there was my answer.'

'You needed more evidence than that,' said Columbanus. 'What else drew your attention to the steward?'

'His service to the Earl of Hereford.' He turned to Golde. 'My wife garnered that crucial piece of information. It gave me a motive for Edric. If someone cuts off your leg as an act of wanton violence, you tend to nurse a grievance.'

Golde grimaced. 'Is that what happened?'

'The bishop sounded holy enough in that church this morning but there was not much Christian spirit about him when he helped to put down the revolt of the earls. Edric was not the only prisoner crippled that day. By the time the bishop rode away, a lot of crutches were needed.'

The monk crossed himself. 'The horrors of war know no limit. Blessed are the peacemakers.'

'What else convinced you, Ralph?' asked Gervase.

'His absence from the race at Woodstock,' said Ralph. 'Edric raised that colt and trained its rider. Would he really miss a chance to see them compete against such fine horses?' He shook his head. 'Not unless he had a good reason. That reason was the murder of Walter Payne.'

'Was he certain the man would be in the race?'

'Completely, Gervase. He watched him in the earlier races, remember, and noted his line of running. Then Edric and the boy practised for many hours over that course.'

'So he could pick exactly the right place for the attack.'

'He proved that in the hall last night,' said Golde.

Ralph grinned. 'Almost proved it.'

'You were the bishop's guardian angel,' said Columbanus.

'There is nothing angelic about me!' he denied hotly.

'Yes, there is,' teased his wife.

They strolled across the bailey towards the keep. Oxford Castle seemed oddly silent and deserted after the dramatic events of the previous day. Gervase recalled that Hyperion was still stabled there.

'How do you know that Edric was the horse thief?'

'I don't, Gervase.'

'Then why suggest it?'

Ralph shrugged. 'A guess. Hyperion is a spirited animal. Only a very experienced horseman could ride him. Ordgar told me how expert Edric was even with his disability.'

'It does not seem to have been a disability,' said Golde. 'In some ways, it spurred him on.'

'It did, my love.'

'We all have disabilities,' confessed Columbanus.

'Yours robs you of *both* legs,' noted Ralph.

Puce with embarrassment, the monk came to a sudden halt. The others stopped to laugh at him but there was great affection in their mirth. Brother Columbanus was quick to point out that his fondness for strong drink was not without an incidental benefit.

'Arnulf the Chaplain had noted my weakness,' he said.

Ralph chuckled. 'You are the patron saint of every brewer and vintner in England.'

'We are all fallible, my lord Ralph.'

'Tell us about Arnulf,' encouraged Gervase.

'That was what confirmed my suspicions about him,' said Columbanus. 'When I saw him with Bristeva, I felt this faint shiver. Something was not quite right in that relationship.'

'A masterly understatement,' said Ralph.

'During the banquet, he came across to pour my wine.'

'A friendly enough gesture.'

'That's what I thought, my lord,' said the monk. 'Then I asked myself why he had made it. I have a chamber close to his. He wanted to make sure that I would hear nothing in the night and be in no position to interrupt him. The way to do that was to tempt me with wine. As you have seen, I cannot hold my drink. Arnulf knew that. If I'd sipped wine all evening, I would not have heard the end of the world, let alone the cries of a young girl being molested. So I held back.'

'You turned your weakness into a strength,' said Gervase.

'Yes,' added Golde. 'Were she here, Bristeva would preach a sermon of thanks to you, Brother Columbanus.'

'And to Gervase. He wrested the chaplain from her.'

'I am just grateful that you alerted me in time,' said Gervase. 'In all the commotion, nobody saw Arnulf slip out of the hall with the girl.'

Columbanus straightened. 'I did.'

'Poor girl!' sighed Golde. 'Bristeva has had to do a lot of growing up in the last twenty-four hours. It must have been a profound shock to learn that the chaplain lured her into the choir in order to take advantage of her.'

'He did the same with Helene,' Gervase reminded her.

'Innocent girls, both,' said Columbanus.

'Bristeva is the lucky one. She survived.' Gervase was rueful. 'Helene was his real victim. The chaplain exercised complete power over her. She was so flattered by his attentions that she could refuse him nothing. But there were dread consequences for Helene. An unwanted child.'

'She must have been demented with fear,' said Golde. 'I cannot find it in my heart to condemn her. Arnulf the Chaplain is the one I condemn. Thanks to him, Helene will be buried in unconsecrated ground, a shameful outcast with nobody to mourn her passing.'

'The bishop was right in his sermon,' said Columbanus. 'He called Arnulf a holy devil. How many other girls would have fallen under his spell if that devil had not been stopped?'

A clack of hooves directed their attention to the stables. Milo Crispin was about to depart with his wife and his escort. Hyperion was leaving with them, towed along by Milo himself on a lead-rein. Golde was astonished.

'That black stallion is being stolen again,' she said.

'No, my love,' explained Ralph. 'Bertrand Gamberell came to his senses.'

'What do you mean?'

'Milo told me this morning. One way or another, Hyperion has landed Gamberell in a vast amount of trouble. He is so disenchanted with the horse that he has given him to Milo

Crispin. In return, Milo has agreed to drop his claim to that disputed land near Wallingford. It is formally ceded to Bertrand Gamberell.'

'But Wymarc also has a claim,' Gervase reminded him.

'Not any more,' said Ralph. 'Recent events have left him with no stomach for a fight over a piece of land. He, too, is willing to let Gamberell's claim take precedence. In other words,' he added, 'the problem has been solved amicably and we will not have to deal with the dispute in the shire hall.'

'That is a relief,' said Gervase. 'We all gain by this.'

'Including Ordgar.'

'In what way?'

'With Hyperion in his stable, Milo will not need to take the chestnut colt away from Ordgar's son. A pleasing solution for everyone. It all stems from that beating Gamberell took.'

'We still don't know who administered that.'

'We never will, Gervase.'

'Why not?'

'What man will admit that he was caught in a bedchamber by an angry husband? Bertrand Gamberell has his pride. He will be more careful in his choice of mistresses from now on. And there is some compensation for him.'

'Yes,' said Gervase. 'He gains that disputed property without having to fight over it in the shire hall. That means we can move on to deal with the smaller disputes which brought us here.'

'Leave those to Canon Hubert.'

'When will he arrive?' asked a worried Columbanus.

'He will be here some time today on that long-suffering donkey of his,' said Ralph. 'For once in my life, I will be glad to see him. Hubert will ride in through the castle gates as if he is entering Jerusalem. And I, for one, will be there to scatter palms in his way and to sing hosannas.' He gave a chuckle. 'His donkey will win no races but I'll wager that it causes us far less trouble than the stallions of Woodstock.'